"Damn, this is ridiculous," Downing said. "We shoulda used a little common sense. I shoulda listened to you, Whit. No way are they gonna come out on a night like this."

From behind them, the floor creaked. In a simultaneous reaction, all three of them snapped their heads toward the sound. An immense form, silhouetted in the glare from the Buick's headlights, took a single step toward them. "Wrong," the shadow said. "We're here. . . ."

B.O.L.O.

Dave Pedneau

BALLANTINE BOOKS • NEW YORK

Library of Congress Catalog Card Number: 88-92828

ISBN 0-345-35718-3

Manufactured in the United States of America

First Edition: May 1989

B.O.L.O.

**In official police jargon,
a message for all units to
"Be On The Lookout."**

PROLOGUE

TROOPER FIRST CLASS E. K. CLARK could think of several places he'd like to be at 2:00 A.M. on a summer-warm November night. The forsaken stretch of mountain highway known as the River Road didn't appear on his list of choices. He could also think of a lot of people with whom he'd like to share the evening. The rookie trooper on the passenger side of the cruiser wasn't among them, especially given the nature of the complaint they were dispatched to answer—an alleged brawl in Tipple Town.

Clark was the new kid's training officer—T.O. in the department's jargon. The burden had fallen to him after a request for volunteers had received no positive response whatsoever. Not that the rookie—his name was Sam Mahoney—was any worse than the usual state police academy virgin. In fact, he was one hundred percent typical, which explained why no one wanted to be his or any other rookie's T.O.

Eddie Clark gingerly guided the cruiser over the narrow tortuous highway, cursing every foot of it—and the rugged and desolate terrain it traversed.

Even in the late twentieth century, the stumpy but steep mountains of southern West Virginia continued to obstruct civilization. In western Raven Country, at the southernmost point of the state, a spine of just those kind of ugly and hostile ridges separated the agricul-

1

tural region of the county from the coal-rich lands to the west. The mountains themselves, reaching an average and meager height of 2,500 feet, had been found rich in anthracite coal. They still were; it just wasn't profitable any longer to mine the dirty fossil fuel.

That hadn't always been true. Clark, himself not yet forty, hadn't even been an urge in his father's loin during the boom days, but a kid didn't grow up in southern West Virginia—as Clark—without hearing how prosperous things had been. In those days coal mining was labor intensive, and the operators imported droves of starving immigrants and southern blacks to the homely coalfields of Raven County. The industry took more from the state than it gave, but a few improvements were necessary. So the operators built company towns centered around company stores. They issued their own money called scrip to be spent at those stores, just so most of the dollars would stay in the family. There wasn't much retail competition. The miners either bought at the company store or they did without.

Since the out-of-state coal barons owned the state's politicians, it wasn't any problem to get roads constructed to serve the multitude of coal camps. In Raven County, its western coal seam offered more than adequate reason to build a narrow and winding artery along the unfriendly mountain slopes to the coalfield communities on the other side.

Engineered about midway up the mountain slope, the road bed had been blasted from coal-blackened rock. Decades later, a handful of people still lived at each extreme of the River Road, but for most of its length it was bordered on one side by the rock wall created during its construction and on the other by a sheer drop of several hundred feet to a north-south waterway, a tributary so obscure in the scheme of things that it didn't even warrant a name.

Few folks dared its serpentine ten-mile length in the daytime, much less after nightfall. In places, chunks of the pavement itself had fallen into the creek. At those junctures where other unpaved arteries branched off the River Road, always on the high side and always leading to an abandoned strip mine site, mud and water and rock washed across the road and undermined the pavement. Strip mining—surface mining to those who practiced and defended it—had been a coalfield plague during the boom years. Whatever beauty the wretched mountains might have possessed had been erased by the blades of bulldozers as they scraped away the very summits themselves to recover the burning earth.

Mahoney had his window down, allowing the warm night air to refresh him as it rushed into the car.

"It's hard to believe," the rookie was saying.

Clark's fingers threatened to cramp from his choking hold on the steering wheel. He squinted at the road ahead, trying to judge his speed as he headed toward a vicious turn. "What's that?"

"They say it's gonna be a bad winter, but here it is November and still in the sixties at night."

Clark braked before he reached the curve and allowed the cruiser to glide through it. "Hell, kid, last year it was eighty-two one day and snowing like hell the next. That's West Virginia for ya. I hear we got a cold front bearing down on us now. When it passes, the temperature could drop fifty degrees in a couple of hours."

The car swayed as it exited the curve. Mahoney leaned with it. "This road's not so bad."

The state police academy put a macho edge to the rookies who completed it. Nothing was to frighten or deter them—not even the River Road.

Clark glanced at his untried partner. "That so? Lemme tell you something, Sam. I say a special prayer ever' time I cross it. The damn thing could drop right out from under us any minute.''

''So, if it's so damned dangerous, why don't they close it?''

At that moment a man-size shadow sprang from the driver's side of the road and into the beam of the headlights. Clark jammed his foot down on the brake. Tires squealed. Mahoney's hands shot forward to brace himself on the dash. The dark figure vanished into the woods on the up-slope side of the road.

''What the fuck—'' Mahoney's hands maintained a white-knuckle grip on the padded dash.

''A deer,'' Clark said, bringing the cruiser back up to speed.

''Jesus!''

''Now, what were you saying about the road?''

''Hell, that could have happened on any road.''

Eddie smiled and shook his head. ''You can bet your cherry ass on one thing, boy. If that complaint hadn't sounded so damned needful, I'd have gone the long way around. That's how much respect I got for this road's reputation.''

Lizzie McOwen, the dispatcher, had radioed them a few minutes before about the alleged brawl in Tipple Town, a small and all-too-often lawless community at the other end of the River Road. The call had come from the chief of Tipple Town's two-man police force and had gone first to the Raven County Sheriff's Department. Its units were tied up, so the call had been transferred to the ''states,'' as the state troopers were called. From the point at which Clark received the transmission, the road—as infamous as it was—provided the shortest response time . . . a lousy road to a lousy town.

Mahoney was relaxing back into the seat. He had grown up in Parkersburg, a city located in the relatively flat northwestern part of the state. He had been pleased when he received a placement in the state's rough-and-tumble southern end. "I think these mountains are kinda pretty," he said.

"That's because it's dark. In the daytime, they look like the bombed-out mountains I saw in Nam."

"Bombed out?"

"You ever seen a high wall, Mahoney?"

"A what?"

"A high wall. It's what's left of the side of a mountain when strip miners have had their way with it. In these hills, we're lucky to even have high walls. They've gouged away the friggin' tops of most of them."

Mahoney eased his head toward the window.

Clark shook his head at his partner's naivete. "You can't see 'em in the dark, for Christ's sakes."

The veteran cop braked again as he approached another curve. "Up ahead, we got the only straight stretch along the entire road. When I first was assigned down here, kids used to come out here and drag-race. They thought it was a real thrill runnin' full out on this narrow son-of-a-bitchin' road. One night a carload of 'em went over the goddamn side. It took us two days to pull the bodies up out of that goddamn piss stream of a creek."

"Two days?"

"We had a hell of a rain, and the creek—" The cruiser completed the curve and entered the straightaway. Clark stopped his story as he gaped at the odd scene framed by his headlights. "What the hell—"

A hundred yards down the straightaway the heretofore negligible berm widened into a pulloff formed over the years by people who used the location to dump household garbage over the mountainside. It created an eyesore, but the practice continued to flourish in spite of the halfhearted efforts of law enforcement authorities to put a stop to it. On this night two vehicles occupied the small parking area. It didn't require Eddie Clark's twelve years of experience to know the circumstance was out-of-the-ordinary. Sam Mahoney, just a couple of months out of the academy, sensed it, too. Unattended vehicles, one a car and the other a van, would have been suspicious enough to warrant an investigation, but that wasn't all the two cops saw. A large group of people milled around the two vehicles.

Clark glanced at the digital clock centered in his instrument panel. "Its two-fifteen in the goddamn morning. I'd bet next month's pay they're not just dumping trash."

Mahoney already had a hand on the butt of his revolver. "Whadaya mean?"

"They're parked at a dumping site—an illegal one, but don't let that fool you. I'd say we got a bunch of drunks, kid—or maybe a bunch of dopers or glue sniffers."

Mahoney straightened his posture. "Let's check 'em out."

Clark was slowing down as he approached the gathering. Specific details emerged. "Check out that fancy van."

"Awesome!"

Mahoney's choice of a word caused the veteran to do a double take. His sixteen-year-old daughter called everything "awesome." The rookies were either getting younger, or he was getting older . . . much older.

"Some paint job," Mahoney said.

Customarily, vehicle color was difficult to judge at night, but in this instance the van's hue was undeniably fire-engine red. Flame decals decorated the side that was visible to them.

"Keep your guard up," Clark warned as he eased the cruiser to a stop.

Mahoney pulled his pistol.

The veteran caught the movement from the corner of his eye. "What the hell do you think you're doing?"

"What's it look like, goddammit?"

"Put the gun back."

"Christ, Clark—" He returned the sidearm to its holster.

"When your sidearm clears your leather, you'd best be on the verge of pulling the trigger. I'm your T.O., and I don't need all the bureaucratic bullshit that goes along with a drawn gun. I'm gonna radio in our position. You stay put until I'm done."

As Clark slid the cruiser into PARK, he half expected the group to make a panicky break for their cars. In a way, he wished they would. Burdened as he was with a gung-ho but untested rookie, he didn't relish the idea of a confrontation with a drunken mob. Not a single member of the party appeared to be fresh from a late-night revival meeting.

Redneck hippies . . . that was the description that came to Clark's mind.

He counted at least ten of them, all of varying shapes and sizes and only one of which was indisputably female. It was hard to tell about the others. Several wore their hair long, and only a few sported telltale beards. Most of their faces were turned toward him, but a few seemed otherwise occupied. At what he couldn't be sure . . . too damned many for him to watch.

Clark had the radio transmitter in his hands. Both of the vehicles faced him, so there was no way he could comply with a regulation that required him to radio a tag number to the dispatcher before he exited the cruiser. West Virginia only required a tag on the rear of the vehicle. Just another example of the kind of legislative ignorance that frustrated cops.

"Keep your eyes on 'em, Sam."

"Will do."

The senior officer depressed the key on the mike. "Unit 280 to station."

Several long seconds passed as they waited for the dispatcher, located some twenty-five miles away, to acknowledge. Clark kept his eyes on the group, and several of them were looking at the cruiser. The radio remained silent. It was possible his transmission wasn't even reaching the station. The rugged terrain often devoured radio signals.

"The big guy's heading this way," Mahoney warned.

With a quick flick of a button, Clark shifted the transmission of his voice from the radio to a small but potent loudspeaker installed in the cruiser's grill.

"Stay where you are," he commanded. "All of you, remain in sight—in the open."

The giant of a man who had been approaching the cruiser stopped. His knees curved in toward each other, as if bent by the weight he carried. He wore a red plaid shirt and bib overalls. A floppy, sweat-stained hat drooped down over the upper portion of his face, and a full unkempt beard concealed the lower portion. He held up his skillet-size hands in a signal of amiable confusion. The gesture did nothing to ease Clark's anxiety. The man in the floppy hat, along with the rest, looked about as guilty as folks could look, which prompted Clark to reach down to unstrap the hammer guard on the regulation .357. That simple act of preparatory self-defense violated no regulations.

"Where the hell's Lizzie?" Clark asked aloud. He flipped the mike back to RADIO and repeated his call to the station.

Immediately a female voice said, "Station to Unit 280. Go ahead."

Clark cleared his throat, trying not to sound too nervous. "We'll be out on the River Road with two suspect vehicles and a group of individuals. At this time, plate numbers are unknown.''

A moment's silence, then the dispatcher responded, ''Repeat your traffic, 280. Did you say *two* vehicles?''

''Affirmative.''

''Do you need assistance?''

Clark had to smile. Lizzie McOwen had been a dispatcher for the local state police detachment for a very long time. The question was her way of asking Clark if he might be biting off more than he could chew. As far as she was concerned, Sam Mahoney represented useless baggage to her veteran unit.

''Lemme check it out, Lizzie. I don't know what I've got.''

''Give me a better location, 280.''

''Jesus Christ,'' Mahoney said, anxious to exit the car.

Clark gave his young cohort a chilling look as he returned her traffic. ''I'm approximately five miles southeast of Tipple Town at the off-road dump site.''

''Ten four, 280.''

Mahoney's fingers were on the door handle. At that point, he clicked it open. The dispatcher, though, wasn't finished.

''Please follow with a description of the vehicles,'' she said.

Mahoney grumbled in frustration, but he remained in the cruiser.

Clark was studying the vehicles. ''Be advised that one is a customized red van, a Dodge maybe . . . with flame decals. The other appears to be a very old and very rusty Chevy, maybe a Malibu. Let us check 'em out, Lizzie. I'll get back to you.''

''Be careful,'' she cautioned.

Clark dropped the transmitter in the seat.

"Jesus," Mahoney was saying, "is she always like that?"

"Lemme tell you one thing, kid. She's worth ten damned pistols. She's the best protection you got out here, and she knows her job. Once we're out, you stay by the car—behind the cover of the door. I'll do the talking. Understand?"

"Sure, Eddie—"

Clark's jaw set. "I mean it, Mahoney. Don't get trigger happy."

"Yes, sir."

The suspects had ceased much of their movement after Clark had spoken to them over the loudspeaker. As he exited his cruiser, his mind was on his wife and two kids. That's the way it always happened when he was in a tight spot, and he often wondered if it was the same with other cops, those with families at least. The guys with whom he worked never compared those kind of notes. Each man came to grips with his apprehension—his fear—in his own silent fashion . . . except maybe for the rookies, who were too stupid to be afraid.

In this instance, he had to depend upon a rookie to cover his back. It wasn't the best of feelings, but that's the way it was. A guy had to play the hand he was dealt. He placed the palm of his hand on the revolver's grips as he moved toward the front of the cruiser and closer to the man who had started to approach. In his other hand Clark carried a long flashlight.

The man raised a welcoming hand. "How ya' doin', sir?"

Clark stopped. The subject's body spread so wide that it obstructed his view of the others. "Just stand where you are, friend."

The suspect held out his hands to demonstrate they were empty. "Hey, officer, no problem. We're just shootin' the shit . . . passin' the time of day, so to speak. No trouble here at all."

Clark could tell nothing about the man. Even in the point-blank glare of the cruiser's headlights, the drooping hat brim and wild beard concealed his face.

"Kinda late for a roadside picnic," Mahoney said from behind Clark.

Dammit, kid! Shut up! Clark would reprimand him once they were clear of this.

The suspect shrugged. "It's a nice night. We just saw some friends and started chewing the fat. Nothing wrong with that. Surely we ain't botherin' nobody way out here. There ain't no house within several miles."

Of that Clark needed no reminder. The isolation of the place—and the odds—weighed heavily on the veteran trooper's mind. Clark wanted to get a closer look at the faces of the other people. Maybe he knew some of them? Maybe one or two would be on the list of folks wanted for some violation or the other? Eddie Clark had been a cop in Raven County long enough to know most of the repeat offenders.

He had a gut feeling that they were somehow up to no good. They appeared just a little too antsy, almost frightened. He caught sight of one shadowy figure—a man judging by the bulk of the figure—inching away from the revealing reach of the headlights.

"Move back with your friends, pal."

The man in the overalls shrugged. "Whatever you say, officer."

The words were polite, but Clark recognized the smug contempt in the coarse voice. It was a tone you heard frequently once you put on a uniform. Usually it came from someone who knew the system from the wrong side. He kept a wary watch on the man as he backed toward the group.

"Take it slow and easy," he heard Mahoney say.

The damned kid. The rookie couldn't stand it. He had to get in on the act.

Clark noticed the girl as soon as the big man moved back beside her. She stood rock still, almost rigid, her eyes wide and ripe with fear. A lot of folks were frightened by cops, but her appearance went beyond that. If he'd been pressed to describe her look, he would have called it the face of terror—the same kind of look that must seize a face in that horrible split second before a head-on car crash. Her eyes gleamed with what appeared to be tears. He gazed deeply into them and saw the plea for help.

At that instant, a whining cry—muffled and seemingly distant—electrified the air.

"What the hell is that?" Mahoney said, stunned by the strange sound.

Clark tensed, too.

"A baby," the man in the overalls said quickly. "It's in the van here. Must need changing or something."

Clark's instinctual antenna vibrated. The atmosphere was taut, like a big rubber band stretched far beyond its limits, ready to snap at any time. Something was wrong. Not a single member of the party appeared to be drunk, at least not to the degree that they could be charged with public intox. The guy in the rear nagged at his experience, the one who seemed to be working so desperately to stay out of sight. He'd get to him in just a minute. It was the woman who intrigued him. He fixed his attention on her. She was willing him a message with her frantic eyes. He flicked on the flashlight and aimed it squarely at her face. Her lower lip trembled; her flat manly chest heaved. The beam of light lifted back to her face for a second. He waited, hoping she would speak. When she did not, the beam returned to the face of the behemoth of a man who had stepped forward to greet them. There was no fear in his eyes—just a cruel smile of amusement.

"I need some ID, pal," Clark said.

"You bet, sir." He started to come forward.

"Stay put!" Mahoney commanded.

Clark stiffened as he struggled to contain his fury. He wanted to pistol-whip the smart-mouthed rookie. Instead, he spoke to the suspect in a firm and unemotional tone. "Just pull out your driver's license and hand it to the young lady there. She can bring it to me."

The huge man smiled, revealing tobacco-stained teeth. "Yessiree. It's in my hip pocket."

"Reach for it slow and easy." Five years ago, Clark would have already pulled the .357. Not these days. Like he'd told Mahoney, nowadays you didn't even pull a gun unless you had cause to use it.

As the man reached back to his hip pocket, Clark watched the others. Some were grinning; others appeared almost as stiff—as frightened maybe—as the girl. The beam of his flashlight roamed in search of the elusive figure in the rear of the crowd. Finally, it isolated the troubled face of its quarry—the man who had so stubbornly sought concealment. Clark squinted. The man obliged by stepping forward.

"Jesus," Clark said as recognition dawned, "what the hell are you doing here?"

From behind him, Clark heard the sharp intake of breath. He turned to look back. Mahoney's hand was full of gun. That's when all hell broke loose. The sheer force of an explosion—its sound lost to the agonizing shock—impelled Clark back against the grille of the cruiser. The vehicle's hood ornament gouged into the flesh of his back. Then the pain was everywhere, searing and consuming. An incessant thunder warped the night air. In those short tormented moments, he caught sight of the passenger door of the cruiser flying past

. . . Mahoney, too. The very last thing Eddie Clark heard was the frantic wailing of the baby.

Lizzie McOwen drummed her fingers on the surface of the desk as she waited for a response from Clark. He and the rookie had been out of the car—at least off the radio—for a good ten minutes. According to policy, she was to wait five more minutes for traffic from him. Then she was to radio him. This time, though, she didn't wait five minutes. Clark had had more than enough time to obtain the vehicles' tag numbers and radio them to her. That, too, was policy, and Clark was one of the few troopers who routinely followed policy. He was at that age when life's value tripled.

"Station to Unit 280." Lizzie paused for him to reply. Thirty seconds turned into an eternity without so much as a crackle of static.

"Station to Unit 280. Please respond." Her voice now possessed a sense of urgency. Perspiration from her hand trickled down the mike stand she clutched.

She'd been dispatching for the department a decade. She'd lost her husband five years before, and her own two children had long since relocated. It wasn't surprising that she became so attached to "her boys"— her words for the troopers with whom she worked. Many young men in green came and left during her years with the detachment, but she had yet to bury one of them. Those who had left the department or who had been transferred to another detachment stayed in touch with Lizzie. She sent each one a small container of homemade candy at Christmas and considered them family, and a few, such as Eddie Clark, were almost as dear to her as her own children.

More than likely he was too far from the car to hear her transmission. She hoped that was it. Clark was the only unit she had patrolling that night. She decided to try one more time before dialing the number of the Raven County Sheriff's Department for assistance.

She pushed down the key on the mike. "Darn you, Eddie. You answer me. Right now!"

ONE

ANNA TYREE GRABBED THE PHONE on the first ring—
the first ring she had heard anyway. She mumbled a
sleepy "hello" into the mouthpiece.

"Anna?"

Even handicapped by a groggy mind, she recognized
the familiar voice of Tony Danton, Raven County's
prosecuting attorney.

"Jesus, Tony. It's late."

"Sorry to bother you, but I need to talk to Whit."

Anna sought out the digital alarm clock on the other
side of the room. Her eyes struggled to focus. "What
time is it?"

"Three A.M., Anna."

Her reporter's instinct took hold, and her mind shifted
into gear as she righted herself in the bed. "What's
going on, Tony?"

The man beside her stirred and turned toward her.
The bedroom was dark, but she knew he was awake—
that his eyes were open.

"Just put him on the phone, Anna."

She ran a hand through her long, auburn hair. "Come
on, Tony. If you're calling Whit at this hour, I know
it's gotta be something big. I'll find out sooner or later.
Why make it hard on you and me, too?"

"Dammit, Anna. I need to talk to Whit. Now!"

"What's gotten into you, Tony?"

16

"I didn't mean to snap, Anna. May I please talk to Whit?"

Before she could reply, a hand shot out of the darkness to rob her of the phone.

Whit Pynchon, the investigator for the Raven County prosecuting attorney, rolled rudely over top of her and settled down on the side of the bed. "What the hell's up, Tony?"

"Can Anna hear?"

She had bounded out of bed and was turning on the bedroom light.

Whit glanced at her. "I don't think so, but whatever it is, she's right. She'll find out sooner or later."

"Let's make it later this time. We've just had a massacre out on the River Road. Five bodies at least, and two of them are state troopers, Eddie Clark and a rookie."

"Oh, sweet Jesus—"

"Yeah. It doesn't get any worse than this."

"A shoot-out?" Whit asked. At once, he was sorry he had spoken his thought aloud. Anna went rigid with militant curiosity, poised to read his reaction to the reply from the prosecutor.

"I dunno, pal. That's what you and I need to find out. Pick me up and we'll head out there."

Whit's head drooped. "I'm on my way."

"Hold it a second. I'm serious as hell about not telling Anna. The last thing we need is a bunch of reporters out there until we know what the hell went down. This is one crime scene I want frozen in time. From what I understand, it's a goddamn bloodbath."

"My oath of silence." Whit hung up the phone.

"Your oath of silence!" Anna's youthful face was ripe with outrage. "Just who the hell do you two think you are? I know something's happened. If there's been a shoot-out of some kind—"

Whit dropped back on the bed. "Jesus, Anna, it's too early in the morning for this."

"Dammit, Whit. I'm the editor of the newspaper. I can't just pretend I didn't hear any of this. We have a right—"

Whit, his face rosy with his own escalating anger, catapulted himself from the bed. "I swear to God I'm gonna quit this job. I've had a curdling gut full of reporter's rights. I've read the Constitution. The word 'reporter' isn't there, Anna. This job's bad enough as it is without having to go through this every time I get a phone call."

She pursued him into the bathroom. "What do you expect me to do?"

"Behave."

"What does that mean?"

He was standing over the toilet. "I apologize. It was a tasteless, highly offensive thing to say. Actually, I'd be tickled pink if you would take 'no comment' for an answer just once in a while. Try it sometime. You might discover that the gods of yellow journalism won't automatically revoke your press card."

"Very funny."

The pressure in his bladder was intense. "I'd also like to take a leak, which I can't seem to manage in the middle of an argument."

Anna's pretty face flushed a deep red as she turned away from him. "I'm sorry. I wasn't thinking."

Whit had to laugh. "You're still the prettiest woman I ever woke up with."

"Go to hell." She slammed the bathroom door shut on him.

Whit finished at the toilet and then went to the mirror where he groaned at the reflection. His thick, graying hair stuck out in all directions, and his face—itself just beginning to show its first wrinkles—was shadowed by stubble. Each time he looked into a mirror he saw another new sign of middle age, which was a nice way to say impending old age. He took some comfort in the dark halo around his chin. His beard hadn't turned to gray yet. Maybe this would be the day he started to grow the beard . . . just in case it made him look a year or so younger. He used a wet comb to tame the hair as much as possible and decided to disregard the stubble. After all, it was 3:00 A.M. in the frigging morning. He could decide about the beard later.

Sounds of feverish activity—a closet door slamming, drawers opening—penetrated the closed bathroom door. He took a few moments to load his toothbrush with Colgate before he opened it to investigate.

By that time, Anna sat on the bed, dressed in a bra and panties, struggling with a pair of worn blue jeans.

"Just what the hell do you think you're doing?"

"Getting dressed. What does it look like I'm doing?"

"If you think you're going to follow me—"

"The last I heard it's still a free country. You remember reading that in the Constitution?"

Whit slumped against the door frame. "No, not specifically, but then I haven't read it since eighth grade civics."

"It shows."

"C'mon, Anna. You sound like some punk kid nabbed on the street after curfew."

She stood and hiked the jeans up to her waspish waist. "Yeah, well, I know the smell of something big, and that's how I make my living—making sure that the *Journal* doesn't miss something big."

Whit finished brushing and then went to the bed. He sat down beside where she stood. "You're putting me in a hell of a bad position."

"Only because you insist on putting me in one first. I've got no choice."

Whit shrugged. "Okay, neither do I then."

She had stepped to the closet and was searching for a blouse. His words made her turn. "What do you mean?"

Whit had the phone in his hand and was jabbing buttons.

A baffled frown formed on her face. "What are you doing?"

He ignored the question. When the unknown party he was calling answered, he said, "This is Pynchon. I'm getting ready to leave my house. Send a unit over here. If Anna Tyree attempts to follow me, arrest her for obstructing justice."

"You jerk!" Anna shouted.

But Whit's attention was still on the phone conversation. "I *know* she's the goddamned editor of the paper. Do it on my authority—and tell that unit to hustle."

He reeled off the address and hung up the phone. "You're off the hook, hon."

"What the hell does that mean?"

"I just resolved your professional dilemma." He rose from the bed and marched into the hall where he opened a closet, withdrawing a pancake holster containing a 9-mm automatic. He slipped the weapon in his hip pocket.

She followed him. "Whit, you're making one hell of a mistake. I swear to God I'll spread this all over the front page—and the editorial page, too."

"Won't bother me a damned bit. I never read the paper, remember?" He pulled a worn corduroy sports coat from the same closet. "Once I get a handle on things, I'll try to fill you in."

"Don't try to humor me, Whit Pynchon." She was in his face, the beauty of her blue eyes intensified by cold anger. "You're going too far this time! So help me, Whit—if you have me arrested—"

"If you try to follow me, you'll be arrested, Anna. You can make book on it. On the other hand, you can go back to that soft, warm bed. I promise to give you the details in time for your edition day after tomorrow . . . or today, I mean. No way can you get a story in this morning's paper anyway."

"That's not the point."

"It's not? I thought getting the story was the entire point, and I'm promising that you'll have it for your very next edition." He didn't wait for a reply. He marched to the front door and opened it. Uncommonly mild autumn air drifted into the house as he watched for the unit from the Raven County Sheriff's Department.

At least winter was being held at bay. Whit despised the cold weather and spent most of the months between October and March in what Anna called his arctic doldrums. This would be his last winter in West Virginia. This time no one, including the voice of his own common sense, would dupe him into staying.

Anna had vanished into the bedroom. He heard her talking, probably to Kathy Binder, the new publisher of the *Milbrook Daily Journal.* He didn't want to hear what she had to say, so he slipped out onto the front porch and closed the door behind him. A gentle breeze filtered through the skeletal, leafless trees that lined the street. Bright stars twinkled in the night sky. Whit gazed up at them. For the first time, his mind was able to turn to the reason for his conflict with Anna.

A massacre. That was a word Tony Danton had used. *A bloodbath.* He said that, too.

Raven County's prosecutor wasn't given to overstatement.

Whit's mind focused on Eddie Clark. He was a vet-

eran trooper—a pretty decent officer in Whit's opinion.
He didn't know much about the trooper's personal life
other than that he had a family. He knew that much.
The killing of a cop, especially in the line of duty, always escalated into a super-murder. The details of the
death would be teletyped to every police agency in the
country that had one of the machines. Shift command-
ers would run several copies, post them on bulletin
boards, stick them into faces of their rookies . . . just
to prove it can and does happen.

A second message would issue from Raven County
sometime during the coming day, announcing the time
of the funeral services and inviting officers to attend
who wished to pay their department's respects. When
received, that, too, would be clipped and posted and
saved. Departments from across the country would reply by teletype, sometimes by phone, offering condolences and assistance. Many officers would attend the
service, some of them from miles away. Even if they
didn't know Eddie Clark, they all shared with him the
potential for violent death in the line of duty. It made
them spiritual friends if nothing else. More than that,
it underscored the all-out effort that law enforcement
agencies exerted when a killer dared to claim one of
their own.

The approach of a car brought Whit back to reality.
The gray sheriff's cruiser rolled to a stop in front of the
house. Whit hurried down the steps, but he heard the
door open, then Anna's voice.

"Kathy told me to call your bluff. Neither she nor I
think you—or that deputy—have the stones to arrest
me."

The deputy was getting out of the cruiser.

Whit motioned for him.

As the deputy approached the house, Whit turned to

Anna. "I don't want to do this, and I won't if you give me your word that you won't follow me."

Anna crossed her arms. "You know better, Whit Pynchon."

"Yeah, I guess I do."

The deputy was at the steps of the house. He was a baby-faced officer, fresh enough on the job that Whit didn't recognize him.

"You know who I am?" Whit said to the confused officer.

"Yes, sir. I do."

"And your dispatcher told you who she is?"

The deputy nodded.

"I plan to get in my car," Whit was saying, "and if she tries to follow me, place her in custody for obstructing justice and take her down to the courthouse. Don't—I repeat, do not—book her. Just detain her until you hear from me."

Anna moved down the steps. "Listen, officer, I think you should know that the Milbrook paper plans to sue if you follow Whit's orders."

The deputy, his virgin face tortured by indecision, looked at Anna and then to Whit, who was on his way to his car. "Come on, folks. I don't like gettin' involved in these kind of domestic matters."

Whit stopped. "This is no goddamn domestic matter, kid—and it beats the mortal hell outa getting on the bad side of the prosecutor's office."

"Yes, sir."

Two

THE DEPUTY PLACED A GENTLE HAND just above Anna's elbow as he escorted her to his car. "I'm sorry about this, ma'am. I'm just following orders."

"That's what Hitler's Nazis said."

"I don't know much about politics—Nazis and such—but I can't afford to have the prosecuting attorney mad at me."

Anna glared at him. "You might change your mind once the newspaper's been mad at you."

He led her to the front seat on the passenger side of the cruiser.

"I don't guess there's any need to put you in the backseat behind the cage, ma'am. You can ride up front with me."

As irritated as Anna was, his comment forced her to suppress a smile. The poor kid was doing his best to mitigate his guilt. She let him off the hook just a little. "I appreciate that, Deputy . . . what's your name?"

"Frank, ma'am. Frank Wilshire."

Besides, Anna's mind was busy, and a scheme was beginning to materialize. She polished it as he circled the cruiser. He opened his door and crawled in under the steering wheel.

"How many died in the shoot-out?" she asked. "Whit didn't say."

He turned to look at her, curious about how much

she knew. Since she was going to be in custody, he saw no harm in answering her as best he could. Maybe she wouldn't be so mad at him afterward. He started the car and pulled away from the curb before answering. "I don't know what all happened. I wasn't out there, but they requested at least three ambulances."

"Three?"

"Yes, ma'am. So I'd say there's quite a few casualties. I think they're all dead."

"All of them?"

"Our guy at the scene said to tell the ambulances there was no need to run a code call. That means no need for emergency lights and sirens. Plus, we were told to call the local medical examiner and a photographer. I hear the state police lab in Charleston has already dispatched a forensic team."

The cruiser rolled through residential Milbrook. At that time of night, the streets were lifeless. Fallen leaves, dancing across the pavement on the arms of the southwesterly breeze, provided the only visible movement.

"I didn't think anything motivated the troops that fast."

The deputy shrugged. "You know how it is when one of your own gets it."

Be careful, Anna told herself. "I can't place the officer who was shot."

"One? There were two—Clark and Mahoney, a rookie. Clark was one of the older guys . . . a trooper first class, I think. I never met him, but the dispatcher said he was a nice guy."

"Oh yeah. What was his first name? I forget."

"They called him Eddie."

Anna made mental notes. "I don't think I knew the rookie."

"Mahoney . . . Sam Mahoney. At least they think he's dead. They haven't found the body yet."

"What?"

"That's how I understood it, ma'am."

"Exactly where did it happen?" In asking the question, Anna employed a tone of voice that implied she had some general notion as to the answer, which—of course—she did not.

"I'm kinda new at this job, ma'am. I'm still not real familiar with the entire county, but I heard them say it was several miles east of Tipple Town on the River Road—around some trash dump."

"The River Road?" Not many weeks before, the *Daily Journal* had done a feature on the dangerous condition of the highway. School bus drivers had been refusing to drive over it until some portions were reinforced. One of the photos that was published with the story showed the notorious trash dump. The following day, Anna's front page editorial had scalded the state Department of Highways for disregarding public safety in the matter of the River Road.

"You know it?"

"I sure do. Anyone in custody yet?"

The deputy chuckled. "Are you kidding? It's an honest-to-God mystery. From what I hear, the troopers' car is even gone, like maybe the culprits fled in it. We got a B.O.L.O. out for the cruiser."

"I'll be damned," she said.

The deputy glanced at her. "Hey, now you can't use any of this."

"Oh, of course," Anna said.

"What the hell took you so long?" Tony asked as he slid in Whit's car.

"I had to wait on a deputy sheriff."

"What the hell for?"

"To arrest Anna."

Danton's sharp intake of breath made Whit laugh.

The prosecutor wasn't amused. "Jesus, couldn't you have handled it some other way, Whit?"

"Hell, Tony, you know Anna as well as I do. She loves to play the part of a crusty newswoman. She's in seventh heaven when she can sacrifice herself for her journalistic principles."

"Yeah, but you're something of an authority on role-playing, too."

Whit, by then back on the road, sneaked a quick look at his boss. "What the hell does that mean?"

"You like to play the strong silent type. I bet you've seen every damned movie John Wayne made."

"Like hell. Spencer Tracy maybe, but not John Wayne. Besides, getting back to Anna, I didn't have the time to argue with her. It'll give her something to write about other than . . . well, other than whatever we've got here. What about this massacre? That's a loaded word to use."

"Five bodies is a load of death."

Whit glanced at his boss. "Five for sure?"

"At least—maybe more. Hell, we've got a situation here with a body count. I gave strict orders for the ambulance crews to leave them as they are."

The comment produced a wry laugh from Whit. The last murder he'd worked had been a drunken shoot-out in one of the local beer joints. When he'd arrived at the scene, he'd found a paramedic, encircled by a crowd of drunks, trying to give artificial respiration to a corpse with a hole the size of a grapefruit through the chest. Every time the paramedic exhaled into the body, bloody bubbles oozed out of the chest wound.

"Public relations," the paramedic had explained when Whit had chastised him for disturbing the crime scene. "Folks get mad if you don't try to do something."

After that, the prosecutor himself had written to the

various emergency medical units in the county, admonishing them against such misplaced heroism on behalf of crime victims in need of resurrection rather than resuscitation.

A full forty minutes after Whit had met Tony, they reached the isolated scene. Police vehicles and ambulances clogged the straight stretch of mountain highway.

"My God," Whit said, "I can tell this is gonna be fun. Half the damn county is here already."

"Just stay cool," Tony said. "Emotions will be running pretty high."

Whit parked his car behind an ambulance, and the two men got out. Most of the police vehicles still had their engines running, and the night air was heavy with exhaust fumes. Beneath the aroma of oxidized fuel, Whit detected the sweet stench of the garbage dump. A tall but slouching figure—a man dressed in denim jeans and a pullover sweater—approached Whit's vehicle.

"We tried to keep 'em from moving Clark's body," the man was saying, breathless from the excitement, "but we've got a division lieutenant from the state police here. He insisted." Captain Ross Sinclair, recently promoted from his lieutenant's rank where he had been in charge of the civil process and service of warrants for the sheriff, appeared overwhelmed by the magnitude of the incident.

"Jeez, Sinclair! You mean they've moved Clark?" Tony asked.

"We don't leave our men lying dead in trash dumps," a stern voice announced. It issued from a uniformed officer who came up behind the captain. He probably wasn't any taller than Sinclair, but his rigid posture certainly created the impression that he was. He sported the insignia of a lieutenant on the expertly pressed green uniform of the West Virginia State Police. "We don't leave our men lying in trash piles," he repeated.

"This is Tony Danton," Sinclair told the lieutenant. "He's the county prosecutor."

Danton had no interest in introductions. He ignored the trooper's outstretched hand. "Dammit, in this county you don't run the show."

The lieutenant maintained a cold, official smile as he pulled back his hand. "This county or any other, it's the same, Mr. Danton. We respect our dead. We did take some photographs to preserve the scene."

Whit had been hanging back from the conversation, but he stepped forward at that point. "At least he's not a total incompetent, Tony."

The smile vanished from the officer's face. "Who the fuck are you?"

Sheriff Ted Early, himself no great admirer of Whit's, had joined the group and tried to offer an introduction. "That's Whit Pynchon—"

"I've heard of you," the trooper said. "The sheriff here was saying that you'd probably want to handle the investigation."

"It's not a matter of what I want. I didn't catch your name."

"Slack. Just for the record—" With those magic words, he turned back to the prosecutor. "We'll handle this investigation. The cooperation of the sheriff and your office, Mr. Danton, will, of course, be appreciated."

Whit found Tony looking at him, the hint of a cruel smile on the prosecutor's swarthy face.

"Slack, is it?" Tony asked.

"Yes, sir. John Slack. I'm from division headquarters up in—"

"I know where you are from. I also know that the prosecution of crime in Raven County takes place under my direction. We'd best reach a meeting of the minds here and now."

Slack shrugged. "There's really not much use to discuss it. We have certain policies—"

"—which don't make a damn to me," Tony snapped. "I have policies, too, and in this county they supersede."

Tony closed the distance between himself and the state police lieutenant, who towered a good foot above the short lawyer. "Among those policies is an iron-clad rule. Whit Pynchon investigates all homicides in Raven County, and it doesn't make a tinker's damn whether the victim wears the green of a state trooper or the rags of a pauper. Do I make myself clear, Lieutenant?"

Sheriff Early and Sinclair were giving the two warriors plenty of room. Whit had been keeping his eyes on the trooper, just in case he lost his cool. He had to give the trooper credit. He didn't wilt under Tony's verbal assault. Instead, he stood there, the anger flashing in his eyes. "Under such circumstances, sir, my instructions are to contact the superintendent of the department who in turn contacts the governor—"

Tony wasn't moved by the threat. "Friend, you can call God himself if you know his number. I've told you how it's gonna be."

By that time, paramedics and cops alike had been attracted by the heated exchange.

The trooper's eyes narrowed. "You have an attitude problem I can't understand, Mr. Danton. Our men are perfectly competent to—"

"Sometimes they are. Sometimes they aren't," Tony interjected. "It doesn't matter. In Raven County, a law enforcement agency doesn't investigate crimes committed against one of its members—or for that matter crimes committed by one of its members. And, in Raven County, Whit Pynchon heads all homicide investigations. If you can't live with that, Lieutenant, then I suggest you tuck tail and haul ass back to division head-quarters so the rest of us can get busy on the case.''

Tony's eyes locked with those of the lieutenant for a brief moment. He then said, ''Come on, Whit. Let's see what they've managed to screw up.''

The two officials from the prosecutor's office pushed their way out of the crowd. Whit's eyes happened to catch sight of Al Downing, a corporal with the local state police detachment. Downing's face was downcast, grieved by the loss of one of his closest friends, but in spite of the pain he managed a friendly wink.

Whit gave Tony a slight tug, and together they approached Downing.

''Glad you're gonna handle it,'' the corporal said softly. ''Slack there's a real asshole.''

''Whatcha got?'' Whit asked.

''A gut-wrenching mess. There were five bodies in the trash dump, including Eddie's. Four of them are still there. At first we thought they took the cruiser and Sam Mahoney. He's the rookie. Now we're not so sure. We think we've found it.''

Whit was puzzled. ''How do you mean? The cruiser's gone, isn't it?''

Downing shrugged. ''Yeah, but it looks like it went over the side of the mountain.''

They approached the van. Its condition drew a stunned whistle from the prosecutor's investigator. ''Damn, Al! What the hell did that?'' He surveyed the tight pattern of ugly holes that peppered the ornate finish of the van.

Downing reached up to touch one of the punctures. ''We'd say double-ought buckshot. It looks like that's what got Eddie and the rest.''

''Buckshot?'' Tony said. ''Jeez, I've never seen damage that extensive, even from double-ought.''

Downing nodded. ''Wait'll you see the victims.''

But Whit was still examining the van—in particular a dark fluid seeping from one of the round holes down near the frame, just below the sliding door on the passenger side. "Have you searched it?"

"We took a quick look inside to see if anyone was there. We didn't see anything."

Whit smeared his forefinger through the liquid and brought it up for them to see. "Maybe we'd better take another look. This looks like blood."

The corporal closed his eyes. "Oh, hell. Maybe it's Mahoney."

"Which door did you open?"

"The rear," Downing said.

"Let's open this one."

"Bring some light over here!" the corporal shouted.

Whit had his hand on the door handle. "It's so badly damaged it might not open."

Tony took a step back. "Give it a try."

It opened with surprising ease.

The lifeless body of an infant rolled out onto the surface of the road.

THREE

As SOON AS ANNA WAS INSIDE the jail, she asked to make a phone call. The young deputy who had arrested her was momentarily speechless. When he did speak, his voice was weak with uncertainty. "I dunno. That guy—Pynchon?—he didn't say you could make any calls."

"C'mon, Frank, the law says I can make a call. I have a right to a phone call."

A second deputy sat at the radio console. He had looked up when Anna used the deputy's first name. "Yeah, *Frank*. We give everybody a phone call. That's the rule . . . unless we got a court order saying otherwise."

Wilshire was shaking his head. "I just don't know. That fella with the prosecutor's office might not want—"

The dispatcher made a face. "If you mean Pynchon, the hell with him. Give the lady her call."

Anna suppressed a laugh. Good ol' Whit—he sure didn't know much about winning friends and influencing people. "If that's how you feel," she said, "why was this department so willing to accommodate him?"

The deputy at the console dropped his eyes to the magazine he was reading. "Just make your call, lady. If it's long distance, it's gotta be collect."

"This phone?" She was staring down at one beside the radio.

"Can't you read? It says Official Use Only."

"So—"

"Down the corridor there."

Anna saw it hanging on a dirty wall. She moved toward it. The deputy who had arrested her started to follow, but she wheeled on him. "I'd like some privacy."

The deputy looked back to the dispatcher, who was obviously his superior.

"She ain't gonna escape, kid. Let her be. As soon as she finishes the call, book her in."

Anna started to object, but the arresting officer beat her to it. "That Pynchon guy said not to book her—"

"I done told you!" the dispatcher snapped. "Screw Pynchon. He doesn't run this department."

Anna couldn't help it this time. In spite of the prospect of being booked, whatever that involved, she laughed a little as she hurried down to phone Kathleen Binder. The *Journal*'s publisher answered on the third ring.

"Have I got a story," Anna said. "I'm about to be booked in jail—"

"Jail?" the sleepy voice said. "He really did it?"

"I'll get to that in a minute. First, I'm going to tell you where to send a reporter—and be sure it's one that knows how to use a camera."

"A drug deal gone sour," Whit pronounced.

Tony, still shaken by the sight of the dead infant, nodded in sullen accord as he and Whit examined a residue of white powder on the bloody-damp carpet of the van.

Downing stood behind them. "According to our dispatcher, Eddie radioed that he was stopping to check out two vehicles, a van and an old Chevy.''

"Did you put out a B.O.L.O. on the Chevy?''

Downing shook his head. "We did on the cruiser. I started to issue one on the other vehicle, but Slack overruled me. He said the description was too vague.''

Whit sighed. "Issue the B.O.L.O.—the hell with Slack. Let's go take a look at the rest of the carnage.''

"The lights!'' Downing shouted as he led them behind the van. "Bring 'em back over here.''

A battery of flashlights was aimed down at the sprawling clutter of trash. The bodies were piled in the center. As the lights fell on them, three cat-size rats scurried away into the dark woods.

"Jesus,'' Whit said, "did you see that?''

Slack had come up behind them. "That's why I got Clark's body out of there.''

"You coulda just put a guard down there with a light,'' Whit said. "Let's go take a closer.''

No one—not even Slack—rushed to join Whit. The odor from the dump site was bad enough. The thought of plodding through it, especially after seeing the size of the rodents, was enough to make the toughest cop think twice. Whit, though, didn't hesitate. Slack, accompanied by Downing and the prosecutor, was compelled to follow.

"They're ripped apart,'' Whit said, stunned by the extent of the mutilations.

As disturbing as the sight of the infant had been, the frail and limp body hadn't been savaged. Death had resulted, it appeared, from a single wound in the diminutive chest. The casualties in the trash dump hadn't met with death quite so gracefully. Whatever the killing weapon had been, it had reduced portions of its victims to bloody mush.

Three men and a woman, Whit decided.

The bodies of the men had each suffered extensive damage, but the woman's injuries were restricted to her abdominal and pelvic regions. In a way, she was the worst of them all—except for the child . . . her child? To Whit's mind, nothing was worse than a dead child, not even a mutilated mother. Whit couldn't take his eyes from the woman's gray and pasty face. It didn't look real, more like a grainy photograph, frozen in time by the terror the eyes had witnessed. If it had been her child, had she known of its fate before she died? Whit realized he didn't even know whether the infant had been male or female.

As he knelt over the woman, he saw that a chunk of her right ear was missing—chewed away, it appeared, by one of the damn filthy rats. No matter what she had been . . . what her character had been, he hoped that she hadn't known the fate of the child.

He glanced up at Tony. "I don't see a lot to be gained by leaving them here."

The prosecutor frowned. "The state police have their crime scene van on the way. They might find something."

Whit's gaze roamed around the area in which they stood. It was covered with aluminum cans, bottles and fragments of bottles, stained grocery bags flecked with old coffee grounds, soiled Kotex. That's what he called them anyway, in spite of the actual brand. "Do you really think they're gonna be able to do much of a crime scene investigation in this?"

Defeated by the sheer volume of human debris, any or none of which might be trace evidence, Tony shook his head. "Naw. I guess not. They sure as hell picked an ideal place to pull this one."

The prosecutor glanced at Slack, whose chest ballooned over what he perceived to be a vindication of his decision to move Clark's body.

Downing quickly ruptured the lieutenant's nonverbal gloating when he called their attention to an area on the edge of the dump. At that point, the woods themselves vanished as the slope dropped away to the creek bed several hundred feet below.

"It looks like a car went over the side there," Downing explained. "See those tire running tracks through the edge of the dump site? We've tried to look over the edge, but you can't see a goddamned thing down there."

Whit abandoned the bodies and moved toward the area indicated by the corporal. Tony headed back up to the highway.

Just a few feet beyond Downing, the mountainside turned into a cliff. "That'll have to wait for dawn. I just hope to hell Mahoney's not down there alive and injured," Downing said.

Whit moved as close to the precipice as his fear of heights allowed. "Me, too."

Tony stood with Captain Ross Sinclair behind the van. "How far is it to the bottom of the ravine?"

"Several hundred feet, Tony."

"What miserable country," the prosecutor said. He glanced at the officer with the sheriff's department. "How's your wife, Ross?"

Most of those involved in any way with law enforcement knew that Sinclair's wife continued to suffer from a long bout with cancer. If you believed the scuttlebutt, the big C was about to win.

The droop to Sinclair's shoulder became more pronounced. "I just brought her back today from another treatment in Roanoke. Those things are worse than the . . ." His voice trailed off. As his wife's illness had progressed, it had become increasingly difficult for him to use its proper name. "The doctor says that's just about the last time they can do it."

"I know how rough it is. My father had it."

"I just hate to see her suffer so."

Whit rejoined Tony. "It'll be hell pulling a vehicle out of there."

Sinclair looked back at the ravaged van. "This one's got North Carolina plates on it."

"That fits the pattern," Whit said. "Most of the big drug traffic—at least the cocaine—is filtering up from Carolina."

"I'd say there was a delivery set for here," Tony said. "The buyers—or the intended buyers—saw a chance to get a lotta dope free."

Downing, who had followed Whit, nodded his agreement. "And Eddie and the Mahoney kid arrived at the wrong time."

"The lieutenant there—" Downing nodded toward his lieutenant, who stood just outside his own unmarked cruiser with the mike cord stretched to the max. "Well, he's gonna make trouble. He's on the radio, having them patch him through to Charleston."

But Tony showed no concern. "What kinda trouble can he make, Al?"

"You can be damned sure of one thing. He'll take his best shot. He's one of the super's favorite guys. Didn't you notice all that brown on his nose?"

Whit smiled. "And I thought all the smell came from the trash pile there."

The prosecutor's investigator turned his attention back to the bodies. About eight police officers held flashlights on the scene as the ambulance crews moved cautiously down toward the remains. Disgust twisted the faces of the paramedics. Not so much because of the gore—that was their stock and trade—but rather because of the odorous refuse through which they walked. Their feet stirred the trash, releasing deep and potent pockets of stench against which they had developed no tolerance.

Whit moved to intercept them. "As you load each of them, check for a wallet."

They started to work first on the woman. The process went slowly. Most folks who had never tried to lift a body had no idea how ponderous it could be—something not unlike a sack of half-full potatoes. The weight seemed always to shift away from the point at which the body was grasped. If they could have simply hauled the bodies by their limbs from the refuse pile, it would have been easier. It didn't work that way. Crime scene procedure demanded that the cumbersome bodies be placed in a sealable plastic bag before they were carried the short distance up the slope to the waiting ambulances. It minimized the chance of losing valuable evidence—anything from bullets to body parts and even hair. The occurrence of a crime didn't suspend the law of gravity. Whit could remember shooting cases in which the bullets had actually dropped from the victims' wounds as their bodies were moved.

The woman's body yielded no identification, so they tagged her as Jane Doe. Tony had moved up to the highway and was talking with some of the officers. Whit remained ankle deep in the noxious trash pile, shaking his head at the wobbly crew of ambulance attendants as they wrestled with the remains of a woman who hardly could have weighed more than a hundred pounds soaking wet. Even in death she resisted their efforts to slip her into the dark black cocoon of waterproof disposable plastic. What the hell would they do when they got to the bulky bodies of the men?

"It's easier once they get stiff," one of the attendants said to Whit.

"You take as long with the next one, and the rest will do just that."

"Funny," the paramedic grumbled.

While one team carried the woman to the ambulance, another went to work on the first of the three men. The blast had ripped away most of the guy's features. His clothes were soaked with blood. The attendants who worked with him wore rubber gloves, a direct result of the AIDS scare. While two of them tilted the limp body, a third fished for a wallet.

"No billfold here," he said, pulling his hand from a pocket.

"Make him John Doe one," another said.

Another body lay facedown in the debris. Whit moved over top of it and immediately noticed the outline of a thick wallet in his back pocket. He bent down to pull it out.

"Hey, you got no gloves on!" an attendant cried.

It startled Whit into a brief flare-up. "Don't shout at me, goddammit. I'm not gonna catch anything from a friggin' wallet."

He angrily wrestled it from the pocket. Its thickness shocked him. He opened it and thumbed through a stack of cash. Whatever the motive had been, it wasn't simply robbery. Or at least the culprits weren't interested in cash. A window in the interior face of the wallet revealed a North Carolina operator's license. A dark-haired man of about forty stared back at Whit. He read the information on the license and learned the man was—had been—thirty-six. According to the license, the victim was Ernest Felty. It gave his address as a rural box number in the postal vicinity of North Wilkesboro, North Carolina.

As Whit climbed up to the road, he counted the money. "The killers abandoned a small fortune," he said as he approached Tony. "I estimate there's about two thousand in here."

"You're kidding!"

He offered the wallet to Tony. "Count it for yourself."

The prosecutor ignored the thick wad of bills, choosing instead to read the name from the license. "Ernest Felty from North Wilkesboro. Pretty far from home. There's a purse on the seat of the van. I'd love to yank it out."

"Go ahead," Whit said.

"I'd best wait on that crime scene crew. I wouldn't wanna taint some evidence, not as much as I fuss at these guys for it." He was nodding toward the gathering of police officers.

Lieutenant Slack emerged from a segregated group of troopers and marched toward them.

"Here comes the chief greenie weenie," Whit said.

"The superintendent communicated with the governor." A slight twitch just above his right eye marred the trooper's professional demeanor as he addressed Raven County's prosecutor. "I'm directed to cooperate with you, Mr. Danton."

Whit laughed. "In other words, he *communicated* to you the score."

The lieutenant tensed; the twitch intensified.

Tony headed off a confrontation. "Ease up, Whit. I'm sure the lieutenant here sees the wisdom of it . . . now that he's had some time to reflect."

The trooper's tone remained coldly official. "I'm also advised that the crime scene van has just left the turnpike. I'm going to send one of the local officers to meet it. I suspect they'll have difficulty finding this location."

The prosecutor nodded his approval. "A good idea, Lieutenant."

"Is there anything else the prosecutor's office wishes us to do? As I said, we stand ready—"

"We got a car coming!" Ross Sinclair shouted.

The men turned. A beam of light foreshadowed the arrival of the vehicle, which itself was still around the bend and several hundred yards down the road.

"That can't be the forensics van," Whit said, "not if it just left the turnpike."

Two troopers hurried to block the road.

"Turn whoever it is around and send them back the other way," the lieutenant shouted.

The vehicle—a civilian compact—rounded the curve and jerked to a stop at the direction of the two troopers. They approached it. After a brief conversation, one of the officers headed back to where his superior officer stood with Whit and Tony.

"It's a newspaper reporter, sir."

"I'll be damned!" Whit cried. "If it's Anna—"

"It's a male, sir."

"Send him packing," Whit said.

The trooper, whom Whit didn't know, looked to his lieutenant for orders.

Tony was shaking his head. "Hell, Whit, the game's up. We might as well face it."

"We'll be happy to exclude him from the crime scene," the lieutenant said.

Tony waved off the suggestion. "No. I'll talk to him." He headed to meet the reporter.

Whit fell in beside him. "I wanna know who leaked the info."

FOUR

THE EDITOR OF THE *Milbrook Daily Journal* had endured worse places than the holding cell at the Raven County jail. In her college days, the basement apartment she shared with a flighty music major made her present accommodations palatial by comparison. There was a difference, though. She had opted to live in the roach-infested basement—a choice constrained by her meager resources, but a choice nonetheless.

Most women would have been permanently disenchanted by a lover who had ordered their arrest. Disenchanted, hell—they would have been livid! If the man had been anybody other than Whit Pynchon, Anna, too, would have fled the relationship as fast as her legs could carry her. However, when you lived with Whit Pynchon—when you loved him—you made allowances.

All too often, his mood transformed him into a self-righteous egotist who really didn't care about stepping on toes, even toes attached to someone he loved. Above all, you always knew where you stood with him. The man had an obsessive romance with truth, at least what he perceived to be truth. He found it impossible to be civil to people he didn't like, particularly when those people insisted upon some type of confrontation with him. She attributed his abrasiveness to the unusual nature of his job, which he claimed to despise. Almost all cops, Whit included, felt misunderstood by the public they served. Because of that, they found great comfort in the company of other cops. Whit, though, was excluded from the special fraternity. Not only did he investigate all homicides and many of the more serious felonies in Raven County, he also conducted inquiries into allegations of police misbehavior—anything from brutality to corruption. It made him a maverick—a man truly without peers.

But not all of his eccentricities were job-related. He despised West Virginia, especially its weather, and was infatuated with the coast of South Carolina. For him, that underscored his purpose in life. He wanted to be a beachcomber the same way other men aspired to public office or corporate presidencies.

As maddening and unpredictable as his character sometimes was, it also provided him with a blunt, cockeyed charm. His determination to leave West Virginia was his one attribute that bothered Anna the most. She really didn't know what would happen when the day came that he decided to move to his low-country paradise. It would happen, just as surely as the next West Virginia winter would come; knowing him as she did, he would announce the decision in the morning and be on the road by midday. Would she go with him? The answer to that question probably wouldn't be known, even to her, until that dreaded day came. For that reason more than any other, they had a kind of silent contract in which they avoided the issue of marriage. She loved her work with the *Daily Journal*. It gave her life purpose, and she wouldn't likely find the same opportunity in Whit's southern nirvana.

So Whit Pynchon was one of a kind, and Anna wasn't at all surprised when he had carried through with his threat to jail her. Nor would he be surprised by the ruse she had pulled off to outflank him. It had become something of a game between them, a contest that had started

earlier that year when Anna was still just a reporter
assigned to the *Journal*'s police beat. Kathy Binder, her
employer and confidante, likened them to Siskel and
Ebert, the quarrelsome pair of film critics.

She looked around the freshly painted cinderblock
walls of the small cell, half expecting to see the begin-
nings of a new growth of obscene graffiti. The walls,
though, were unmarked. The reason came to her. She
was in a jail for God's sakes. Presumably, no one came
into the cell carrying anything with as much dangerous
potential as a pencil or a pen. Even absent the traditional graffiti, the place reminded her of a public rest
room. It had that same odor, emanating no doubt from
the stainless steel commode that appeared to sprout
from the painted cement block of the wall.

The door consisted of a metal frame covered by what
looked to be oversized chicken wire. According to Wilshire, the deputy who had arrested her and who had so
apologetically guided her inside, the cell only housed
inmates for short time—until they could be transported
up the elevator to the main jail atop the courthouse.

"The toilet's disinfected daily," he claimed, as if that
attested to their efficient concern for sanitation. She
would have felt more comfortable if he'd said it was
disinfected after each use. Unless her situation turned
desperate, she had no intention of availing herself of
the facility. It's silver-steel surface looked painfully
chilling.

A metal cot, bolted to the wall, constituted the only
other concession to comfort. It offered no mattress, and
its surface, peppered by large holes, proved more painful than agreeable.

Black fingerprint ink, a souvenir from the booking
procedure, discolored the crevices around her well-kept
fingernails. Her hands looked like they belonged on the
local service station attendant. *Damn you, Whit!* Some-

times she wanted to choke him, not because of this incident alone but rather because he steadfastly refused to acknowledge the crucial role the press played in the conduct of an open government. By taking that attitude, he demeaned her career. When they had first met, her opinion of cops had been just as biased as his opinion of journalists. Because of their association, her views had moderated. It irked her that his opinion of those in her profession remained so narrow-minded and negative.

Anna shook her head at herself—at the troublesome thoughts she had conjured. How could anyone with a modicum of intelligence survive an extended stay in a jail? She'd been in the cell for just a few minutes and already she was thinking herself to death. What else was there to do but let the mind wander? The devil's workshop . . . wasn't that what they called an idle mind?

Footsteps, accompanied by voices, approached the door of the cell. Seconds later, Kathleen Binder, the owner and publisher of the *Journal*, smiled in at her. "You look like you've made yourself at home, Anna."

"I trust you're here to get me out—bail me out or whatever it is you have to do."

Anna wondered—hoped, actually—that she looked as out of place within the walls of the jail as Kathleen Binder did. While her friend and editor had been languishing in a cell, the *Journal*'s publisher had taken time to prepare herself for public viewing. Anna knew how sensitive the young woman was. Without makeup, Kathy Binder considered herself ugly—pale, washed out, a lackluster study in the absence of contrast. The young widow wouldn't even answer the door of her home when she was her "plain self," as she liked to say. Standing on the other side of the bars in the wee hours of the morning, she might have been a model from the pages of *Vanity Fair*. Her long blond hair, just a shade shy of platinum, shimmered. The blue of her irises was accentuated by a matching eyeliner. Delicately applied blush highlighted her high cheekbones.

Both Anna and Kathy Binder—in spite of her inferior self-image—were beauties. They were in their midthirties. They both considered themselves liberal feminists. For all of their similarities, they couldn't have been more different in appearance. Anna's auburn hair looked best when it was a little mussed, and she spent very little time worrying about makeup. Her skin boasted a perpetual tan. Where Kathy was willowy, Anna was well endowed.

Kathy was brandishing a white sheet of paper. "Our lawyer woke up Judge O'Brien. To say the least, he's not a bit happy with your boyfriend. In fact, there's a good chance he may be destined to take your place."

Anna laughed. "I'd love it—just for a short stay, of course."

"Anyway, you're a free woman, my dear."

"So, where's the guy with the keys?"

Kathy's smiled broadened. "They tell me the door's not even locked."

Anna couldn't believe it. She pushed the door open. Then she remembered the events that preceded her brief incarceration. "They fingerprinted me and took a mug-shot," she said as the two women headed for the jail lobby. "Everyone should go through that humiliation once—just once."

"No thanks. Whit's gone too far this time, Anna. Our attorney was incredulous, and, as I said, Judge O'Brien was furious."

Anna was admiring the dress, striped in muted earth tones, that her employer wore beneath the light outer coat. "You're overdressed for a trip to a jail."

Kathy was always dressed to the hilt, giving the same

attention to her clothes that she did to her makeup. The death of her husband, the former publisher of the *Journal*, had left her well heeled. She loved clothes and was able to afford the best. A quick-paced metabolism kept her skinny-thin, but she was able to select those fashions that made her appear sleek rather than bony.

"I threw on the first thing I found," she said.

"Some people might not believe that, but I do. I've seen your closet. Who'd you send out to the River Road?"

Kathy shrugged. "I wanted to send Norm Goodson, but no one answered at his house. It's late for him not to be home. Anyway, I had to settle for Bobby Harrington."

Anna moaned. "Not Bobby?"

"It was the best I could do."

"I hope he remembers to take the lens cap off the camera this time."

"I gave him an adamant warning."

"Let's drive out there ourselves just to make sure."

The *Journal*'s publisher laughed. "And maybe to rub a little salt in Whit's wound?"

Anna smiled. "He'll have apoplexy."

Whit towered over the stunted frame of Bobby Harrington. "For the last time, I wanna know who tipped you."

Harrington, on his tiptoes to muster the last inch of height he had, did his damnedest to sound defiant. "Like I've told you already, my publisher called me. She didn't tell me the source of her information. Even if she had, I wouldn't reveal it."

The prosecutor put a hand on his investigator's shoulder. "Forget it, Whit. What's done is done."

"Friggin' reporters," Whit mumbled. "They oughta be an endangered species."

Harrington, relieved to have been rescued, was extracting his camera from its case. "Can you give me the details, Mr. Danton?"

"It's still pretty sketchy. What did you say your name was again?"

"Harrington, sir. Robert."

"I haven't met you before."

"I'm kinda new. Mostly I've been writing some sports stuff. This is my first opportunity to get into general news." The novice reporter with fiery red hair watched an ambulance crew as it lifted a body into the back of one of the vehicles. "How many are dead?"

"Five we know of, including a state trooper."

Harrington whistled. "What was his name?"

"We'll have to get you those specific details later. I don't really know his full name."

The reporter's face dropped.

Tony put an arm around the young man's shoulder. "Look, Mr. Harrington—Robert—I'm not trying to withhold information from the press. I knew the trooper as Eddie Clark, and we both can agree that this story will hit the wire services—and radio—as soon as you file it. I'm sure his family would appreciate knowing about this before everyone else does. Most of the other victims appear to be nonresidents, and at this point the identification we have is shaky at best. We just don't really know what went down. You'll find it's often like that at the scene of a major crime—chaotic, confusing, not at all like what TV makes it out to be."

Loud voices from a couple of officers on the other side of the road snagged their attention. Tony turned to see one of them running toward him.

Whit, who had eased away from the conversation between Tony and Harrington, was trying to head the cop off. Whatever had been found, he didn't want it displayed in front of a reporter. He didn't make it in time.

The officer—a Raven County deputy—brandished something in Tony's face. "Look at this. It's an ammo clip of some kind."

Tony threw up his hand. "Jesus Christ, man! What the fuck about prints?"

The sudden realization of his mistake prompted the deputy to drop the large metal object to the ground. "I'm sorry. I was thinking—I mean . . ."

Whit squatted down over the mammoth ammunition clip. For the moment, he'd forgotten all about the reporter as well as the deputy's reckless disregard for what almost certainly was crucial evidence. "My God, what kinda damn gun uses something like that."

One of the deputies—a weary veteran—didn't even need to take a close look. "It's from a scatter gun, a .12 gauge. From the looks of that damned van, I'd say somebody around here has laid his hands on an automatic shotgun."

Whit was staring up at the county cop. "They make automatic shotguns?"

Sinclair prodded at the magazine. "Nobody around here would have one of those."

"No one around here should have one," the deputy said. "It's against the law—even the semiautomatics with that kinda clip."

Whit whistled. "Christ, I didn't know that."

Tony was staring with refreshed horror at the tight pattern of holes in the surface of the van. "You mean to tell me there's a shotgun that shoots like a machine gun?"

"I'd say it's worse than a machine gun, Mr. Danton." The deputy went over to the van. "That clip holds about a dozen shells, and each one of those shells has nine pellets about the size of the tip of my little finger. If that ain't enough for you, they also make a friggin'

drum you use instead of a clip. It'll hold thirty damned
shells.''

"What the devil would you use something like that
for?'' Tony asked.

The deputy inserted a tip of a finger into one of the
holes. "Killin', Mr. Prosecutor. It ain't worth a shit for
anything else.''

FIVE

DAWN IMPOSED A NEW PERSPECTIVE on the sprawling
crime scene on Raven County's River Road. Whit stood
with State Police Corporal Al Downing on the edge of
the mountain as it fell away toward the creek below.
With the aid of the spreading daylight, they had inched
far enough down the slope to gain a view of the actual
creek. Downing's face was grim as he gazed at the un-
derside of a vehicle—a state police cruiser that rested
on its top in the actual creek bed itself.

"I guess we can cancel the B.O.L.O. on the cruiser."

Whit's knuckles rubbed his weary eyes. "Yeah, I
guess. Get your boys to round up some strong rope, a
lot of it. I'd say it's at least two hundred feet down
there."

"Ten four."

As Downing used the trunks of the small trees to pull
himself back up to the road, Whit took time to settle
down on a rock. The bodies had departed the scene an
hour or so earlier, all except the rookie state cop who
was presumably in the car at the bottom of the ravine.
One of the ambulances was on the way back to the
scene—just in case.

For the past hour, Whit had been assigning both deputies and troopers to a variety of tasks. Ted Early's deputy sheriffs were still securing the scene and manning
roadblocks at each end of the River Road. The state

police had been delegated to contact North Carolina authorities about the victims. Lieutenant Slack had driven back to the local detachment headquarters to handle that detail himself—a convenient way to escape the embarrassment he'd suffered when he lost the power struggle with Tony, Whit suspected.

Up on the road, the crime scene team from the state capital continued their tedious scrutiny of the van. When finished with the gross examination, they planned to tow the vehicle all the way to Charleston, where they would enshroud it in plastic. Then they would introduce a liberal dose of Super Glue inside the plastic tent. The glue would evaporate, its fumes eventually hardening on exposed surfaces both inside and outside of the van. The process would reveal, they hoped, every fingerprint on most of the vehicle's smooth surfaces.

As front-line criminal investigators, the state police hadn't done much in the past to earn Whit's respect. Although there were individual exceptions, they lacked the finesse a good detective needed and were far more suited to road patrol. On the other hand, the forensics division, centralized in South Charleston, West Virginia, was a damn good resource when you could get its full and immediate attention. Trouble was, it took the death of one of their own to warrant that kind of service. If the victims had just been dope dealers from the Carolinas, Whit would have had no luck getting the crime scene van dispatched at all, much less immediately. It would have taken days to get prints from the van processed, assuming they would have wanted to waste that much Super Glue. Such was the nature of law enforcement. It was the same everywhere.

He heard the sound of heavy feet on dried leaves. Downing had returned. ''The crime scene guys have about three hundred feet of rope. Sinclair and a couple of the deputies are getting it.''

Whit rolled his eyes. "I don't know if I want deputies holding on to my lifeline."

"If you weren't such an asshole toward your fellow cops, you wouldn't have to worry about such things."

"That makes me feel a lot better, Al. Very reassuring."

Downing shrugged. "You know what they say, pal. If the foo shits—"

A pair of deputies came down the slope to join Downing and Whit.

"Damn," one said, "that's a friggin' long way down."

Whit didn't dare look too closely. He had a deep phobia of heights. Downing had noticed already his reluctance to take a long look down at the inverted cruiser. "One of the deputies might go, Whit. Might be better if you stayed up here."

"Hell, no," one deputy said. "I mean, I know the Mahoney kid may be down there, but my balls shrivel up just being this close to the edge."

The other deputy didn't say a word, which meant he wasn't about to go either.

"Just cinch me up good," Whit said. "I'll go first."

He wrapped the rope around his midsection, fingering it in the process. "Is this the heaviest we've got?"

"It'll hold," a deputy said.

Whit glared at the county officer. "I don't notice you offering to test it."

He turned to Downing. "Wait until I get to the bottom, Al, before you start."

The state cop winked at Whit. "Don't worry, big guy. I'll make sure these guys don't drop you."

One of the deputies laughed. "The sheriff was up there when we got the rope. He said it might solve a lot of problems around here if it broke."

Both Downing and the other deputy laughed. Whit

didn't. He concentrated on retaining the fluid in his bladder as he eased himself over the edge, his eyes riveted on the men who held his life in their hands.

The sun had risen high enough to spill its direct light on the River Road when Anna and Kathy Binder finally reached the scene. Tony recognized Anna's car and went up to meet the two women.

"Your damned cops are a bunch of jerks," Anna said as she wearily climbed from beneath the wheel.

Tony had to smile. "What's wrong, Anna?"

"They wouldn't give us directions even when we knew the location. I've been driving all over these damned mountains."

Kathy looked even more fatigued than Anna. "She honestly means that, too. There were times we weren't even on roads, at least not what I'd call roads. Cowpaths maybe."

Tony was shaking his head. "How'd you do it, Anna?"

"Do what? Find this place?"

"No, dammit. How did you manage to get a reporter out here so damned quick this morning?"

Anna had been looking around for Harrington. She finally spotted him shooting a photo of the forensics team as they searched along the edges of the road.

"Ask me no questions, Tony, and I'll tell you no lies. Let's just say it started when the sheriff's department gave me my obligatory phone call. I assume your highhanded investigator told you that he had me arrested. I was booked, fingerprinted, the whole nine yards, Mr. Prosecutor."

"How were the accommodations?"

His quip made Anna smile, but the publisher of the *Journal* found no humor in his remark. She was trying to exercise the cramping muscles of her back. "You should know, counselor, that Judge O'Brien issued an order releasing Anna. He wasn't thrilled over being disturbed so early in the morning. Did you have any part in her arrest—an illegal arrest, I might add? At least, according to my lawyer.''

Tony held up his hands in a gesture of helplessness. "I plead innocent, Anna. That was Whit Pynchon, pure and simple.''

"I know it, Tony. Speaking of the bastard, where is he?''

Tony turned and pointed to the ravine. "Hanging on a rope over the side.''

Anna's eyes widened. "Whit?''

"I might as well fill you in." Tony turned to Kathy Binder. "On the other hand, we really do need to withhold some information, at least from the general public. It might be crucial to the success of our investigation.''

Anna started to protest, but her employer stopped her with a hand gesture. "As long as you understand, Tony, that we—Anna and me—will make the final decision on what to print and what not to print.''

Anna was shocked. "But, Kathy—''

"I'll trust in your judgment," Tony was saying, ". . . and Anna's.''

Kathy's attention had been trapped by the appearance of the van. "What happened to that?''

"We think the damage was caused by a shotgun.'' Tony remained silent about the unusual nature of the weapon. Other than that, and his suspicion that it was a drug deal turned nasty, he told the two women most of the known details. For the moment, he also withheld the information about the dead child.

The three of them ambled over to the side of the road near to the point where Whit had descended into the gorge. "How are you going to get the car up?'' Anna asked.

Tony was trying to peer over. "We'll bring the trooper's body up first—if it's down there. Then, I'd say they'll have to get some kind of crane to haul the car out of there."

Anna heard Whit's voice crackling over a walkie-talkie.

Al Downing, who was preparing for his descent, turned and called to Tony. "Whit says Mahoney's down there. I'm going down."

Tony sighed. "Everyone's accounted for."

"How many in all?" Anna asked.

Silently, Tony counted. "Six in all."

The editor of the *Journal* pondered his answer. "Three civilians in the garbage dump and Trooper Clark. Trooper Mahoney at the bottom of the ravine. That makes five, Tony."

The prosecutor slowly nodded. "There was a sixth, Anna. He was found in the van."

"Four men then?" Kathy asked.

"Not exactly. It was a child—"

The publisher gasped and covered her mouth with her hand.

"An infant, a baby boy hardly a year old," Tony added, his voice cracking.

"Were you going to tell us that?" Anna asked.

"Yeah—when the time seemed right."

For Kathy, whose lifelong desire for a child had died with her husband, the bright sunny day turned incredibly dark. She struggled not to cry. "How can people be so cruel? It can't just be greed."

Tony shrugged. "I'd like to believe that whoever turned that shotgun on the van didn't even know the kid was in there."

Anna had taken her friend's hand. "That doesn't make him any less dead, Tony."

SIX

"CAN YOU GET HIM OUT?" The voice on the walkie-talkie belonged to one of the two troopers who remained at the murder scene, probably ordered by Lieutenant Slack to stay behind to be certain the body of the rookie was handled with appropriate departmental decorum.

Whit stood back to allow Al Downing to make that determination. He'd seen all he wanted to see of young Sam Mahoney anyway. The blast from the souped-up shotgun had struck him in his midsection. That much was obvious. The ride down the mountain, though, hadn't been kind to the rookie cop's remains. As Whit had descended, he noted several places on the mountainside where the fallen cruiser had made violent contact. Small trees jutting from the steep slope had been splintered. Large chunks of rock had been chipped away.

Downing's jaw muscles flexed as he leaned down to peer into the car. At the same time, he tried to keep the seat of his pants out of the trickling stream of ice-cold water. The cruiser rested crossways in the stream on the rock ledges that flanked the waterway. The atmosphere around the vehicle reeked of spilled gasoline, most of which had flowed into the creek itself. By some minor miracle, nothing had ignited the fuel.

Downing slammed the side of the overturned cruiser

with disgust. "Tell 'em that I doubt it. I'd say we best try to wrench this whole damn car up there. The poor bastard might come out in pieces if we try to pull him free."

Whit put the hand-held radio to his mouth. "Downing doesn't think so."

The prosecutor's investigator agreed with Downing's conclusion, but he knew it was better if the other state cops heard it from one of their own. They wouldn't have put a lot of credence in Whit's opinion.

The walkie-talkie was silent for several minutes. When it crackled back to life, Tony Danton was on the other end. "Whit, we've got a wrecker on the way with some kind of high-powered winch attached to it. It'll be an hour or so before it arrives. You wanna come on back up?"

Whit looked to Al, who said, "I'm gonna stay. No sense going through that twice . . . or having somebody else go through it who doesn't have to. Regarding that wrecker, I think we're gonna need more than a wrecker to haul this thing out of here."

"I'll stay with you. I've seen those big wreckers do some amazing things." Whit keyed the walkie-talkie. "Al and I will wait down here on the wrecker. You might be thinking about another alternative, though, if the wrecker can't handle it."

"Okay. Listen, we're gonna lower some hot coffee to you," Tony then said. "We have some breakfast biscuits if you want them."

"Sounds like they're having a real picnic up there," Downing said.

Whit heard the hostility in the cop's voice. "I expect they're just hungry, Al. I am, too. I'll have 'em send something down."

Al was still peering inside at the body of the young

man who had only been assigned to his detachment a few weeks earlier. "Suit yourself, Whit."

The corporal stood and waded out of the stream to a large rock painted with bright sunlight. Whit told the prosecutor to send the food and drinks on down and then went to sit beside Downing.

"You oughta take those shoes and socks off."

"They'll dry."

Whit nodded toward the broken body crumpled in the cruiser. "You know it's a chance we all take, Al."

Downing removed his hat—a baseball style decorated by an official insignia and issued by the department—to reveal sandy, thinning hair. A tremor, barely perceptible, rattled down his thin, wiry frame. "You and I know about the chances, Whit. Anybody that's been in the business knows. It's a little different with a rookie. They still think it's like a kid's game of cops and robbers. They haven't seen yet just how ugly-dead a person can really be. About a quarter of them wash out in the first year—the ones that realize it ain't worth the bullshit or the risks. Besides, it's Eddie as much as it is the kid there. He and I were at the academy together. That was a lot of years ago. We got together again when they assigned me to Raven County. We socialize with his wife and his kids."

"You're just making it harder on yourself."

"Hell, Whit, knock it off. You know there's no way I can't forget about all this. I'll tell you something ironic. Eddie was afraid his youngest kid—a fourteen-year-old-boy—was fooling around with drugs. He was on my ass to get some kinda undercover effort going here in Raven County. Nobody around here believes we've got much of a drug problem. Eddie thought different."

"Maybe Eddie was right. I think it'd be a good idea to organize something. Besides, we need to know who's the big dealer here in Raven County. I'd bet next month's pay that it's the same person or persons responsible for this.''

Al looked up at the investigator. ''I was thinking the same thing.''

''I think I can convince Tony. He and I were talking about it just the other day. One of the school principals came into the office claiming that some kid was selling dope in plain view from a car at the high school parking lot.''

''I've never had any problems with you, Whit, but a lot of the guys say you're a first-class asshole. I think they're wrong.''

Whit shook his head. ''Nope, they're not wrong. I like being an asshole, and I'd better not hear that you're out doing any public relations on my behalf. I got a reputation to maintain.''

Downing managed a smile.

They heard the rustling of brush and looked up the mountainside. They were startled to see Ross Sinclair easing himself down at the end of the rope. He had a canvas bag over his shoulder.

''Here's breakfast,'' the sheriff's department captain announced. ''I expect a pretty damned good tip for delivering it.''

Anna and Kathy Binder left the scene around 8:30 A.M. She had missed her opportunity to goad Whit, who remained at the bottom of the ravine, probably unaware that Anna had even been there. On the way back to Milbrook, they had discussed the approach the *Journal* would take with the story but reached no final decisions. Anna had dropped the publisher at her home and had driven back to the house she shared with Whit Pynchon, where she had showered and dressed for work. By the time she arrived at the offices of the *Milbrook Daily Journal*, it was almost 11:00 A.M. The paper published in the mornings, so even at that time the newsroom was quiet. The main team of reporters wouldn't report until after lunch. One young woman sat at a terminal, a phone to her ear, typing an obituary being called in by one of the local mortuaries. Anna paused at the obit desk until she was finished with the call.

"Has Harrington made it back?" Anna asked of the obit writer.

The girl nodded. "He's in the darkroom."

"Alone?"

"I guess."

Anna closed her eyes to quell her panic. Harrington wasn't one of her favorite staffers—even when he was just covering high school sports. He was even less impressive as a photographer. She prayed he wasn't trying to develop the film himself. She hurried to the darkroom. A red light above the door warned her not to enter. She rapped instead.

"Yeah?" a voice cried.

"Harrington, this is Anna Tyree. Are you trying to process that raw film?"

"It's developed," he shouted back.

"You'd better not screw it up, Bobby."

The young reporter didn't answer.

"Bobby? Did you hear me?"

The door opened in her face, and the stench of chemicals rushed out at her. Bobby Harrington held up a long strip of 35-mm film. "Here it is, Miss Tyree. I got some great shots."

Anna scowled at the freckled baby face. "Bobby, the next time you have film to develop—especially on something as critical as this—you wait and let the staff photographer handle it."

"But I know—"

"You heard me, Bobby. It's not open for debate."

"But—"

"Dammit, Bobby!"

He dropped his head. "Okay, I understand."

Bobby Harrington shared a common prejudice with the majority of the news staff, both male and female. They didn't give Anna the same respect that a male editor would have received simply by virtue of his position. In that regard, and in many others, Raven County remained a victim of cultural lag. Anna understood the prejudice, she just didn't tolerate it.

"I hope you have some good shots of that van."

"Great ones. Oh, and I got a shot of them with that baby. It's covered—"

"No way," Anna said. "We won't use that."

"Okay. Here's the van—"

"Just get me a print of it. In fact, I want a print of everything you shot."

"Everything?"

"Not the baby. On second thought, wait for Lou Miller." He was the staff photographer. He could have Anna a set of proofs in no time.

"I don't mind trying, Miss Tyree."

"There's no need. Go write your story. I want to see it as soon as it's finished."

Harrington turned anxious. "I'm not sure I have enough details yet."

"Then go get the details. That's your job. You're a reporter first. You should have left the film for Lou and gone after the details."

She left him standing in the darkroom, choosing not to tell him that she intended to give the story to Norm Goodson, a veteran reporter, as soon as he arrived at work.

"You know how I feel about those kind of undercover operations," the Raven County prosecutor was saying. "You used to feel the same way."

Whit didn't feel up to a debate as he sat in Tony's office. His jeans and jacket were stained with mud and clay. The shirt he wore smelled of sweat. Traces of dirt streaked his face. His thick, gray hair was windblown and still decorated with bits of leaves. The climb down the mountain and then back up had exercised muscles Whit didn't know he had. A little beyond forty, he wasn't in the best of shape. Not that he was a physical wreck. In a way, he was more than a little proud that he had been able to manage the climb without having a heart attack.

"I know," Whit said, "but we need to isolate the dealers in this county. That's where we're going to find our killer."

"I'd say we only need to find some son of a bitch with an automatic shotgun. There couldn't be too many of those damned things circulating in the county."

"You can forget ballistics, Tony—they won't be a bit of help. Besides, I can guarantee you that kind of gun wasn't obtained legally. We'll have no chance of tracing it. This is one time we need an undercover operation."

But Tony was shaking his head. "They're nothing but trouble. You remember last time."

Whit remembered it very well. A year and a half ago, Tony had succumbed to a request by the chief of the Milbrook Police Department to fund an undercover drug operation. The city cops had a new kid, a stranger to Milbrook, joining the department, and they wanted to use him for a few weeks undercover. The kid had made a handful of petty buys, nothing bigger than a nickel bag of grass or a single Tylox pill. Once the cases reached the point of trial, the kid, who was by then a uniformed cop, balked at testifying. It turned out that he had been banging a female druggie, and the trial was certain to reveal that fact. The cop, of course, had been married at the time.

Undercover drug operations, especially in rural communities like Milbrook, tended to fail just because of such problems. Tony, though, had insisted on trying several of the cases and had been ambushed with testimony that his undercover operative had purchased more drugs than he had reported and had used those drugs to procure sexual favors from a half-dozen girls, some of whom were under the age of consent. All the cases had gone down the tubes. So, too, had the undercover cop's career and marriage.

"Downing thinks his department can send a pretty decent undercover man down here."

"There's no such thing, Whit. Once a guy goes undercover, he's got to get dirty. I'm as down on drugs as anybody, but I don't think undercover operations solve the problem. All we end up bagging are the kids that sell a joint or a handful of pills to each other. In the process we sometimes ruin a good cop. It makes for good press, and too often not even that."

Whit persisted. "The circumstances are different this time. Trust me, Tony, Let me run the operation."

Tony had been emphatically shaking his head, but Whit's last comment produced a sarcastic laugh. "This kind of thing requires a high degree of interagency cooperation. Just how does Whit Pynchon—who is hated by most of the cops in Raven County—hope to acquire that?"

"I'll let Downing serve as liaison with the state boys. Sinclair agreed to do the same for the sheriff's department. Just think about it, Tony. That's all I ask."

Danton's phone rang. He answered it quickly, glad to be let off the hook. Whit heard only one side of the conversation, and Tony said nothing to reveal its nature until he hung up.

"That was Slack. We're right about the drug involvement. The North Carolina authorities knew Ernest Felty. They say one of the other John Does is more than likely his brother, Cleveland Felty. They suspect both of them of moving fairly large quantities of cocaine up from Atlanta into the Carolinas and the Virginias."

"How soon can we get a positive ID?"

"Pretty damned soon. A cop who knows both Felty brothers is on his way up here. In fact, he knows them pretty damned well—he's their brother."

Whit grinned. "Let's see. We've got a couple of dead drug dealers, killed by some kind of super shotgun, with a cop for a brother."

Tony nodded. "The plot thickens, as they say."

"And the bullshit deepens."

SEVEN

WILLIE MACK SMITH LOVED THE ODOR of gunpowder solvent. It provoked fond memories that went as far back as his eighth birthday. That's when his paw had given him his first gun. Before Guthrie Smith had handed Willie Mack the compact single-shot .410 shotgun, he'd first given his son a box with two bottles, two dozen pieces of white cloth, and several metal sticks that screwed together to make a cleaning rod. Willie Mack had known exactly what purpose the strange items served. He'd seen his paw use his own gun cleaning kit often—almost daily in fact. After lecturing for a good thirty minutes on the need to clean a weapon after every use, Guth Smith had pulled the used .410 from a closet.

"It's yours, boy. If I find it dirty, you're in for a thrashing."

Guth Smith had found it dirty a few times, and, true to his word, Willie Mack had gotten a beating each time. But as Willie Mack grew into his teens, he reached a point where he could clean a gun as fast and as thoroughly as his paw—and was a better shot. He had been thirteen when his paw first let him guard the moonshine operation located inside the worked-out mine on a mountain slope to the rear of their property. There had been a day, his paw had told him, when the still operated all year long, but by the time Willie Mack was old enough to appreciate the peanut-buttery taste of the mountain liquor, the operation was mainly just a side-line. Store-bought liquor had become too cheap and too easy to get, and people had become leery of homemade liquor . . . what with the TV and newspapers talking all the time about lead poisoning from 'shine condensed in old car radiators. Guth Smith never used the corroded guts from a radiator. He depended on a tightly coiled condenser of copper tubing, made for him by a fan of his liquor. It squeezed the best out of the fruity mash. The condenser was still way back in the mine, tightly covered with a musty old tarpaulin.

As he thought about those days, Willie Mack soaked a cleaning patch with the sweet-smelling aromatic solvent and attached it to the heavy cleaning rod. He hoisted the automatic shotgun up between his knees, inhaling deeply as he inserted the swab into the barrel. The perfume of the solvent mingled with the odor of spent gunpowder as he forced the cleaning rod up and down the large barrel of the weapon. He held the weapon by the sturdy handle made a part of its body. The gun, almost as heavy as a .50 caliber machine gun and even more deadly, was the pride of his arsenal and well worth the half-ounce of coke he'd traded for it down in Georgia.

He first had encountered drugs in the army. For his own part, he had no taste for heroin or cocaine, preferring instead a cold beer and an occasional smoke of pot. On the other hand, he'd been raised in a family that boasted a long history of running and making liquor. His old man had always kept a box full of cash around the house, most of which he derived from his moonshining. Only once had Guth Smith served any time for it, and then it had been because he got nabbed selling it to a hardware store in Milbrook. It amounted to a couple of weeks in the county jail. They'd never found the still itself, hidden in the old mine. The shaft hadn't been mined since the early twenties, and nobody but family even knew it existed.

If the market value of the 'shine had held, Willie Mack would have been perfectly content to continue the traditional family enterprise. It was easy to make, and nobody got too bent out of shape about it. Drugs, on the other hand, meant dealing with a lot of people, which increased the exposure. Because of that, the profits were enormous. Besides, the cocaine was small and damned easy to move. It meant, too, a lot of heat, although Willie Mack and his younger brother Didimus had been lucky on that account, at least until last night.

The automatic shotgun was heavy—it weighed a good ten pounds—but he casually lifted the muzzle to his eye. Willie Mack Smith himself was a big man, made to appear even bigger by his bulging beer gut and his thick hair and heavy beard. The bib overalls he wore only served to accentuate the pregnant appearance of his belly. He twisted the thirty-eight-inch weapon in his large, callused hands as he sighted down the barrel. A few flecks of residue remained. He replaced the end of the cleaning rod with a brush, which he saturated with the fragrant solvent, and began thrusting it into the barrel.

Willie Mack hadn't minded killing the guys from Carolina. They had been shorting both sides of their game, the suppliers and their customers. The suppliers had contacted Willie Mack and made him an offer he just couldn't refuse. Everything the Feltys had on them was his if they didn't leave Raven County alive.

"No problem," Willie Mack had said. They weren't the first people he'd killed.

He hadn't counted on the cops showing up—pure, fucking, bad-luck coincidence. Willie Mack knew that killing cops was like jamming a short stick into a big hornets' nest. If you had to do it, you had best be prepared to suffer some. The cop that worked with Willie Mack wasn't too fuckin' happy about it, but he was in too deep to do much about it.

Once the barrel was spotless, he moved to the breech, where he went to work with a smaller brush, using copious amounts of solvent, which he worked into every joint and crevice.

Nope, no doubt about it.

He'd rather have not killed the cops, but it had happened. Whatever followed, Willie Mack could handle it.

Thirty minutes after he started on the huge, complicated weapon he was finished—except for the clips. He started to look around and found one full clip and another empty one. There was a third somewhere—another empty one. He lifted himself from the couch to see it if had slipped under his ass.

The house itself was quiet. His kid was at school, and the old lady had gone to the store in Tipple Town. Didimus was somewhere, probably sleeping off the booze he'd drunk after last night's excitement.

"Didimus!"

He paused for a reply. There was none.

"DI-DI-MUS!" Willie Mack's voice rattled the walls of the farmhouse.

"Here," he heard a raspy voice cry.

Feet hit the floor above him.

"GET YOUR ASS DOWN HERE!"

He heard his brother stagger out of his room on the second floor and pad barefoot down the hall.

"MOVE IT!"

"Whatsa matter?" Didimus Smith came slowly down the creaking steps. He was a smaller release of his brother. The hair was just as full and black, so, too, was the beard, but Didimus had no gut on him, never would the way he craved liquor rather than good solid food.

"I got a clip missing."

"Why blame me?" He reached the bottom of the staircase, his eyes aglow with the effects of the spirits he had consumed the night before.

"Did you pick up that clip from the road last night like I told you?"

"Huh?" Didimus gaped.

"You fuckin' drunk! You left it!"

"You told me—"

Willie Mack jerked the weapon to his shoulder. His brother threw himself back against the wall, colliding against it with such force that a framed 3-D portrait of Jesus Christ—it had belonged to their mother—clattered to the floor.

"GOD, WILLIE MACK! DON'T!"

His older brother squeezed the trigger. "You're good for fuckin' nothin', asshole."

"PLEEEASE, WILLIE MACK!"

The action clicked, and Willie Mack grinned. Didimus gagged and then, cupping his mouth, rushed for the front door. Willie Mack followed and caught him bending over the front porch, throwing up into the yard. With a single well-placed foot, he sent his retching brother head first into the yard.

"I oughta feed you to the goddamned hogs, little brother."

Didimus righted himself but stayed on the ground. "It's just a clip, Willie Mack."

"Sure, with whose friggin' goddamn prints on it?"

His younger brother paled. "Honest to God, I didn't hear you say—"

"You were drunk! Like always!"

"Jimmy shoulda—"

"I didn't tell Jimmy to get it. I told you. Jimmy does what he's told."

Jimmy Carr was a cousin and the third member of the Smith family who worked in what they called "the operation."

The steps sagged under Willie Mack's weight as he stepped down into the yard. "Lemme tell you somethin', little brother. If I catch any grief 'cause you fucked up, I'm gonna take a ball crusher to you."

Didimus Smith was starting to weep. "We shouldn't oughta have killed them cops last night. That's what's gonna cause the grief."

"I ain't worried about no cops, little brother. I'm worried about you. Just remember what I said."

Anna moaned as she hung up the phone. Kathy Binder was sitting in one of the chairs in front of Anna's desk.

"What's wrong?" the publisher asked.

"That was Norm Goodson's wife. You were wondering why he wasn't home last night?"

Kathy nodded.

"He's in the hospital."

The publisher sat up. "What?"

"They had to take out his gall bladder this morning."

"His gall bladder? Is he all right?"

"Yeah, but he'll be off for a while."

"You were going to assign him to the killings. What now?"

Anna rose from her chair and walked to the window that looked out over the newsroom. "I guess that leaves us with Bobby Harrington."

"He's not a bad kid," Kathy said.

"No, just a bad reporter."

"Oh, Anna."

"I don't mean 'bad'—just inexperienced. Well, he's going to get his experience in a hurry." She opened the door and called to the young man who was hunched over the keyboard of his word processor.

"Be gentle," Kathy said.

It made Anna laugh as the toothsome reporter entered the office.

"We need to talk about the story on the shooting," Anna said as he nodded a greeting to the publisher.

"I'm on top of it," Harrington said. "The state police are supposed to call me back with some personal information about both officers."

"What about the case itself, Bobby? Have you talked to Tony Danton again?"

"He's supposed to return my call, but—"

Anna sighed. "Bobby, if you wait for Tony Danton to call you back, you'll be waiting until Christmas. You need to go down to the courthouse. Park yourself in the prosecutor's office until you have those details."

With his tightly curled red hair and face full of freckles, he looked like a kid to Anna. "I'm going to be candid with you, Bobby. I was waiting for Norm Goodson to get here. I was going to turn the story over to him."

Bobby looked from Anna to the publisher. "You don't think I can handle it?"

"It doesn't matter now. Goodson's just had emergency surgery. He's fine, but they had to remove his gall bladder. It looks like you get the story after all."

"I'll really do my best," he said.

"I'm just not sure that's good enough, Bobby. I'm going to stay on top of this story—and your case, too. I'm giving you fair warning."

There was a mischievous twinkle in the young man's dark eyes. "I was going to talk to you about something, Miss Tyree. I was thinking about doing something special—"

"Let's just keep this one straightforward and simple," Anna said. "It's going to be difficult enough without us complicating—"

"Please, hear me out."

Both Anna and Kathy were a little shocked at his insistence. They traded glances.

"Okay, Bobby, what did you want to say?" Anna asked.

"The police think this thing's drug-related. Right?"

"That's the consensus of opinion."

"Why don't we go beyond this incident and actually do a series on the scope of the drug problem in Milbrook and in the outlying areas of the county?"

Anna frowned. "Is there a drug problem? I don't think we know that."

"I know it," Harrington said.

Kathy Binder looked hard at the reporter. With his red hair and white skin, his eyes should have been sky blue. They weren't. They were brown and big as saucers. When she had first hired him, he reminded her of a character from a kids' cartoon—all eyes, hair, and teeth. "What does that mean, Bobby?"

"Well, I have friends who use cocaine. They live right here in Milbrook, and from what I hear them say there's an awful lot of it around."

"I've never seen much evidence of it," Anna said. "I don't think the police have either."

Harrington shrugged. "That's because they haven't been looking. I can get some inside information. I really can."

The publisher was shaking her head. "That sounds like police business to me. We'd better stick to publishing a newspaper."

"What sort of inside information?" Anna asked, much more interested in what he was saying than her employer.

"Maybe some leads on who the big dealers are, Miss Tyree. I won't spill the beans on my friends, but they may be able to guide me."

"Why on earth would they want to do that?" Kathy asked.

"Well, they won't—knowingly."

"Absolutely not," the publisher announced.

Anna, though, eyed Bobby Harrington with a new interest. "Bobby, excuse us for just a moment. Let Mrs. Binder and me talk about it."

EIGHT

"WHAT'S THE SHIT-EATIN' GRIN ABOUT?" Whit asked the question of his boss as he entered Tony's office. Ross Sinclair was already there.

"You might like to know, Whit, that Ross agrees with me about your idea on an undercover drug operation."

"You all have been teaming up on me."

"Not at all," Sinclair said. "I just share some of Tony's reservations."

Whit eyed the sheriff department's second-in-command. "Does that come from your many years of experience with drug operations?"

Tony's face clouded. "Come on, Whit. None of us have all that much seniority dealing with drug operations."

"My point exactly," Whit countered. "You had one undercover operation go down the tubes, and it's turned you against the idea itself."

"More than one," Tony said.

Sinclair eased forward in his chair. "My objections, Whit, are based on something else. I've done a lot of reading on the subject, and I've talked with officers in other areas. The story's always the same. You get the two-bit kids on the street, but the biggies get away. The top dogs don't sell to people they don't know. It's hard as hell to nab them."

Whit settled into a chair. He didn't know Sinclair

well enough to have formed any opinion about him as a cop. He liked him as a person. In his former rank as lieutenant, Sinclair had been responsible for supervising three civil process servers and for managing the constant string of misdemeanor warrants issued from the county's magistrate courts. The sour-grape vine in the department circulated the word that the sheriff promoted Sinclair because of his terminally ill wife. They ignored the fact that he was the only eligible officer smart enough to pass a civil service test, and that alone put him in line to be captain.

Whit leaned back and said, "Just because they're hard to nab, Ross, that's no reason not to try. Dammit, we had a couple of state police officers gunned down last night. It's obviously drug-related. I don't think we're going to get to first base treating this like a typical homicide. We've got to go at it from the perspective of motive. That's dope."

"I don't disagree," Sinclair said. "I just don't think bringing an undercover cop in is going to lead us to the big-time dealers. We'll end up nailing the same penny ante streetpeople we always do."

"I wish I had your crystal ball," Whit said.

The prosecutor reentered the debate. "Let's wait and see what the forensics team finds. Who knows? Maybe we'll have a clear set of prints somewhere in that van—or maybe on that ammo clip."

Whit chuckled. "Sure, Tony, and there really is a Santa Claus, too. You know one of Ross's deputies has already ruined any chance of getting prints off the clip."

"That still leaves the van," Tony said.

Whit threw up his hands. "Any port in a storm, eh, Tony?"

At that moment, a large figure filled the doorway of Tony's office. The bouquet of a hard drinker's hangover accompanied the newcomer.

"Sinclair, I wanna see you."

The harsh voice—and the odor—belonged to Lenny Barker, chief of police in Tipple Town. His ragtag department was composed of the chief and another man. Barker was as rough as the town in which he worked.

Sinclair was startled. "You sound mad, Lenny."

"Damn right I'm mad. I got a crow to pick with you, and I might as well do it here and now. The prosecutor there oughta know about it."

"What's wrong?" Sinclair was asking.

"Last night, I phoned your department for some goddamn backup. I had a bunch of drunks raising hell and fighting right on the main street. I got no help at all. Nobody showed."

The chief's comments stunned the other three men. Whit broke the shocked silence. "Jesus, Barker, where the hell have you been all day?"

"What the fuck's that s'posed to mean?"

Sinclair elaborated. "We got your call, Lenny. Both of my units were tied up on the other side of the county. Our dispatcher turned the call for assistance over to the state police—"

"They didn't show neither," Barker snapped.

"We know that," Whit said, impatient with the blustering attitude of the small-town cop. "They were killed on the way."

Barker's face exhibited the high color of a man whose love for booze had turned to an obsession. When he heard about the troopers, the crimson drained from his face. "A car accident?"

"Murdered, Barker. Gunned down on the River Road."

"Who?" Barker asked.

"Sam Mahoney, a rookie, and Eddie Clark."

"Eddie?" Baker asked. "They killed Eddie?"

Tony studied the shaken officer. "I'm surprised you didn't know."

"I rounded up those drunks and got them in jail," Barker said. "It was late when I went to bed. I got up and came right straight over here."

"When's that two-bit town going to invest in a police radio?" Whit said.

Barker looked at him but didn't answer. His face was still pale. "Uh . . . if there's anything my department can do, Tony, we wanna help. Sorry I made such an ass out of myself."

"From the smell of you," Whit said, "you had some assistance from a bottle."

Barker clenched his fists, but Tony quickly stood up. "That's enough, Whit."

The investigator nodded his agreement. "You're right, Tony. Sorry I said that, Lenny."

Tipple Town's chief didn't seem appeased by the lukewarm apology, but Tony had approached him and was guiding him back into the hall.

"We're going to have a meeting tonight here at the courthouse with a lot of the law enforcement units in the county," Tony said. "I guess you might say we're going to form some kind of task force on this thing. You and your officer are welcome."

Barker nodded. "I'll be there. My man'll have to stay in town, though. We both can't leave at the same time."

"It's dangerous," Kathy Binder said.

But Anna remained unconvinced. "Not until we print it, Kathy. If we come up with anything, we can turn it over to Tony and Whit. If Harrington there has some contacts, we should give it a shot. It sounds to me like there's a lot more going on than even the cops suspect. Whatever they find out, they won't share. You know that as well as I do."

"I don't like it, Anna." This time, the publisher stood and started to pace the office. "Let me ask you something, Anna. You know we're friends, and I'm not pulling rank. I won't pull rank. You're the editor, and I'll leave the final decision up to you."

"I appreciate that—"

"Let me finish," Kathy said as she continued to pace the small office. "I get the impression that you're doing this just to spite Whit. In fact, it seems that a lot of your decisions are made on that basis."

"What?"

"Don't get mad, Anna. Just think about it. Like this morning when I told Tony that we might withhold information if there was good reason to do so. You took immediate offense at it."

"I know Whit Pynchon."

Kathy laughed. "I know that. You live with him. I confess, Anna. I don't see how in the world you two ever got together. I don't see what keeps you together."

"We separate our private lives from our jobs."

Kathy laughed again. "Which is why I had to roust the judge out of bed in the wee hours of the morning to get you released from jail. My God, Anna, they could write a book about you two."

"I might write a book. It's something I've always wanted to do."

The publisher settled back in a chair. "You're trying to divert me. Let's get back to the original question. Don't you see what I'm saying?"

Anna slowly shook her head. "No, I really don't. I know the relationship Whit and I have seems, well, odd, but I love him. I could kill him sometimes—a lotta times—but I do love him. He loves me. He can be a bastard, especially when he's in his winter doldrums, but he's exciting in a quiet, moody sort of way."

Kathy was holding up her hand, trying to stop Anna.

"That's not really the point, Anna. If you can stand to live with him, that's your problem. I'm trying to get you to assess your job decisions—to get you to think about whether those decisions are made purely as an editor or rather to get Whit's goad. One-upmanship. Is that a word?"

"I'll look it up," Anna said flatly.

"Please, Anna. Don't be mad."

Anna leaned toward her friend and employer. "Let me say this, Kathy. I met Whit because I was an aggressive reporter. I'm now an editor—an aggressive editor. I don't see anything wrong with a reporter trying to uncover a drug problem, especially a broad-based one in a small town like this. It's a good investigative story, the kind that wins press awards. If I had never met Whit Pynchon, I'd still want to do this story myself. Hell, Kathy, I'd love to get out there and do it myself right now. No, I don't think it has a thing to do with Whit."

"You know he'll be furious."

"I'm going to let Harrington follow up on his idea. I'll stay on top of it daily, Kathy."

"And Whit?"

"If he gets upset, that's just a little icing on the cake."

Kathy Binder threw up her hands in a friendly gesture of consternation.

"Between the news media and other police agencies, I've been on the phone all day." A weary Tony Danton was replacing the telephone's handset. "That was a conference call with the governor and the superintendent of the state police."

"I'm impressed," Whit said.

"Like hell you are. What have you been up to this afternoon?"

"Going through our files for suspects."

"If I didn't know you better, Whit, I'd have to believe you called them and coached them."

"What's that supposed to mean?"

"The superintendent wanted to send me this hotdog undercover man of his. The governor wanted to say that he thought it was a good idea."

Whit chuckled. "I'd say Al Downing was behind that. I talked with him right after lunch and told him you vetoed the idea."

The intercom on Tony's desk buzzed again. "Damn, I'm about ready to rip it out of the wall."

He pushed a button that put the voice on the other end on the speaker. It was his secretary. "There's a Curtis Felty here to see you, Mr. Danton."

"Felty?" Danton said.

"The brother from North Carolina," Whit said.

"Oh, the cop. Send him back."

"I'll go get the photos," Whit said.

The bodies from the River Road massacre had been dispatched to the state medical examiner's office in Charleston that morning. The police officer from North Carolina would be asked to identify the remains based upon photos taken at the morgue of the local hospital where a cursory examination had preceded the trip for a complete postmortem. The photos were in the file Whit had opened on the case.

As he returned to Tony's office, Whit heard a subdued voice that he did not recognize. He presumed it belonged to Curtis Felty since it was distinguished by the broad southern dialect common to so many North Carolinians. The photos were in his hand. As many times as he had handled similar situations, he was never comfortable with them. How did you handle it? *Here, take a gander at these. Do you know any of them?* It was just too cold—too uncaring. He had paused outside the door to Tony's office. The prosecutor was explaining West Virginia's system to the man.

"Our local medical examiner simply performs a visual examination of the bodies," Tony was saying. "We have one central medical examiner's office for the entire state that performs detailed autopsies. It gives us a much more highly trained forensics effort, but it also slows down the process a little."

"How soon before the bodies are released?" the man asked.

Whit stepped into the office.

The man turned.

"This is Whit Pynchon. He's my investigator. Among other things, he handles all homicides."

Curtis Felty stood and extended a hand. As tall as Whit was, Felty was taller. Big and barrel-chested with a rugged and tanned face, the North Wilkesboro cop had dark brown eyes that were weary and a little sad. He wore faded jeans, scuffed cowboy boots with sharply pointed toes, and a light blue jacket. As Whit shook the strong hand, he was reminded of James Arness, the man who played Matt Dillon in the old *Gunsmoke* TV series.

"Pleased to meetcha, Pynchon."

"Whit has the photos," Tony said. "I was explaining to Officer Felty how our system worked."

"Half-assed," Whit quipped. "Like most systems."

"Whit's also our resident cynic."

Felty managed a weak smile.

"You're a city officer?" Whit asked.

Felty nodded. "A detective. You have a photo of the child?"

Whit hadn't expected that question. "Uh . . . yeah. I brought all the photos."

"I'd like to see the child's photo first."

Whit glanced at Tony, who shrugged. He fumbled

through them until he came upon the one photo of the infant. The local pathologist had taken photos of the adults from several different angles. He had taken only one photo of the infant boy. He handed it to the burly North Carolina cop. The man bowed his head as he gazed at it. When he handed it back to Whit, a sheen of moisture glistened in the man's dark eyes.

"Now the others," Felty said.

He shuffled through the balance of them quickly, this time displaying no emotion in spite of the grisly mutilation the camera had captured. "What kind of weapon was used?" he asked.

"We found an unusual clip at the scene," Whit said. "One of our deputies said it looked like it came from an automatic shotgun."

"Figures," Felty mumbled.

He gave Whit a single photo. "His name is Cleveland Felty. This" —he extended another photo—"is Ernest. The girl is . . . was . . . Ernest's wife. The boy—his name was Nathan, by the way—belonged to them."

"Do you know the third subject?" Whit asked.

Felty boldly examined a full-front snapshot of the ravaged features. More skull than face showed. "I can't recognize it, but I can make a pretty good guess. I'd say his name is Tommy Panchino. He's the right size and the hair's the right color. He was involved with my brothers. If they were into something, he was usually right there with them."

He gave the photos back to Whit.

"Can I get you some coffee?" Whit asked. "Maybe a soft drink or something?"

Felty nodded. "A Pepsi."

"Be right back."

Tony had waited on Whit's return before going into details with the visitor from Wilkesboro.

"I don't know how to say this," Tony then said, "but it looks like—"

Felty interrupted the lawyer. "No reason to be delicate. I know what my brothers were into."

Whit wasn't surprised, but he feigned astonishment. "You did?"

"Sure."

"Do you happen to know who they came here to meet?" Tony asked.

The big cop shook his head. "They didn't share that kind of information with me."

Whit couldn't help himself. He couldn't let it go at that. "I don't wanna be nosy, Curtis, but, if you knew about the drugs—"

"Why didn't I do something?" Felty said, finishing Whit's thought for him.

"Yeah," Whit said.

Tony was rapt, anxious for the answer.

Felty's expression remained stone cold. "I don't owe you or anyone any explanation."

"We understand that," Tony said.

"As long as you really do understand that, I'll say this: Before I was a cop, I was a brother—and a son."

Curtis Felty rose to leave. He had the Pepsi in his hand.

"Will you be accompanying the remains back to North Carolina?" Tony asked.

The man's mass was framed in the doorway when he turned and said, "No."

NINE

BOBBY HARRINGTON WAS READY to give up on the phone call when a garbled male voice finally answered.

"Hey, Poo, what's up?" Bobby said.

"Who's this?" The voice on the other ended sounded sleepy, but Bobby suspected otherwise. Poo Kerns was probably whacked out on cocaine—or grass—or whatever pill he'd last put his hands on.

"It's Bobby Harrington, Poo."

"Bobby who?"

Jesus, Bobby thought to himself.

"Harrington, man! Bobby Harrington!"

"Oh, Bobby. Hey, man. How's it hangin'?"

The reporter still didn't believe the guy on the other end of the line knew to whom he was talking.

"Listen, Poo"—Bobby dropped his voice to a whisper—"I need to get my hands on some coke, pal. Think you can give me a hand? I don't need a whole lot."

There was a pause on the other end. "Who's dis again?"

"Christ, Poo. It's Bobby Harrington. We went to school together—all the way from the first grade through high school, man. We used to pal around together when we were in grade school. I just saw you last week."

"Sure . . . sure. Look, man, why doncha call me back t'morrow. You're spoilin' the hell outa my good times. I'm not in any shape to do any remembering, if you know what I mean."

"I need some coke bad, Poo. Why don't I stop by your place? Maybe if you see me, you'll remember—"

"Sure . . . sure, man." The phone clicked dead.

"That didn't sound very promising," Anna said. The reporter had placed the call from Anna's office while both Anna and the newspaper's publisher monitored it on the speaker phone.

"He was high as a kite," Bobby said. "Don't worry, though. I'll get the stuff. He was trying to give it to me just last week."

Kathy Binder's face displayed obvious distaste for the deception. "I don't like this, Anna. I think we should abandon the idea."

"You're the boss," Anna said, "but I think we've got an opportunity here we'd be naive to pass up. Just trust me on this one, Kathy. I'll see that Bobby here plays it as cautiously as possible."

"Sure, Ms. Binder. Give me a chance."

Anna's phone rang. She punched the button that put the caller on speaker.

"Yes?"

"Anna, Whit here."

"Oh, how are you?"

Anna and Kathy exchanged glances.

"You sound like you're in a barrel," Whit said. "If you've got me on that goddamned speaker phone—"

Kathy laughed as Anna hurried to lift the handset. "Okay, Whit. Is this better?"

"I just wanted to let you know that I'll be home late."

"I thought you were calling to update me on the investigation."

Whit chuckled. "Not too damned likely, but I do love you."

"You're in too deep for that to work. Besides, being charming doesn't become you." She winked at Kathy. "What's going on with the investigation?"

"The investigation is continuing," he said. "Beyond that, I have the customary no comment."

"Beyond that," Anna replied, "you really mean that the forces of righteousness haven't uncovered any additional information. Am I correct?"

"No comment, my dear. I'll see you later." Whit hung up the phone.

"You were brusque with him," Kathy said as her friend replaced the handset.

"He's accustomed to it. You might call it our official stance with each other. Besides, he gives new meaning to the word 'brusque.' "

"What should I do?" Bobby Harrington asked.

Anna looked to the publisher of the *Daily Journal*. "It's your decision, Kathy."

She sighed. "Okay, do it. But, please . . . please, be careful. I think we're sitting on top of a powder keg."

"Yes, but in this case," Anna quipped, "the powder in the keg is white and very expensive."

Tony Danton shouted the meeting of law officers to order. At least thirty cops—deputies, state troopers, and city officers—filled the first few rows of seats in the spacious courtroom. Only a handful wore their uniforms.

The turnout astonished the prosecutor. "I hope we don't have an armed robbery tonight. I'd bet there's not a single police unit in the field."

The sheriff stood. "We thought of that, Tony. I left one of my men on patrol to answer any complaints. If he needs help, he knows where we are."

Whit stood off to the side at one of the doors to the

courtroom. As the sheriff finished speaking, Whit winked at Tony.

The prosecutor smiled. "Well, I hope that's good enough, sheriff. Every one of you knows what the situation is in this case. We've had two police officers murdered along with four other people, including a small infant. Raven County isn't accustomed to hosting this form of criminal activity. This is the kind of case we all want to solve—very badly. Because of that, it's also the kind of case we can screw up. I'm sure many of you are feeling some pretty potent emotions over this case, but I want to be heard loud and clear on this: Don't lose control of those emotions. This is the last case we want to lose because we played fast and loose with the rules."

The door behind Whit opened. Curtis Felty, dressed the same as he had been that afternoon, stepped inside the courtroom and nodded to Whit.

Every face in the courtroom was turned upon the intruder. Raven County was small enough that each officer in the room knew the stranger wasn't a Raven County cop.

His unexpected appearance at the gathering momentarily left Tony speechless. He saw the hostile curiosity on the faces of the local officers. "Uh . . . gentlemen, the man who just entered the room is Curtis Felty. He's a detective from a municipal department in North Carolina. He's also a brother of two of the victims in the incident."

A heavy murmur traveled through the room.

Under his breath, Whit said to Felty, "Some entrance."

"You all shoulda told me about the meeting."

"Maybe you aren't welcome," Whit whispered.

Felty's eyes narrowed. "Maybe I don't give a damn whether I am or not."

Meanwhile, Tony had resumed talking, outlining the case to the Raven County officers.

He concluded with a stern warning. "We have reason to believe that the killers are in possession of some pretty deadly firepower—an automatic shotgun, in fact, equipped with clips and maybe even an ammo drum. Obviously, they have no qualms about killing cops. So be careful. Any questions?"

Felty stepped toward the front. "I got somethin' to say."

Tony looked at Whit, who just lowered his head.

"Go ahead," the lawyer said.

Felty marched back and forth across the front of the courtroom as he spoke. "I lost two brothers this morning. Now, I'm not gonna paint halos over their heads. They were big-time drug dealers. I know what you're thinking—that maybe I am, too. Well, I'm not. I don't really care whether you believe that, but it needed sayin'. As bad as my brothers were, they were still my brothers. I wanna add something to what the district attorney there said. I've had some contact with the type of folks you're gonna be lookin' for. The firepower doesn't stop with automatic shotguns. They might have grenades, Uzis, even maybe a bazooka or two—though they don't call 'em that these days. Down in my jurisdiction, we stopped a vehicle in the middle of town that was carrying M79 grenade launchers along with a stash of coke."

The faces of the officers were rapt with attention—with concern.

"I know what I'm talking about," Felty was saying. "My brothers got started dealing grass. They were forced into the coke trade. They were trying to get out of the scummy business, and they had come to me, scared to death. You didn't know my brothers, but I can tell you this. No matter what else you can say about 'em, it'd take the devil himself to frighten either of 'em. You're dealing with terrorists, pure and simple. Most of the cocaine dealers in this part of the country don't care who they kill. Babies or cops, either way they seem to get a kick out of it. I'm hopin' you guys can apprehend the culprits, but you got a right to know what you're facing.''

To Whit, it seemed as if the husky cop from North Carolina had something else to say, but he stopped there. He paused for a moment, then walked back to a position beside Whit.

''Bazookas, huh?'' Whit said.

''Like I said, they call 'em something else these days. LAW missiles or antitank guns, I think. Something like that. They're becoming very popular.''

A cop dressed in the blue uniform of the city raised his hand and stood. ''What makes you think the killers are even from Raven County?''

Tony looked over to Whit. ''You wanna answer that?''

Whit knew what Tony was doing. He was easing up to the fact that Whit was going to head the task force. Not that everyone in the room didn't know that already.

''They may not be,'' Whit said, ''but it's the only place we can look. We'll have to depend on other departments—or other detachments of the state police—to look beyond Raven County.''

Tony stepped beside Whit. ''Investigator Pynchon will be in charge of the investigation. I ask that you give him every cooperation.''

''Will he do the same in return?'' someone called out.

Tony started to answer, but Whit jumped in ahead of him. ''Probably not, but that's the way it is.''

Sinclair mounted his feet. ''This is the time for us to put aside all our interdepartmental quibblings. You all know that Whit Pynchon is a damned good investigator. I, for one, am glad he's handling this situation.''

Ross then looked directly at Whit. "I can assure you that our department will cooperate in every way that we can.''

Whit glanced at the face of the sheriff. He didn't seem especially pleased with the commitment made by his second-in-command.

"Outline the plan for the investigation,'' Tony said to Whit.

"Okay, here's what I'll ask you to do.'' He lifted a stack of papers from the desk. "This is a copy of the sketchy description we have of the other vehicle that was involved. You'll also find a general description of the weapon that we think he used. You won't find many weapons like that. Keep your eyes and your ears open. Also, I want each department here to go over its arrest records with a fine-tooth comb. Make a list of any and all suspects in drug cases. Add to that list any and all individuals who you may think are capable of multiple murder. If you have a doubt, put the name on the list.''

"That'll be a hell of a list,'' someone said.

Whit nodded. "That may be true, but, if you do your job and if the killers are locals, then I'll bet my ass the names of our killers will be on that list. We'll meet later this week and go over those lists. Each department will be assigned a number of names. If it becomes necessary, we'll question every single person on the list.''

Chief Thomas Wampler of the Milbrook PD was shaking his head.

"You got a problem with this, chief?''

"I don't, but the city council might—if it involves any overtime. My budget's mighty tight right now.''

Whit shook his head. "I know that'll be a great comfort to the families of Trooper Clark and Trooper Mahoney.''

Wampler's fleshy face reddened. "Dammit, Pynchon, you're—" He stopped. "We'll do what we can. That's all I can say."

Al Downing, dressed in a sweater and jeans, stood. "You know we want to nail these bastards, Tony, but my department favors some type of undercover operation. I don't know whether they'll go along with anything other than that."

Tony nodded. "I've already talked to your superintendent and the governor. They were in favor of an undercover operation, but they promised to assist with whatever action the local officials elected. He's promised his cooperation—reluctantly, I might add."

Whit used the opportunity to escape the limelight. He ambled back to the door. Felty's clear blue eyes were on him as he leaned back against the rich wooden panels of the wall.

"I get the feeling, Pynchon, that I'm more welcome in this room than you are," he said.

Whit smiled. "Yeah, you probably are."

Tony was bringing the meeting to a close.

"Let's step out in the hall a second," Whit said.

Whit led the out-of-town cop to the water cooler at the far end.

"What's on your mind, Pynchon?"

"I get the impression you plan on doing some police work of your own in this case."

"Maybe. What if I am?"

The cops started exiting the courtroom.

"I can't talk you out of it?"

"Nope."

"Then at least keep me up-to-speed on what you find out."

Before Felty could answer, Lenny Barker came up to them. "I'm Barker, chief of police in Tipple Town.

That's a wide place in the road on the other end of the county. I just wanted to pay my respects.''

"Obliged," Felty said, shaking the man's hand.

Other officers were lining up to do the same thing.

"How 'bout it, Felty?'' Whit said.

"Do I get the same guarantee in return?''

Whit thought about it before he answered. "Yeah, but I reserve the right to change my mind.''

"So do I, Pynchon.''

Whit departed, leaving Felty to receive individual condolences from the officers of Raven County. He found Tony still inside the courtroom with Ross Sinclair.

"Felty might be trouble,'' Tony said.

"He also might be a big help. For some reason, I like that guy,'' Whit said.

Sinclair was shaking his head. "He's a hot dog. I can tell by the way he acts.''

Tony tended to agree. "Keep a close eye on him, Whit. We don't know a damned thing about him. Let's face it. For all we know, he could have been in it with his brothers. If he's on the level like he says, he can still screw us up just as quick as one of our guys.''

"Somehow I doubt that,'' Whit said.

TEN

PAUL KERNS AND BOBBY HARRINGTON actually had been best friends from the third to the sixth grade. They had both enjoyed their respective collections of little plastic cowboys and Indians and could sit for hours staging gigantic mass battles that were fought over the length and breadth of their bedrooms on a cold or rainy day. On nice days, the engagements took place on a knoll behind the Kernses' upper crust home in North Milbrook.

The friendship didn't end when they moved to the Milbrook Junior High. It simply cooled off. Once they decided they were too old to play ''Custer's Last Stand,'' they discovered that they didn't have that much in common anymore. Paul Kerns—who somehow got the name of Poo once he arrived at the junior high—fell right into the high society clique. He still waved at Bobby when they passed in the halls, but Bobby had been compelled to find new friends, kids whose parents didn't live in North Milbrook, as the high society part of town was called.

Bobby had last seen Poo two years ago at the funeral of Poo's mother. Kerns's father had passed away a year before that. Bobby had somehow missed the news and hadn't even known about the death of Mr. Kerns.

As Bobby drove toward the ritzy home Poo had inherited, he remembered how depressed he had been after the services for Mrs. Kerns. It wasn't so much her death. That was the kind of sadness a person could handle. You prepared yourself for it before you arrived, rehearsing what you would say to your old friend when you hugged him and shook his hands. Bobby had been well prepared to tell Poo how sorry he was and how he was willing to do anything to help Poo.

The words, though had never been spoken. After Bobby had viewed the cosmetized remains of Mrs. Kerns, the funeral director had guided him to a room reserved for the family. There were several older people Bobby hadn't known—and there was this gaunt, ashen-faced skeleton that Bobby didn't even recognize.

"Bobby? Is that you?"

The voice had astonished Bobby Harrington. It belonged to Paul Kerns—to Poo Kerns, but it issued from a wasted shadow of a person whom Bobby didn't even know.

"Poo?" The young man looked worse than his dead mother. Bobby would never have even recognized him on the street.

The walking corpse, its eyes sunken and blackly rimmed, hugged Bobby. It reeked, smelling as if it hadn't been washed for a century or more.

"Sit with me during the service," Poo had said. "Mom's folks don't have much use for me."

They've probably been downwind, Bobby had thought.

But what could he say—but yes?

That had been two years ago. What did Poo look like now? If his decline had continued for those two years, what in God's name would he smell like? Bobby remembered when Poo had started drinking. There had been an arrest or two before his boyhood friend had graduated from high school. After that, he'd heard, it had become booze all the time and grass, too—so much abuse of both chemicals that the boy's brain had geared down to half-speed. Bobby didn't know at what point his old friend had turned to hard drugs.

After the funeral two years ago, Poo had sniffed some coke in front of Bobby. "I'd offer you some," Poo had said, "but my supply's a little light at the moment."

Bobby Harrington had never been a prude about such things, and he enjoyed a beer or an occasional drink as much as the next guy. He'd even tried grass several times. As with anything, Bobby figured it was a matter of moderation, a concept Paul "Poo" Kerns wouldn't know if it ran over him on the street.

It had been a decade at least since Bobby had driven by the Kerns home. In the darkness of the warm November night, he wasn't even certain he would recognize it. The houses in North Milbrook hadn't changed, but Bobby didn't remember all the trees and shrubs that had sprouted around the foundations and in the yards of the rambling homes. Some landscape contractor with a hell of a sales pitch must have passed along the block some years back. The neighborhood looked vastly different than the image he retained in his memory.

As Bobby's car approached the block in which he remembered Poo living, he slowed down. The spilled glow from his headlights partially illuminated the well-kept lawns and recently trimmed trees and shrubs that decorated the yards. That much hadn't changed. North Milbrook remained the snobs' haven, the breeding ground for—

"Ohmigod," Bobby said aloud.

Even in the glare from his headlights, the condition of the Kernses' yard jumped out to shock him. The grass hadn't been cut in months. With the coming of fall, it had yellowed and was laying in thatches over the gently ascending slope. A strong southwesterly wind racing along an approaching front tossed litter about the shabby

yard. The shrubbery looked more like a thicket of wild
rose—so dense that it prohibited even a glimpse of the
Kernses' ranch-style home that Bobby remembered sitting atop the slope's summit.

So much for breeding, Bobby thought as he pulled
his car to a stop along the curb.

"The wind's picking up," Whit said as he stepped
into the house.

Anna sat in front of the television, waiting for the
eleven o'clock news. It had become a ritual since she
had been promoted to the position of editor. Each night
her anxiety mounted as news time approached. It was
bad enough that the pretty faces they hired to deliver
the newscasts could so easily scoop her paper. What
made it worse was that they were so damned inept at it
when they did. No matter how significant the story . . .
no matter how many man-hours print journalists had
spent on it, the TV folks gave it a few spoken lines and
a staged interview, nothing more . . . wham-bam-thank-
you-ma'am—"and now a word from our sponsors" journalism.

And the personalities! Many times, she had watched
them work as they did an on-camera interview. The
subject of the interview, intimidated by the camera's
cold eye, mumbled and stumbled and somehow bum-
bled through it. Once the news team was finished with
the actual interview, the reporter did a dozen takes of
the lead-in and staged repeats of most of the questions,
just to be sure he or she looked good. The helpless
victim of the interview became a sacrificial counter-
point to the poise of the interviewer. TV journalists
were bad actors, nothing more.

"Am I going to get any surprises?" she asked.

Whit's brow knitted. "What's that mean?"

"I have this terrible feeling that Miss Jolly Smile on

Channel 11 will announce an arrest in the River Road killings.''

She hadn't been home long, but she hadn't wasted a second in changing from her skirt and blouse to her battered robe. She sipped a cup of hot chocolate, her eyes pleading with Whit to put her mind to ease.

He approached the overstuffed chair in which she was sitting and settled down on the worn arm. ''Would I do that to you?''

''Damn right you would. You had me arrested this morning.''

Whit shrugged. ''Yeah. That did me a lot of good, didn't it? By the way, how did you manage to get that freckle-faced photographer to the scene so damned quick?''

''I don't reveal professional secrets.''

''That makes two of us,'' Whit said, mounting his feet. ''I think you'll enjoy the news tonight.''

''Dammit, Whit! If you've screwed me with this story, I'll—''

He stepped into the bedroom and closed the door on her—so she couldn't see or hear him chuckling. The story would be on the news, but they wouldn't have any more information than the *Daily Journal*. God knows he wished he could have announced an arrest in the case. His gut instinct told him that there would be more lost blood—and maybe lost lives—before the River Road killings were cleared.

The interior of Poo Kerns's home wasn't quite as bad as Bobby Harrington had anticipated. He had prepared himself for a noxious pigpen, but he received a surprise. The living room in which he stood was sparsely furnished, and the thick rug didn't look too clean, but it didn't especially smell bad.

The young woman who had answered the door probably had more to do with the home's acceptable condition than did Poo, who sat google-eyed on the floor, his back wedged into a corner.

The female—Poo's live-in girlfriend, he decided—hadn't been too anxious to let him inside. She had opened the door only a few inches. Bobby had identified himself, but that had done little good. At that point, he hadn't been able to see anything of her but the center of her face—deep chocolate eyes, a long and pointed nose, and a mouth full of what he'd always called "buckteeth."

She had whispered back to someone—Poo, he assumed. Seconds later, the door had opened. That's when he saw just how wide the girl was. She had to tip the scales at two hundred pounds—half of which hung in two bulbous sacks from her chest and the other half of which was gathered around her hips.

"Hey, Bobby baby."

Poo sat in the corner.

"I thought you'd forgotten who I was," Bobby said.

"Aw, hell, you know me—I got this aversion to reality. Meet Princess, Bobby."

The woman managed a smile that made her overbite all the more prominent. She wore one of those things Bobby's mother had called a muumuu. In her case, the name was appropriate.

"Princess takes care of me," Poo was saying. "Come over . . . put your ass down here, Bobby baby."

The only light in the living room came from a low-wattage bulb in a floor lamp. Bobby couldn't really tell much about Poo until he sat down in front of him. He was surprised for a second time. Poo didn't look quite as bad as he had at his mother's funeral. As Bobby worked his legs into a comfortable position, he noticed the small mirror on the floor in front of Poo and the faint shadow of white dust on its surface. A small straw rested on the grimy carpet beside the mirror.

"You're looking okay," Bobby said. That was a lie. Whereas Poo didn't look—or smell—as bad as he had at the funeral home, he still looked more dead than alive.

"Like I said, Bobby baby, Princess takes care of me. 'Course I take care of her, too—don't I, Princess?"

Princess smiled. "Can I get you a beer, Bobby?"

"Sure."

"Bring me one, too," Poo said.

She vanished into the rear of the house.

"That girl's like a mother to me," Poo said. "And she fucks like a bitch dog in heat."

"So, how you been doing?"

"Floatin' most of the time. Did I hear you right on the phone? You wanna buy some stuff?"

"Yep. I figured I could count on you. I was afraid you might have forgotten that I called."

Poo's glassy eyes widened. He leaned his back against the support of the corner. "I remembered it. Excuse me for saying so, Bobby baby, but you ain't the type. You gone and turned into a narc or somethin'?"

Bobby felt his face turn hot. "Who me? Christ, Poo, we used to be best friends. I wouldn't do something like that to you. I work for the newspaper here. You can check on me."

"The newspaper, huh?"

"Yeah, I'm a reporter."

"Maybe you wanna write about me then?"

At that point, Poo smacked himself squarely in the cheek. It startled Bobby.

"Sorry, man, but I was killin' a flea. Princess there's got a dog. The son'bitch is a regular fucking flea farm, man."

Bobby's skin started to crawl.

"When'd you start usin'? I always had you pegged as a straight arrow."

"I'll be honest, Poo. I don't use that much, but I have this girl. She likes to indulge sometimes. I'd like to get her some—sorta like a birthday present, you know."

"She fuck good?"

A vague sense of nausea started deep in the pit of Bobby's stomach. What the hell was he doing here?

"Sure, Poo, she's okay."

"But a lot better, I bet, after a snort or two. Huh?"

Princess reappeared with three beers—some cheap brand Bobby had never heard of before.

"Bobby here wants to buy some stuff for his girl, Princess. Says she fucks better when she uses."

Princess giggled.

"If it was anybody but you," Poo said, "I'd kick your ass right outa here, but for old times' sake . . ." He left the sentence unfinished and tried to snap a finger at Princess.

The gesture failed because of a lack of coordination, but the girl must have gotten the message anyway. "Be back in a second," she said.

Poo started to snicker. "Princess there . . . she fucks better when she's drinking . . . she snorts and all she wants to do is talk. Her mouth runs on about a mile a minute."

"Hey, Poo. I appreciate this, but how much is it gonna cost me?"

"Not a fuckin' thing. It's on me . . . like I said . . . for old times' sake."

"C'mon, Poo. At least let me reimburse—"

Poo waved both hands. "Forget it, goddammit. Tell you what you can do, though."

Somehow—maybe it was the edge to Poo's voice—Bobby knew the coke was going to cost him. Maybe not in money, but it *was* going to cost. "What's that, Poo?"

"Bring your lady to a party tomorrow night."

"A party? Gee, Poo, I don't know—"

"You want the stuff or not?"

"Sure."

Princess waddled back into the room. Her fleshy hand was closed tightly on something.

"So, just come to the fuckin' party. It's right here in the neighborhood. Tell him where, Princess."

She provided a street address.

"Gonna come?" Poo asked.

"I'll come," Bobby said, "but I don't know about the girl. She's got a mind of her own."

That made Poo laugh. "Man, you gotta learn to be the boss, Bobby. Show up alone if you can't do any better. We gotta get you back into the swing of things. Princess there'll be your date."

Bobby looked up at the round face and saw her smiling.

"We got a deal?" Poo asked.

"Yeah. Sure."

"Give him the stuff, Princess."

She offered a small glass vial containing a few pinches of white powder.

"That ain't much," Poo said, "but it's free. Let's call it a reintroduction to each other."

Bobby turned the vial over in his fingers. "It's plenty, Poo. I really appreciate this."

He stood, anxious to leave.

"You best show up tomorrow night, Bobby baby—and bring that bitch of yours along."

Princess followed him to the door. She put a hand on his shoulder. "What's your girl look like?" she asked.

* * *

Didimus Smith eased open the heavy curtain that covered the living room window. In the country darkness, the headlights of a car illuminated the massive figure of his brother, Willie Mack, as he lumbered down the driveway toward the waiting vehicle.

"Who the hell is it?" Didimus asked.

Jimmy Carr jammed a handful of popcorn into his mouth. "Willie Mack's cop."

Didimus squinted. "Which cop?"

"I reckon if he wanted you to know that," he mumbled, "he'd tell you."

The younger of the Smith brothers wheeled on his first cousin. "You know?"

"Nope, and I don't wanna know," Jimmy said. It was easier to lie to Didimus.

Sometimes, though, it didn't work. "The hell you don't, Jimmy. I'm getting sick and tired of being left outa things around here."

"You'll have to settle that with Willie Mack."

"I'm gonna. You can bet on that."

"Here's your chance," Jimmy said, smiling.

They heard the bulk of Willie Mack Smith hit the wooden porch. The door flew open.

"You fuckin' asshole," he bellowed.

Didimus backed away from his brother's fury.

Since Willie Mack's eyes were on Didimus, Jimmy wasn't quite so intimidated. "Whatsa matter?"

Willie Mack didn't answer. Instead, he reached out for his brother. "They found the gawdamn clip!"

"I'm sorry," his younger brother whined.

"Sorry! If they get fingerprints off that—"

"Willie Mack!" The sharp voice belonged to Jerilyn Smith. She had come out of the kitchen. "The boy's sleepin'."

"That kid's gonna have to get used to some hell-raisin'!'' he shouted back . . . then under his breath to Jimmy, ''she's gonna make him a momma's boy.''

''Maybe your cop buddy could wipe it off for us,'' Jimmy suggested.

''He got no chance,'' Willie Mack said, much more softly but through clinched teeth.

His huge and callused hands reached out and took two fistfuls of his brother's shirt. He pulled Didimus to him. ''You listen good, little brother. The cops are gonna declare war on us. They had a meeting tonight. You best be on your good behavior. One more mistake, and it'll be your fuckin' last.''

Tears rolled out Didimus's eyes. ''No more mistakes, Willie Mack. I promise.''

Still holding Didimus, Willie Mack turned to his cousin. ''That goes for you, too, Jimmy.''

''I'm always careful, cousin.''

Willie Mack released Didimus. ''If those mother-fuckin' bastards want a war, we'll give 'em one.''

ELEVEN

MARY PAPAZOLI WAS READING THE *Daily Journal*'s front page story about the River Road killings when the big man in the western outfit entered the circuit clerk's office. She did a double take. Most of the traffic that entered her area of the office consisted of attorneys, occasionally an insurance claim adjuster, and none of them dressed like a cowboy. He took off his Stetson and leaned over the counter.

"I need some help, ma'am."

She stood. "Uh . . . yes, sir. What can I do for you?"

"I'd like to see all the indictments over the past year."

"All the indictments?"

"Yes, ma'am."

She looked him over a second time. She hadn't ever remembered seeing him before. "May I ask your reason?"

He smiled. It gave her a chill.

"Where I come from, miss, court records are public records. I'd bet that's the way it is here, too. I don't think it really matters why I want them."

Mary bristled. She had worked in the office of the circuit clerk for over twenty years. Most folks—the ones who mattered anyway—considered the office an extension of the circuit court. They showed its personnel the same respect that they extended to the judge's court reporter and secretary.

"I'll have to clear it with the judge," she said.

"I'll wait."

"He's on the bench. I won't be able to see him until he recesses. Usually, that's about eleven. Sometimes he goes right on through until lunch."

The man reached into an inside pocket of the denim jacket he wore. He produced a badge case and flipped it open. "I'm Detective Curtis Felty. I'd appreciate your cooperation."

Felty? Felty! She made the connection at once to the newspaper article about the shootings on the River Road that she had been reading just before the man walked into her office.

The cop saw her glance back at the newspaper laying on her desk. "Two of 'em were my brothers," he said by way of a terse explanation.

Mary felt the flush in her cheeks. "I'm sorry. I didn't know."

"No way you could have."

"I still feel as though I should clear this with someone. If you'll wait a minute—"

"I got nothing but time."

She vanished and returned five minutes later. "The circuit clerk sees no problem with showing you where to find the information. However, I won't have much time to help you."

"I can manage."

"Please follow me."

She led him into the records room and to a table piled high with thick books of bound documents. "The indictments for this year are in this book. Those for the prior year are in that book. As you can see, we have quite a few indictments a year—on average about one thousand two hundred."

"Felony and misdemeanor?" he asked.

"Misdemeanors are rarely indicted, Detective Felty. They proceed to trial in the magistrate courts upon a warrant rather than an indictment."

"Where do I find those?"

"Golly, you'll find those records in the office of the magistrate court clerk, but I'd bet there are several thousand for each year."

"Thank you. I'll start here." He pulled a small notebook from his hip pocket. "Are the addresses of the defendants on the indictments?"

Mary shrugged. "Sometimes—if that information was available at the time the grand jury rendered the true bill."

"The true bill?"

"That's another name for an indictment."

She left him to the multitude of legal documents and went to her desk where she picked up the phone. The circuit clerk had given his consent, just as she had told the stranger. He had also told her to call Tony Danton and tell him what the man had wanted.

"That's some damned gun," Dr. Merrill Barucha said. "I've recovered enough lead shot to start a reloading business."

Whit grinned. "You sound sleepy. Did we keep you up all night?"

"Christ, Whitley. When they started rolling those bodies in here, I thought we'd had a natural disaster somewhere. Two of us spent all night with them."

"Did you come up with anything?"

"Wadding from the wounds . . . plastic . . . and, like I said, a hell of a lot of double-ought lead shot. There's not much reason to carry anything over to ballistics."

"I know. Anything else?"

Ross Sinclair sat on the other side of Whit's desk. They had been discussing the case when Whit received the call from West Virginia's chief medical examiner. At the request of the state police superintendent, Barucha had supervised each of the postmortems himself.

"The two adult males—not the troopers, but the others—had been drinking. I've ordered drug screens on all the bodies," Barucha said, "except the troopers, of course."

"In other words," Whit said, "you've got nothing to help us."

Sinclair rolled his eyes when he heard Whit say that.

"Not a thing, Whitley. There are some collateral findings, but it won't do much for your investigation."

"What's that?"

"The infant showed signs of child abuse."

Whit rocked forward in his chair. "What kind of signs?"

"Some bruising of the muscle tissue. At that child's age, it's unlikely to have been caused by anything other than some pretty rough treatment. They're consistent with typical trauma caused in abuse cases. There also appears to have been a hairline skull fracture at some point. It's well healed."

"The world is ripe with creeps, Doc."

"Ain't it the truth, Whitley. Too bad you don't have to be licensed to be a parent. One more thing, Whit. You folks must have some rats down there the size of Dobermans."

"I saw 'em. They could eat Dobermans."

"Should I send the remains of the out-of-state folks on down to the North Carolina?"

"No, send them back to the hospital here. A relative is still in town."

"They need to be embalmed pretty quickly, Whit."

It was Whit's turn to roll his eyes. "Does it really matter, Doc?"

"It might to the folks who are going to attend the services."

"I'll make a note—to quote Mike Hammer, my favorite private eye."

As Whit was hanging up, the prosecutor stuck his head in the door. "I hear you got a call from the M.E. He come up with anything?"

"Nope, nothing to help us."

Sinclair was rubbing his chin. "Do those automatic shotguns require any special kind of shell?"

Whit shook his head. "The same kind that go in any other .12 gauge."

Tony took a seat beside Sinclair. "The circuit clerk just called me. Curtis Felty is upstairs in the records room. He wanted to see all of the indictments over the past year."

Whit frowned. "The indictments?"

"Don't ask me what he's up to," Tony said. "I got a feeling he's going to be real trouble."

Sinclair started to get up. "Maybe I'd better go have a chat with him."

Tony put a hand out to stop him. "Not yet, Ross. Let's give his interest a chance to play out on its own accord."

The phone on Whit's desk rang again. He snatched up the receiver. "What is it?"

Whit's face brightened. "Put him on."

He covered the receiver. "This is the local office manager for UPS. He says he's got a bagful of cocaine to deliver."

The small vial of white powder rolled across Anna's desk. "It's almost as easy to get as marijuana," Bobby Harrington said.

"Just how easy is that?" Anna asked.

Bobby blushed. "You know what I mean."

"No, I'm not sure that I do." Anna retrieved the vial and popped out the small rubber stopper. Cautiously, she sniffed it contents. "It doesn't smell."

"Don't sniff too hard. It might not smell, but—"

Anna sneezed "Damn! My nose is tickling."

"I tried to warn you," the reporter said, smiling.

"Just my luck," Anna quipped. "If I ever decided to become a cokehead, I'd probably be allergic to it."

She sneezed again. She replaced the rubber stopper and rolled it back to the reporter. "Here, get the stuff away from me. Did you obtain it from this friend Poo?"

"Yeah, it was a gift."

"A gift? You mean he didn't charge you for it?"

"No. I guess maybe he's being cautious. Maybe if I was a narc or something, then it wouldn't be so bad on him by him giving it away."

Anna lifted her eyebrows. "That's a thought. How much would that be worth?"

"Maybe ten dollars. Hell, I don't know. I did have to make him a promise to get it."

"What was that?"

"He wants me to bring you to a party tonight."

Anna's jaw dropped. "Me? You told him about me?"

"No, I told him I was getting the stuff for a girl. He just kind of assumed it was my girlfriend, and he made me promise to come to a party tonight—and to try to get you to come."

Anna was frowning. "I don't understand, Bobby. Where did I come into all of this?"

"You're the girl I got this for."

Whit transferred the call from the UPS official to Tony's phone so that it could be placed in "speaker" mode. He, Tony, and Ross listened to the details.

"We received this package with a post office box for an address. The addressee is Tory Appleton," the man was saying. "As you know, we can't deliver to P.O. boxes, only to street addresses."

"What was the address?" Whit asked.

The man read off the box number.

"Did you open it?" Tony asked.

"No, sir, but I was examining it, and I noticed a little white powder sifting out. We've been told to be on the watch for that kind of thing. Apparently, we're handling a lot of illegal drugs—unwittingly, of course."

"What's the return address?"

"It's a post office box in Miami."

"Figures," Ross quipped.

"Anyway, we just got a phone call a few minutes ago from a guy who asked if we had a package for Tory Appleton. I lied and told him it probably hadn't gotten here yet. I told him to call back in a couple of hours."

"Good thinking," Tony said.

"The stuff might be flour or glue or something," Ross said.

"I'm gonna put you on hold for a second," Whit said to the caller.

"You got any field test kits?" Whit asked of the sheriff's captain.

"Sure do."

"I'll run over to the UPS terminal to get the package. We'll test it. If it turns out to be contraband, then we'll figure some way to make a bust when they come to pick it up."

Ross looked to Tony. "Sounds like the way to go to me," the prosecutor said. "I expect the stuff's for real. I know the name of the addressee. If memory serves, we indicted him earlier this year for possession of cocaine—a case from the city boys, I think. We lost the case on a bad search."

"Like I always say," Whit said, "this is one of the few rackets where you get a second shot at the one that gets away."

"The field test kits I have are probably stale-dated," Sinclair said. "We don't do a lot of drug work."

Whit slumped.

"They'll have to do," Tony said. "I'll check around. Maybe the state police or the city has some."

"I sure as hell wouldn't count on that," Whit said. He picked up the phone and told the UPS employee that he was on his way to the terminal.

It was noon when Felty finished with the collection of indictments. He had a list of thirty names of people indicted on drug-related charges. Mary Papazoli was preparing to go to lunch when the North Carolina cop exited the records room.

"Where do I find the disposition on these cases?" he asked, brandishing the list of names.

"I'd have to look them up individually. It will probably take me a week or so."

"A week or so? Could I look them up?" Felty asked.

"No way! I can't turn you loose in my filing system."

"I can't wait a week either."

The aging clerk glanced at the wall clock. "It's my lunch hour, Mr. Felty. I'll be back in an hour."

"All I need to know is whether these people are in prison or not," Felty said, a plea for help in his voice.

The deputy clerk sighed. "Let me have a look at the list. I can probably tell you that from memory."

"From memory?"

"I prepare all of the prison commitments, and we don't have too many of them."

"A bleeding heart judge, huh?"

His comment produced a frown on the woman's face. "Why do you say that?"

"Never mind." He handed her the list.

She scanned it hurriedly. When she was finished, she made a mark beside three names and drew a line through two more. "Those with the marks were committed to prison. They might be out already. Those two that I marked off are dead."

"Dead?"

"A car wreck," she said. "It happened the night before they were to be sentenced. Ironically, the judge was going to put them both on probation. I guess they didn't think so. According to the newspaper, the driver and the passenger were both heavily intoxicated—their last fling, I guess."

"God overruled your judge," Felty said. He took the list, thanked the clerk, and marched from her office.

TWELVE

WHIT CAUTIOUSLY UNWRAPPED THE SMALL cardboard container the UPS man had given him.

"The guy was right," he said, displaying the interior of the box. White powder was sifting out of a second smaller box that had once been a container for photographic film.

"Somebody was careless," Tony said. The three of them—Whit, the prosecutor, and Sinclair—sat around the table in the prosecutor's conference room.

Whit used a single-sided razor to slice open the box within the box.

"Wonder how much of this shit is moved this way?" Sinclair said.

"According to the terminal manager, a lot more than we think," Whit answered. "He was telling me some tales he'd heard from some UPS guys in the big cities. Apparently, their trucks get robbed by addicts in search of drugs."

"It just takes longer for the trends to get here," Tony mused.

A plastic bag was stuffed inside the film box. Whit extracted it slowly. "If it's not coke, it's sure a good imitation. There's the reason for the leak."

An effort had been made to heat-seal the inner bag, but a small gap in the joint had escaped the shipper's attention.

Sinclair had the field test kit in his hand, a two-inch square plastic bag containing two vials of chemicals. Whit eased the bag of suspected coke open and Sinclair used a small spatula to extract a pinch of the substance.

"How outdated is that thing?" Tony asked.

"It expired three months ago. It should still work," Sinclair said.

"It's going to be the basis for our probable cause," Tony said. "I sure as hell hope it works. And I hope some magistrate or judge has the same faith in it that you do."

Sinclair dumped the white powder into the polyethylene bag containing the two vials. He resealed the ziplock feature on the test kit. "We break one vial and then the other. If the stuff is cocaine, we should see blue over pink."

"See what?" Tony asked.

"A color separation. Blue will rise to the top, and the pink will sink to the bottom. The deeper the coloration, the more pure the stuff."

"Give it a shot," Whit said.

Sinclair used his fingers to snap one thin vial inside the plastic container and then the other. The reaction was almost immediate as the chemicals mixed with the powder.

"Damn!" Sinclair said.

Whit squinted at the kit. "It looks pink and blue to me."

"Did you see how fast the reaction was?" Sinclair said.

"Which means?" Tony asked.

"I bet the stuff is ninety percent pure at least."

Whit picked up the larger baggie of powder. "I'd estimate we've got two ounces. What's the street value?"

Sinclair shrugged. "A couple of thousand maybe."

Tony was astonished. "And they sent it by UPS?"

Whit phoned the UPS terminal and talked with the office manager. "When the guy calls back, make arrangements for him to pick it up at three P.M. I'll be there."

"Is this going to be dangerous?" the man asked.

"I doubt it."

The manager, though, wasn't sure. "On *Miami Vice*—"

"It's not like *Miami Vice*," Whit said.

But Tony was worried. As soon as Whit hung up, he expressed his concerns. "You know, Whit, we've got some problems with this case."

"An illegal search?" Sinclair asked.

"No, the search won't be a problem. What are we gonna charge this guy with when he picks up the dope?"

"Possession, at least," Sinclair offered.

Whit, too, was beginning to see the problem. "We've got to be able to prove that the guy knew he was picking up cocaine. If we snatch him when he makes the pick up, he can easily claim he had no idea as to the contents."

"That's bullshit," Sinclair said.

Tony shrugged. "Maybe so, but that's the way it is. No way do I wanna let this guy get away with two ounces of pure cocaine, so we've got to make the arrest before he has a chance to get away."

Whit was nodding. "And if we put too many units out at the terminal, he may get wise and not even show."

"Surely you don't mean this bastard's gonna walk on this?" Sinclair was incensed.

"Just give me a minute, Ross. Let me think it over. This guy's made an ass out of me once. That's one time too many." Tony ran his hands through his short, dark hair. "There's got to be some kind of angle we can work."

"We could substitute flour for the real stuff," Sinclair suggested. "Then we could follow him—find out where he goes and get a search warrant for the premises. If he does give us the slip somehow, we don't lose the contraband."

"And if he's got no other drugs in the house," Tony said, "then we got no case at all."

Whit was shaking his head in exasperation. "Now I see why they use UPS."

Bobby Harrington was writing a story on the Milbrook High "roundballers" when Anna Tyree called him into her office.

He sat down in front of her desk. "I've thought it over, Bobby. I think I'd like to go to that party tonight."

The reporter's face drooped with disappointment. "I don't really think you should, Miss Tyree. I was just kidding you about that this morning."

"Whatsa matter, Bobby? You think you'll get ribbed for dating an older woman?"

Harrington's freckles disappeared in the intensity of his embarrassment. "No, ma'am. That's not it . . . not it at all. It's just the way Poo talked. These things may get a little rough—a little risqué."

Anna laughed. "Trust me, Bobby. I can handle myself."

"But I don't have any idea who might be there."

She stood. "Do you have a girl, Bobby?"

"A girl?"

"A girlfriend! A steady . . . or maybe a fiancée."

"No, ma'am."

"You seemed so upset. I thought maybe you were worried about getting into other-woman trouble."

Harrington's embarrassment turned to a mild frustration. "Look, Miss Tyree, I was being honest. I just don't think it's safe for you to go."

His display of anger, benign though it was, caught Anna off guard. In a way, she was glad to see it. The young man had seemed so—she scanned her vocabulary for the right word—so malleable.

"Look, Bobby, I appreciate your concern, but it's misplaced. You don't spend seven or eight years in this business without learning to take care of yourself. Over the past year, I've had a good teacher. What time is the party?"

"Eightish."

"Fine. You can pick me up at my house." She gave him the address and then started to say something else, but she caught herself and began to laugh.

"What is it?" Bobby asked.

"I started to wonder aloud about what I should wear. What's proper for a druggie orgy?"

The freckles again vanished on Bobby Harrington's face.

Curtis Felty decided to start at the first name on the list. The copies of the indictments had been arranged alphabetically by grand jury session. Thus the first names on the list belonged to individuals who had been indicted during the February term, the first term of the present year.

TORY APPLETON—that was the first name Felty had scrawled in the small notebook. Luckily, he even had an address for Appleton. According to the info sheet attached with the indictment, he lived in apartment 3C at 1408 Main Street. Felty's luck didn't stop there. Main Street was right where most main streets were located. It bisected downtown Milbrook.

The address turned out to be a door that led to apartments located above what appeared to be a flea market shop—a junk shop, they used to be called. Steep and narrow steps led up into squalid darkness. Felty reached down and pulled a .380 automatic from inside the sharp-toed cowboy boots he wore. He jacked a shell into the chamber and slipped the small but powerful weapon into the denim jacket he wore.

As he reached the top of the first flight of steps, he heard the whining thump of bluegrass music, punctuated by the shrill crying of a child. North Carolina . . . West Virginia—it didn't matter. The names changed; that was about all. There were plenty of apartment buildings just like this one in his jurisdiction. If the apartment number meant anything, the apartment he sought was on the third floor. He walked the full distance of the hall to the second flight of steps. His heavy boots rattled the aging hallway floor. Just as he reached the second flight, one of the apartment doors opened and a small child, his face streaked with ketchup, peered out. Felty put a finger to his lip. The little boy smiled and nodded his understanding.

Apartment 3C was right at the top of the steps. Felty withdrew the automatic from his pocket and used the butt of the gun to rap on the door.

"Police! Open up!"

He didn't wait for his command to be obeyed. The solid heel of his right boot exploded against the door just below the strike plate. The door flew open.

Felty heard a commode flush.

He charged the sound and found a frail man-child, his hair closely cropped into linear patterns over the ears, standing over the toilet bowl.

"Hey, man, you got a fuckin' warrant?" The kid talked tougher than he looked.

Felty leveled the gun at the young man's reddening forehead. "This is all the fuckin' warrant I need."

"Jesus Christ, man! Who are you? I ain't never seen you before."

"C'mon, scumbag, let's move out in the living room. I'll introduce myself there."

The man's hands were in the air. The initial color that had flushed his face was gone, drained out by the fear. His skin was white and glistening with sweat. "Sure, mister. Look, I just finished taking a leak. That's all."

Appleton backed out into the apartment's small living room.

"Search the place, mister. I got nothing to hide. I swear . . . nothing at all. Go on. Check it out."

Felty's head moved ever so slightly as his eyes scanned the cluttered living room. "It smells like a pigsty in here."

Appleton's hand shot out for a chipped vase that rested on top of a large television. He swung it toward the intruder's head. Felty saw it just in time to jerk up the arm that was carrying the gun. The vase exploded against his elbow, sending waves of pain up to his shoulder and into his jaw and head. His finger involuntarily tightened on the trigger of the .380. In the small confines of the apartment, the crack of the weapon mushroomed into an ear-shattering roar.

"I don't think the bastard's gonna show," Sinclair said. He waited with Whit in the Spartan office of the UPS terminal manager. They both gazed out a window that offered a view of the graveled parking lot in front of the package pickup office.

The prosecutor's investigator glanced at the wall clock. "It's just 3:15. Let's give him a little more time."

Sinclair was in uniform and planned to remain in the office. The terminal manager, a ruddy-faced replica of Don Knotts in looks and behavior, had found Whit a dark brown jump suit emblazoned with a UPS emblem. The pants legs stopped just above Whit's ankles.

"Any chance he's going to know you?" Sinclair asked.

"I don't think I've ever seen him," Whit said. "I didn't have anything to do with the case earlier this year."

Whit had reviewed the facts behind Tory Appleton's arrest in early January. The indictment had grown from a report filed by the state police. Tony had been wrong about the case coming from the city police, although Whit understood the grounds for his boss's error. The states had made a city cop kind of mistake.

The suspect had been the subject of a simple traffic stop. The trooper had suspected him of drunk driving and had made the obligatory arrest. Later, at the detachment, Appleton had blown a mere .03 on the newly installed Intoxilyzer. Under law, a person had to be .1 for the presumption of intoxication to become operable. In fact, any reading under .05 became evidence in favor of the defendant. Given the defendant's unstable condition, and the apparent lack of alcohol, the trooper had concluded that Appleton was driving under the influence of drugs rather than alcohol, a suspicion supported when a search produced a small piece of folded aluminum foil containing what turned out to be cocaine. Because the case had involved hard drugs, and the prosecutor wanted a supervised probation rather than the half-ass joke of unsupervised probation that would have resulted from a magistrate court conviction, he had exercised his option and proceeded by indictment in circuit court.

Four months later Appleton had walked out of court a free man. The small packet of cocaine had been concealed in Appleton's wallet, which—the court ruled—shouldn't have been the subject of a warrantless search since there was no way it reasonably could have concealed a weapon. The case was just another example of a cop trying to take a shortcut. In the Appleton case, the trooper had had more than enough time to secure a search warrant. It had just been too much of a bother. The charge of driving under the influence of drugs had washed out as well.

The office manager—his name was Carl—paced the small room adjacent to the package pickup area. "I think maybe he got wise. Jesus, guys, what if he comes back later? After you all have gone?"

Sinclair chuckled. "Relax, Carl. If the guy figured something was up, no way would he risk coming back."

"I hate this kind of stuff," Carl said. He lifted a bottle of liquid antacid from his desk and took a long swig. "I got a nervous stomach. The doc says it's on the verge of becoming an ulcer."

Whit felt a little sorry for the agitated terminal manager. He had formed his opinion of police work and involvement with the police from television . . . probably from *Miami Vice* based on his earlier comment on the phone. Because of that, he had visions of a shootout in his terminal, climaxing probably in his own death.

In truth, the real danger to a private citizen came not so much from the criminals as from the criminal justice system itself. The guy didn't know it, but if the bust went down, he'd make at least three court appearances, probably more. Each one of them would tie him up for the better part of a day. The system itself would totally disregard any inconveniences it might cause a witness like Carl while tying itself into knots to address the convenience of the judge first, then the lawyers on both sides, even the court reporter, and after that the defendant. A mere witness had no standing whatsoever in the system's pecking order—a puppet bound by a web of strings, each one in the hands of a different party to the chaotic scheme of the judicial system.

Instead of informing the man of that future misery, he simply said, "This is the easy part, Carl."

"Whadaya mean?" the man asked.

Before Whit could answer, an old Pontiac convertible crunched across the gravel of the parking area. One time, the vehicle had boasted a deep blue finish and a rich cream-colored rag top with matching interior. The blue long since had faded, and the car's body was eaten alive by rust. The rag top was gone, too . . . almost completely. What little that remained of the convertible top hung in shreds from the motorized roof frame, which the driver for some reason had gone to the trouble of raising. Or perhaps the motor that raised and lowered it had burned out in the lifted position. Whatever the reason, the occupant now operated the vehicle without any overhead protection whatsoever. He had all the windows up to provide some obstruction against the autumn-chilled air. The car pulled to a stop in front of the door.

As the driver exited the car, Whit noticed the smear of dark red on the battered bucket seat.

"I'd say that's our mark," he said. "He looks to be alone and maybe wounded."

Carl—the terminal manager—was trembling. "Whadaya want me to do."

"You scoot into the back," Whit said, now much more cautious because of what had appeared to be blood on the seat of the vehicle.

"I'll slip out the loading entrance and meet him on his way out," Sinclair said, his gun already drawn.

"Watch that thing," Whit warned, meaning the gleaming .357 in the deputy's hand.

Sinclair grinned. "Relax, Whit. I won't shoot you.

I'm one of two or three cops in this county who likes you.''

Quickly, Whit stepped out into the pickup area and stationed himself behind the worn counter. The front door swung open and the driver of the convertible stepped inside. He staggered just a little as he crossed the threshold, and Whit saw that he was favoring his left side.

"Can I help you?" Whit asked.

The customer was pale and shaking a little. He was probably in his early twenties and possessed a careworn face scarred and pitted by a raging case of teenage acne. He wore his hair cropped close to his scalp in a patterned style popularized by some college football player. In keeping with current trends, he displayed what appeared to be a diamond earring in the lobe of his right ear.

"I'm s'posed to pick up a package, man."

"Your name?"

"Appleton . . . Tory Appleton."

From his vantage point, Whit couldn't see any blood, but the suspect was in severe discomfort. His jaw muscles twitched against the pain as he shifted his weight.

"Are you all right, Mr. Appleton?"

"Yeah, I'm fine, pal. Look, I'm in kind of a hurry—"

Whit looked beneath the counter that separated him from the suspect. "Do you know how big the package was, sir?"

"I called earlier, and some dude said it was here. Step on it, okay."

Whit saw Sinclair through the front window. The uniformed man lifted up his head so Whit would know he was in place. The young man must have sensed or heard something. He turned momentarily to glance over his right shoulder. Sinclair had ducked beneath the window opening, but the suspect's movement gave Whit a chance to see the dark stain of blood behind his left arm.

"Here it is," Whit said.

He handed the box across the counter. "You look awful, Mr. Appleton. You're bleeding. You oughta see a doctor."

Appleton snatched the box and didn't give it a second look. "You just made me feel a lot better."

He wheeled toward the door. Whit let him go, using the opportunity to slide his own hand into the pocket containing the compact automatic. As Appleton pulled the door open, Sinclair stood and jammed the barrel of his revolver dead against Tory Appleton's chest. The box fell from the suspect's hand.

"What the hell is going on?" he said.

Whit hurried out from behind the counter and latched on to Appleton. From the back, the bloodstain was clearly visible. If Whit was any judge, the kid had been shot.

"You have the right to remain silent . . ." Whit went on to complete the Miranda warnings as he cuffed the suspect's hands behind his back.

"Jesus, watch my arm."

"What caused that?" Whit asked when he was finished with the cuffs.

"I just got shot, motherfucker."

Whit spun him around.

"By whom?"

"How the hell do I know? Some asshole tried to kill me, and he said he was a cop."

THIRTEEN

"IT LOOKS LIKE ONE of Little Mackie's toys to me," Jerilyn Smith said. She turned the strange object over in her hands. Willie Mack had just returned from the small post office in Tipple Town where the package had been delivered.

"Shit, I wish Little Mackie cared about those kinda toys. All he goes on about are them computers they got at school."

"Maybe he'll be the first one to get hisself outa this holler," she said.

"What's wrong with this holler?"

Jerilyn Smith, tall for a woman but also very heavy, tried to hand the device back to her husband. "There are better places, Willie Mack—and better ways to make a livin'. Now what is this thing?"

"It's crossbow, honey—and it ain't no toy. It's even got a scope on it. I wanna see you shoot it."

They stood on the front porch of their house. Willie Mack picked up one of the short arrows that had been supplied with the weapon. His wife tested the tension on the sleek black wire. "Ain't no way," she said.

"You do it like this," her husband said. He took the weapon and positioned it on the floor so he could get some leverage. Carefully, he pulled it back to its cocked position and then inserted the short arrow.

"You wanna try it first?" he asked.

His wife shook her head. "It's your toy."

"I told ya . . . it ain't no toy . . . cost over three hundred dollars."

He aimed the crossbow at an aluminum pie plate that he had nailed to the trunk of the large chestnut tree in their front yard.

"I wish'd you could find somethun' else to use for target practice," his wife said. "You're gonna kill that tree."

As if in response to her complaint, a large starling settled to the ground not twenty feet from where they stood. Willie Mack swiveled the crossbow around, centered the black bird in the scope, and squeezed the trigger. The sound startled the bird to flight. The arrow, though, was too fast for it. The sharp blade nearly cut the starling in half.

Jerilyn gasped. "That's amazin'. Where'd you learn to shoot one of those things?"

"Ain't nothing to it, Jeri . . . just like shootin' a rifle. They had 'em at that gun show down in Georgia last year. I shoulda bought one there. Been thinking about it ever since."

He had cocked and loaded the device again. "You wanna try it?"

"Sure, but I don't wanna shoot at the chestnut."

"See if you can hit that starling again. It's past caring."

She took the weapon from him and brought it up to her ample shoulder.

"Just watch your hand, hon. Don't let the drawstring get you."

whannnnng . . . .

The arrow buried itself in the ground within three inches of the bird's corpse.

"I like it," Willie Mack's wife said. "At least it's

quiet. Sometimes you drive me crazy shootin' around here all the time."

"I'm gonna take it deer hunting this year."

"Is is legal?"

Willie Mack shrugged. "For bow season, I guess it is."

Sinclair and Whit questioned Tory Appleton in the prosecutor's conference room.

"I didn't know what the fuck was in that box," Appleton declared.

"C'mon," Sinclair snapped. "Who the hell do you think you're dealing with? We weren't born yesterday."

On the way to the courthouse, they had stopped by the emergency room of the Milbrook hospital. Appleton's wound had turned out to be little more than a graze. A doctor had cleaned and bandaged it and told the young man how lucky he had been. Throughout the ordeal, Tory Appleton had continually asserted ignorance about the contents of the package. He also refused to say anything about the person who had shot him.

But he had plenty to say about the reason for his visit to the UPS terminal. "This dude called me and asked me to pick up the package. That's the way it happened."

Whit shook his head. "No way, kid. It doesn't wash. A guy doesn't do that kind of favor for somebody moments after he's been shot."

"I wasn't hurt bad."

"So who was the guy that called you?" Sinclair asked.

"I ain't no fink, man."

"So you're gonna take the fall yourself?" Sinclair asked.

Whit decided to try a different approach. "We got a

return address on the package,'' he told Sinclair, loud enough that the suspect could hear. ''I've got a contact with the Drug Enforcement Administration. He's stationed in Miami. I'm gonna give him a call.''

''Call anybody you fuckin' like,'' Appleton said.

Whit rose to leave. On his way out, he heard Sinclair telling the kid, ''You don't know what trouble is until you've had the Feds on your ass. Once he makes that call, then you'll belong to them. You'd better do some quick thinking.''

Not a word of truth to it, Whit thought. Unless you were a public official selling drugs or on the take in one way or another, the Feds really didn't give a damn. At least that's how it had been for the last three or four years in West Virginia. He did have a friend with the DEA who was stationed in Miami. Whit had no hope of getting the local Feds into the case, but he did want to tip his Miami friend about the post office box number in Miami—for what good it would do.

Ed Leslie had started out as a state trooper and had joined the Feds three years before. As with most DEA agents, his first assignment had been one of the agency's hot spots—probably its hottest spot, both climatically and operationally. Leslie hustled up kilos of coke the way local cops rounded up public drunks.

Whit reached Leslie in his office.

''Damn, Whit. How long's it been since we talked?''

''Six months at least. I'm not even gonna ask how the weather is down there.''

Leslie laughed. ''Good! Because it's actually kind of cold and chilly right now. I was gonna call you. I saw the teletype on Clark.''

''That's what we're working on—indirectly.''

Whit quickly told Leslie about the UPS incident and gave him the post office box number in Miami.

"It's probably small potatoes to you guys," Whit said, "but it's a lot for us."

"You say it checks pure," Leslie asked.

"Yeah—with a field test kit."

"If you got around two ounces, I'd say the street value up your way is about three thousand dollars to four thousand dollars. These days, it's hard to say. There's been so much coming in that the law of supply and demand has taken effect. The price is dropping every day."

Whit was still a little shocked. "We figured two grand."

"Not if the stuff's eighty-five to ninety-five percent. They can cut it quite a bit before they sell it. Down here it would bring almost that much. You're not gonna believe this, old friend, but these guys deal in so much cash these days they don't count it. They weigh it."

"Ah, c'mon."

"I'm serious, Whit. A million in twenties weighs in right at sixty pounds. That's how they check it. I gather you think Clark's killing was related to drugs."

"We found some cocaine residue in a vehicle left at the scene. It looks like the dealers were up here from North Carolina." Whit went on to tell Leslie about the automatic shotgun.

"It's become a war, Whit. The big-time dealers have learned that most cops—especially locals—aren't crusaders. They've learned the advantage of a good offense. You *can* indeed scare the authorities away. After all, the buyers and the sellers are willing participants. When you might be facing the kind of firepower these assholes are now sporting, it sure makes some guys wonder if it's worth it."

"Sounds like you live an exciting life down there, Ed."

There was a pause on the other end. "If you wanna know the truth, it's worse on up the pipeline. Most of

the guys we bust are foreign punks. The real tough guys
are the inland distributors. You'd be amazed how many
of them are just good ol' country boys. They come on
like hayseeds, but they enjoy killing. To them, there's
little difference between dressing out a side of beef or
a cop. And they love their weapons, the more exotic
the better. I'll tell you, Whit. I'd rather be down here
busting the Colombians and the other Latinos than up
your way dealing with those hillbilly pipeliners.''

"Gee, thanks."

"I'll check out that address, but don't expect a lot.
Some joker probably just made it up off the top of his
head."

Tony's face appeared in the door.

"Thanks for the advice. I gotta run, Ed. Enjoy the
Sunshine State."

"I miss the snow," Leslie said.

"Then you oughta be committed." He hung up the
phone.

"Who was that?" Tony asked.

"Ed Leslie . . . you remember him?"

"Oh, yeah. Where's he now?"

"Miami. He's going to check out that Miami P.O.
box. We got the bastard. He came in to pick the stuff
up. Just like you said, he claims he had no idea what
was in it."

Tony shrugged. "It figures. We can go ahead and
charge him, but we'll be lucky to get it through a grand
jury. I'd really hate to see this bastard beat us twice.
Where is he?"

"In the conference room. Do you wanna try to cut
some kind of deal with him?"

They headed for the conference room. "I don't know.
Lemme talk to him before I decide. Whichever way I
go, play along with me."

* * *

Didimus Smith drove up to the house just as Willie Mack was putting away the crossbow.

"What's that?" he asked as he exited the car.

Willie Mack didn't even look up. "A crossbow. What have you been up to?"

"I was down at Tipple Town. Ever'body's talking about them two dead cops, Willie Mack."

That snagged his older brother's attention. "Ever'body but you I hope."

Didimus stepped back. "I didn't say nothing. I just listened, Willie Mack. Honest."

Willie Mack eyed his brother. "Hell, Didimus . . . you don't have to say nothin'. You just look guilty. What the hell were you doing at Tipple Town anyway?"

"I had a hankerin' for a beer, so I went into Moe's place."

Willie Mack closed the box on the newest addition to his arsenal. "We got beer here, brother. You were probably sniffin' after some diseased splittail."

"Aw, hell, I was just wantin' some company. Anyway, I might have us a deal. There was this guy in Moe's place—"

The older Smith brother let the box containing the crossbow drop to the ground. He reached out to grasp Didimus by the suspenders on the bib overalls he wore. "Goddammit to hell. I've told you a hun'nerd times that I handle the selling end of the business. Who the hell was this guy?"

"Brucie Jones, Willie Mack. You know Brucie. We've done business with 'im before. He's okay."

Willie Mack did know Brucie Jones, and Didimus was right. They had done business together. But Willie Mack remained angry. "I don't give a big goddamn. You don't talk to nobody about sales. I handle sales. Just like paw used to handle sales when he was cooking 'shine. You got no sense, Didimus—and after two beers you get diarrhea of the mouth.''

Didimus was shaking. "He cornered me, Willie Mack. I didn't say nothing. He just asked if'n we could get some stuff for him. He said he wanted delivery Monday after next—a grand worth, he said."

"And you just listened while he said all that, huh?"

"Honest . . . that's all I did."

Willie Mack released his brother. "So, what did you tell him?"

"I told him I'd let him know."

Willie Mack turned away from him and started into the house.

"What do I tell him?"

His older brother stopped. "Tell him no."

"But he wants a thousand dollars' worth. We can cut some stuff and triple our money."

"He can want a million dollars' worth. The answer's the same, leastways for Monday a week."

"I never seen you turn down a grand before." Didimus was hurt. He had figured he was bringing a pretty good deal home.

"If you can work it out for some other day, fine by me, Didimus, but I'm going huntin' Monday after next. It's the first day of deer season."

FOURTEEN

"YOU GOT NOTHING ON ME," Appleton told Tony Danton.

The prosecutor brandished the bag of coke. "You call this nothing? You had it in your possession. You know what the law says about that, Tory. You face jail time for just having it. And don't forget one thing. I'm damned good with juries. They're made up of folks who like socking it to dope-dealing punks like you. So maybe I can do better than just simple possession. With this much coke, maybe they'll believe you intended to sell it. That's more than simple possession—we call it possession with intent to deliver. That's prison time, Tory. The judge isn't putting dealers on probation. It's getting too near to election time."

"But I didn't know I had it. What about them people at UPS? They had it, too. You ain't rousting them."

"They called us," Sinclair said.

"I'd have called you, too. Just as soon as I saw what it was."

Tony laughed. "Sure, kid. I hope that's what you tell that jury, too."

Whit just shook his head. "You sound like a broken record, Appleton."

"And you sound like a cop without a case."

Tony and Whit traded looks. The kid didn't really know how right he was.

"So tell us about the guy that shot you?" Tony asked.

"Never seen him before in my life."

"Can you describe him?"

"Shit, man. All I saw was the barrel of that goddamn gun. I never got much of a look at the guy. All I know is he said he was a cop."

Whit stood behind Appleton. "Did you believe him?"

The boy hesitated before he answered.

"Did you?" Whit asked again.

"Not really."

The office secretary peeked into the room. "You've got a call, Whit. It's Anna. Do you want me to tell her you'll call her back?"

Whit sighed. "No, I'll take it in my office. I need some fresh air anyway."

As soon as he picked up the phone in his office, he said, "If this is official—"

"Dammit, Whit! Don't be so hard to get along with."

"I've had a rough day."

"Who hasn't? I just called to say I have to work late tonight. I probably won't be home until after midnight."

"Okay. Thanks for calling."

"Hold on a second," she cried, trying to catch him before he hung up.

"What is it?"

"Something's going on. I can tell."

Whit rolled his eyes. "Nothing is going on, Anna."

"Have you got a break on the River Road thing?"

"No comment."

"What about the autopsy?"

"No comment. Look, Anna, I have to go."

"You know where you can go—"

Whit hung up the phone. To him, Anna Tyree was two people. There was the sexy, attractive woman who filled a void in his life. Whit's first marriage had dissolved many years before, and he hadn't become involved again until he had met Anna. A part of her vanquished the loneliness with which he had lived for so long. But there was another part of her—the part that had been a reporter and now an editor. He treated that side of her personality the same way he treated other journalists. That she loved him—and he believed that she did—was something of a miracle. When she stopped giving him as good as she got, then he'd start worrying that he was being too hard. He loved her, in spite of the constant disputes, but more than that he respected her. Whit Pynchon could count the number of people he respected on two hands.

He started back toward the conference room and ran into Curtis Felty.

"How's the investigation going?" Whit asked.

Felty was momentarily at a loss for words. "I thought I was supposed to ask that question."

"Things are seldom the way they're *supposed* to be. The remains of your family members are on their way back from Charleston. You'll want to arrange for them to be transported home."

"I appreciate it," Felty said.

"And I think it'd be best if you accompanied them back," Whit said, his gaze tight on the North Carolinian's face.

"It's a free—"

Whit couldn't help himself. He broke out laughing.

Felty wasn't amused. "What's so goddamned funny?"

"What you were going to say. It's a free country, right?"

"It is, by God."

"That's what people keep telling me. Come in the

conference room. We're questioning a suspect in a drug case.''

Whit opened the door and started inside. Appleton looked up; his eyes locked on Curtis Felty, who was just behind Whit. The suspect's face turned white. ''That's the son of a bitch that shot me.''

Anna stood before a mirror and adjusted the short-haired brunette wig. She had purchased it during her college days for a Halloween costume party and was surprised to find that it hadn't dry-rotted over the years. She pushed the ends of her auburn hair underneath the wig and worked it down on her head. Anyone who knew her well would see through the light disguise. However, she wasn't much of one to socialize. In spite of the fact that she had lived in Raven County for almost two years and now edited the *Daily Journal*, very few people recognized her on the street. Anna preferred it that way. She kept her photos out of the newspaper.

If Whit knew, she thought, studying herself in the mirror.

Satisfied with the appearance of the wig, she dug into a bureau drawer and removed a small makeup kit. As a rule, Anna wore very few cosmetics. She didn't need them. On this evening, she applied them heavily. She darkened her eyebrows to match the hue of the wig and applied a sticky dose of mascara to her eyelids. Then she used the same mascara to alter her facial aspect. It was a trick she had learned in college when she had appeared in several productions put on by the drama department. By dabbing some of the viscous black gop on each side of her nose and working it in, it made her nose look larger. By working a small circle into her cheeks, she also appeared thinner. Each of the steps made her look older. By the time she was finished, she would probably end up looking like an aging Hollywood Boulevard hooker. That was what she wanted. After all, she was going to a party of dopeheads.

"You've got a choice," the angry prosecutor told Curtis Felty. "You can haul ass back to North Carolina or face criminal charges here. You have our sympathy over your family, but we're not going to tolerate vigilante justice in this county, not so long as I'm prosecutor."

Tony made the speech from behind his desk. Felty sat on the other side of the desk. Whit was beside him. They had left Sinclair in the conference room to guard the shaken suspect.

"I didn't mean to shoot at the kid," Felty said, his voice firm and not at all contrite. "The bastard swung a vase at me and the gun went off."

"You don't even have a right to carry a gun in this state!" Tony snapped. "You don't have the right to make arrests. You had no business at that apartment, goddammit!"

Felty maintained his composure in the face of Tony's verbal assault. "Danton, you have no idea what you're up against. You need all the help you can get."

"All the lawful help I can get," Tony countered. He leaned back in his chair. "You've committed a felony assault, brandished a weapon . . . hell, man, even a half-assed prosecutor could make a sound case for attempted abduction. How the hell would you like it if Whit here came down to your jurisdiction and decided to go on his own rampage?"

Felty didn't answer that question. Instead, he said, "Have me deputized, Mr. Danton."

The lawyer just shook his head and turned his face to Whit. "Can you believe this guy? He wants deputized."

"I want these bastards," Felty said. "My brothers,

they deserved what they got, but not the kid. For that someone's gotta pay. That piece of pond scum you've got in there, he knows enough to get us started.''

Tony's voice softened. ''I can understand how you feel, but you've also got to look at it from our point of view. You have an ax to grind, detective. Cops are supposed to be objective and levelheaded. When they become the victims of crime, then they can no longer function—''

Felty sprang to his feet with a grace that didn't seem possible in such a hefty man. ''You people are out of your league! This just isn't some small-time dope deal gone sour. These guys have got one hell of an operation—like Avon or Amway or what have you. Besides, two cops died. Are you gonna try to tell me that most of your guys are objective . . . levelheaded? Bullshit!''

The detective was trying to pace in the small office. He gave up on it and leaned over Danton's cluttered desk. ''My brothers were going to get out. Not because they got religion but because they got rich—and because they knew just how bad things were gettin'. Trouble is, Mr. Danton, they don't let people out. These bastards have a friggin' network. It runs from the swamps of Florida to the hollers of Appalachia. They got distributorships. The local dealers buy franchises. They got arsenals of firepower to protect those franchises.''

''Sit down,'' Tony said. The man was leaning across the desk, glaring down into the lawyer's face.

''When I'm through, counselor. These guys offer their distributors guaranteed bail. Did you hear me? Guaranteed fucking bail! Like the goddamn automobile club! When things get really hot on a local dealer, they encourage him to jump bail and even relocate him. Just like us, they've got their own witness protection program. If a dealer is even too hot for that, they cut their losses and waste him."

On that, Felty eased back down into his seat. "You got no idea what you're up against."

Whit dared to join the debate. "When I talked to Ed Leslie today, Tony, he was telling me about the same thing."

The prosecutor remained unimpressed. "Hell, we've had the mob to deal with for years—"

"This ain't the mob," Felty said. "In our area, and yours, too, I bet, these are the same guys that used to run moonshine . . . the same guys that used to burn crosses on the lawns of the coloreds. These are rednecks, and they don't have shit for consciences."

"Be that as it may," Tony said, "it doesn't change a thing. You're trouble, Felty, and I got enough of that already. I don't need to import it. However bad these guys are, you're not a big enough help to—"

"He might be," Whit said, interrupting his employer.

Tony frowned. "What the hell does that mean?"

"Maybe Curtis here can be a help. Appleton in there is scared to death of Curtis. Let's tell the bastard who Felty is. Let's tell him that Felty thinks he was somehow involved in the deaths of his brothers."

Tony was shaking his head. "I don't like this already."

"Hear me out," Whit said. "We tell Appleton that we've got nothing to hold him on and we're releasing him—but he'd best look out for Felty. Maybe the kid will talk."

"That's extortion," the prosecutor said.

"No, it's not. It's deception. The courts have always allowed us to obtain a confession by trickery and deception."

"It's not the way we do things, Whit. It's coercion any way you look at it."

"Dammit, Tony, you've ruled out an undercover operation. We've got a guy here who probably knows our killers, and right now we've got to let him walk. What harm can it do?"

Tony stood and stared out a window. The setting sun was masked by the thickening clouds that accompanied an approaching storm system. "What makes you think he's more frightened of Curtis here than these redneck dealers? You make them sound pretty damned evil."

"I saw the look on Appleton's face when he saw Curtis. It might not work, but it's worth a try."

Tony turned and addressed the detective from North Carolina. "If I agree to this, do I have your word that you won't go off on any more rampages of your own?"

Felty nodded. "You do, sir."

FIFTEEN

"WHO THE FUCK WAS THAT GUY?" Appleton asked as Whit and Tony reentered the conference room.

"Didn't Captain Sinclair here tell you?" Whit said. He managed a conspiratorial wink at Sinclair who was frowning in his confusion.

"He's the one that busted into my apartment!" Appleton said. "He shot at me! I wanna know who he is!"

Tony had moved to a far corner. He was going to go along with the plan, but he had told Whit to handle it. He wanted no part in the actual implementation.

Whit settled down at the table across from Tory Appleton. "I guess you got a right to know. We had a couple of state troopers killed this week. You hear about that?"

Appleton's face lost even more color. "Hey, man, I didn't have nothing to do with that."

Whit ignored him. "A couple of other folks, and a small infant, were killed in the same incident. They were from North Carolina—"

"What's that got to do with me?"

Whit closed his eyes in a gesture of dramatic frustration. "If you'll keep your mouth shut, I'll tell you."

"Man, I don't know nothing—"

"Shut up!" Whit snapped.

"Yes, sir."

"As I was saying, these folks from North Carolina, they were brothers to the guy you're asking about. He was an uncle to the baby who was killed. We think a drug deal turned bloody."

Appleton held up his hands—as if to indicate they were clean. "I don't know nothing about any of that."

Whit shrugged. "Trouble is, Appleton, he thinks you do."

"Hey, man, you gotta tell him—"

"He's gone," Whit said.

"Gone?"

Whit nodded.

"What's he gonna do?" the young man asked.

"He told us he was going back to North Carolina, but I can't guarantee it. Anyway, kid, I guess you're free to go."

Tory Appleton's eyes swiveled from Whit to Sinclair. "Free? What about that guy? He tried to kill me."

Tony was standing behind the suspect. "Do you wanna press charges against him?"

Appleton turned. "Me? What about you guys? You're the cops!"

"He says he didn't do anything to you," Whit said. "It's your word against his. You're welcome to go to a magistrate and swear out a warrant on him. He'll be charged and arrested. You know how that works, Appleton. I'd say he'll make bail at once."

"Jesus, man, that son of a bitch is crazy. You shoulda seen him when he busted into my place. You saw the gunshot wound! Can't you tell him I don't know nothing about those murders?"

"I think you do," Whit said. "So does he."

Panic produced tears in Tory Appleton's eyes. "I swear to God . . . I swear on my mother's grave, man! I didn't have nothing to do with no killin's. Christ, you gotta believe me."

Whit saw his chance. "Maybe not, Tory, but I bet you know who the big drug movers are in this county."

Appleton's eyes narrowed. "Wait a minute. What is this?"

"It's nothing, Tory. I just think you could help us. If you do, we'll help you."

Tory jumped to his feet. Sinclair started to restrain him, but Whit stopped him with a hand on his shoulder.

"You're jackin' me around, man."

"I said you were free to go," Whit said. "There's the door. Walk out of it."

"But what about that asshole out there?"

"As far as we know, he's going back to North Carolina."

"Like shit he is! What did you tell him about me?"

"Nothing, Tory."

"So what makes him think I know anything about what happened to his people?"

Whit stood and started toward the door. "You'll have to ask him that."

Tory Appleton turned to the prosecutor. "Hey, can't you do something? That guy might kill me."

"I can do my job," Tony said. "If anything happens to you, I promise we'll do our best to catch and convict whoever does it. That's how the system works."

Whit opened the door. "See ya around, Tory."

The boy stared at the door for a long time. Then he sat back down at the table.

Bobby Harrington did a double take when Anna slipped into his car. "Jeez, Miss Tyree. I didn't know you at first."

"I didn't want anybody recognizing me at the party. Don't forget, Bobby. Call me Annie tonight."

"Yes, ma'am."

"And none of that either."

"None of what?"

"Don't call me ma'am."

He sat there, gaping at her. Her features were illuminated by a street lamp. "You really look different."

"Let's get a move on, Bobby."

"Yes, ma'am."

"Yes what?"

"Uh . . . yes, Anna . . . I mean, Annie."

"Do you know where you're going?"

"I have the street address. I think I can find it without any difficulty."

"What kind of car is this?" she asked as he pulled out.

"A 1974 Oldsmobile Ninety-Eight."

"It's huge."

"I like the old big cars. This one's got everything. Velour seats, automatic seat adjustments, air—"

"I don't want to buy it, Bobby."

The young man laughed. "Sorry. I'm sort of proud of it."

She glanced back out the rear window. The long vehicle stretched out forever behind her. "Can you park it?"

"Sure. I bought it several years ago from a little old lady who was in a nursing home. She only drove—"

Anna was laughing.

"What's so funny?" he asked.

"That story. That's a classic. A little old lady who only drove it to the grocery store."

"This little old lady only drove it to the liquor store. I think she had been something of a boozer. One fender had been messed up, but, other than that, it was in mint condition. I only paid eight hundred dollars for it."

Ten minutes later, Bobby pulled the long black vehicle to a stop in front of a sprawling ranch-style home in an upper crust section of Milbrook.

"Here?" Anna asked, incredulous at the location.

Bobby squinted toward the front door. "Doesn't that say 1208 Locust Drive?"

"But this is just a block or so from where Kathy Binder lives."

Bobby slid the car into PARK. "Can't help that. I'm sure this is the place. The front porch light's on, and the driveway's full of cars."

He was right about that. It certainly did appear that something out of the ordinary was taking place inside the exclusive home.

"Poo lives in a pretty good neighborhood, too," Bobby was saying as they exited the vehicle. "Of course, his house looks like hell."

A strong gust of chilly wind buffeted Anna as the two of them started up the long, car-choked drive toward the house. She put a hand to her head to hold her wig, just in case.

"The wig's very becoming," Bobby said, smiling at the prospect that it might blow off.

Anna looked at him to see if he was cracking wise. His face seemed sincere enough. "I regret this already. I was expecting some sleazy apartment somewhere. I look like one of the barmaids at Chilly's Tavern."

"You look fine, Miss . . . uh, Annie—especially for a druggie orgy. Isn't that what you called it?"

"You're right, Bobby. It's silly. Nobody will know me anyway."

They reached the front porch, and Bobby froze. "What do I say?"

"What does that mean? Your buddy invited you. Use his name." She pushed him toward the door just as another icy gust swept out of the northwest. November's warm spell was drawing to an abrupt conclusion.

He punched the doorbell.

"Maybe we oughta leave," he said as they waited for a response.

"Not after I did all this to myself, Bobby. We might as well see what this is all about."

The door opened. A middle-aged woman dressed in a tight sweater and jeans stared out at them. "Were you invited?" she asked, her eyes on Anna rather than Bobby.

Anna pointed to him. "He was."

"Uh . . . Paul Kerns . . . Poo. He invited us."

The woman's puffy face brightened. "Oh, Poo! Yes, he said someone might stop by. Please come in."

She stepped back and opened the door for them.

"It feels like snow," the woman said, taking Anna's jacket. "I'm Martha Wilson."

The woman offered her hand, and Anna took it. "Annie," she said. "I'm Annie Tyson."

"What an endearing name," Martha said.

Endearing? In truth, Anna's full name was Anna Tyson Tyree. When she had started her first job as a reporter, the editor had thought it would be cute to use Annie Tyson-Tyree as a pen name. It had followed her until she became editor of the *Daily Journal.* Hopefully, the abbreviated corruption of Annie Tyson wouldn't be familiar to anyone.

The woman slipped her hand around Bobby's waist. "Come, meet everyone."

He looked over his shoulder at Anna, who was grinning. Obviously, Martha Wilson had already had more than her share to drink—or snort—or shoot. She was bubbling with a chemical-induced enthusiasm. She guided them through a well-appointed living room to a door that led to a set of steps.

"Everyone's down in the family room," she said. "It's our pride and joy. It's a thousand square feet with a wet bar."

"Wow," Anna said as the three of them went single file down the steps.

"Bobby!"

Anna heard the male voice just as soon as Bobby, who was in front of Martha and Anna, reached the bottom. She could hear the sound of music—Bruce Springsteen, she thought—and the dull roar of voices. When she stepped into the room, she saw a young man with thinning blond hair, pulled back into a sparse ponytail, with his arms wrapped around Bobby.

"Where's your lady?" Anna heard the man. She assumed it was Poo.

Bobby turned around to her. "This is Anna."

"Annie," Anna said quickly. "Annie Tyson."

"I'm Poo." His face was thin, washed out, and his eyes were glassy. Nonetheless, he wasn't spaced out enough that he didn't look her over, from top to bottom. Anna shivered.

Poo patted Bobby on the back. "You got great taste, man. What can I get you two? The booze is over at the bar; the other stuff's over there."

He pointed to a corner that was crowded with people. Anna used the opportunity to study the party-goers. Most of them were middle-aged, dressed in casual slacks and shirts—the kind they ordered out of L. L. Bean. As a rule, and true to the social conventions, the women had dressed up more than the men. Martha, in her sweater and jeans, was perhaps the most casually dressed of them all, a prerogative—Anna assumed—of the hostess. Plush sofas ringed the room. Most of the people were milling around or crowded about the corner with the "other stuff." A few stood at the bar, but Anna's eyes settled on two couples on the sofa. They were making out . . . necking . . . right there in front of everyone. A white-haired man actually had his hand inside the blouse of a girl that looked young enough to be his daughter. His distinctive face, the kind that looked to be chiseled from some flesh-colored block of granite, tripped one of Anna's memory circuits. Somewhere, very recently, she had seen him before. But had he seen her?

"Bobby baby!" The voice was high and feminine and came from the corner with the "other stuff."

Anna saw the short, broad figure of a girl emerge from the crowd in the corner and charge toward them.

"That's Princess," Bobby whispered.

"Princess?"

"Poo's girl."

Princess's buckteeth were broadly displayed as she smiled and pushed close to Bobby to give him a kiss. She turned to Anna. "And you must be Bobby's girl."

"Annie. I'm Annie Tyson."

The doorbell sounded again. Martha Wilson brushed by them. "Now I want you all to make yourselves at home," she said, her eyes tightly on Bobby. She patted him on the seat of his pants as she hurried up the steps.

"That's my aunt," Princess said.

Bobby frowned. "Mrs. Wilson?"

"Mrs. Wilson!" Princess cackled, her boobs and belly bouncing in rhythm to her laugh. She wrapped an arm around the reporter. "I like you, kid."

Anna continued to gawk openly at the white-haired man on the couch. Not since her college days had she witnessed such a public display of eroticism. He had the young girl's blouse open, and Anna could see a small pinched nipple. The man's index finger was caressing it. Suddenly she remembered the man's face and where she had seen it—not two weeks before on the Lifestyle pages of the *Daily Journal*. The man's name, if she remembered correctly, was Cletus Wilson—Dr. Cletus Wilson. He was a prominent local surgeon.

"Is that Martha's husband?" Anna asked of Princess.

"That's Uncle Clete," Princess said, smiling at his blatant display. "He's a surgeon. You know what they say about a surgeon's hands. Some operator, huh?"

Her shrill laughter seemed to drown out the rest of the noise, even the voice of Springsteen.

"Who's the girl?" Anna asked. Now that the surgeon's attentions had moved down from the girl's face to her chest, Anna found her face familiar, too.

"Barbie Fields."

"She seems familiar to me," Anna said.

She felt Bobby nudging her with an elbow, but she ignored him.

Princess moved between Bobby and Anna. "Barbie works down at the newspaper. If you're interested, I'll be glad to introduce you."

Anna felt the chill form on her face. It spread downward, all the way to her knees, which had gone weak. That's where she had seen the girl before! At the same time, she felt Princess's large hand come around her rib cage and settle just beneath her breast.

"Whatsa matter, hon?" the fat girl asked. "Somebody just walk over your grave?"

SIXTEEN

Whit assumed Anna was home when he pulled into the driveway of their house. Her car was parked in the street in front. On other hand, the windows of the house were dark. When Anna was home, every light in the place was on in absolute disregard of the costs of electric power. As he entered, he moved quietly, just in case she had fallen asleep. Three steps into the house, though, and he knew it was empty. It had that feel about it.

"Anna!"

There was no answer. He started turning on lights and checked his watch. It was 10:30 P.M. She had said that she would be late, but he had hoped to find her at home. He wanted company that night. He turned on the television in an effort to bring some life to the silent house and then went to the kitchen, where he mixed a stiff bourbon and coke. The muscles of his shoulders and neck throbbed from fatigue and stress. The alcohol, he hoped, would ease the discomfort.

With drink in hand, he picked up the wall phone in the kitchen and dialed the number of the newspaper. After 5:00 P.M., incoming calls to the paper were answered in the newsroom.

"Miss Tyree, please?" he said when a surly male voice answered.

"She's not in this evening."

"This is Whit Pynchon. What time did she leave?"

Everyone at the paper knew about the relationship between their editor and the prosecutor's investigator. As soon as Whit told him who he was, the voice became less hostile.

"Oh, Mr. Pynchon. I don't know where she's been tonight. I haven't seen her since about six o'clock."

He hung up and dialed Kathy Binder's number. The publisher answered before the phone could even complete its first ring.

"Kathy, this is Whit. You must have been sitting on top of the phone."

"Hi, Whit. I was just getting into bed when it rang."

"Sorry to bother you, but I was trying to locate Anna. I guess she isn't at your place."

Kathy chuckled. "No, Whit. I don't know what her plans were for tonight. You know Anna."

"Oh, yeah. I know Anna." He apologized for bothering her and hung up the phone.

What the hell was she up to? And what was her car doing out front? It wasn't unusual for Anna to come home late, but when it happened it was always because she was at the paper working—and she always had her car.

That's when Whit thought about Tressa, his seventeen-year-old daughter. Tressa lived with her mother, Whit's first wife, on the other side of Milbrook. She and Anna were close friends. In fact, it had been Tressa who had played something of the part of matchmaker when Whit and Anna had first met. He phoned the number of his ex-wife.

Julia Pynchon answered.

"Julia, is Tressa there?"

"Where else would she be this time of night?"

A conventional chill infected his ex-wife's voice. They had been divorced for almost fifteen years, but his ex-wife still played the part of the wronged woman. Not that Whit had been unfaithful. It's just that he didn't turn out to be what she wanted, and she had always blamed him for that.

"Can I speak to her?" Whit asked.

He heard the phone clunk down.

Moments later, the cheery voice of his daughter came on the phone. "Hiya, Pops."

"How are you?" he asked.

"I think I'm trying to catch a cold. Are we still going out Friday night?"

"Sure, hon . . . just like we always do." It was something of a standard ritual. They went to dinner together at least one night a week, usually a Friday unless Tressa had one of her rare dates.

"I was looking for Anna," he told her. "She isn't at work, and Kathy Binder hasn't seen her."

"I haven't either," Tressa said, concern edging into her voice.

"I'm sure she's okay," Whit said. "It's just a little bit unusual."

"I guess you're busy on the murder of those policemen," Tressa said.

"Yeah, I am. We think it's drug-related."

"I read about it in the paper. It sounded awful—especially about that baby."

Whit's mind was working in a strange fashion that night. "Lemme ask you something, Tress. Is there much drug traffic at the high school?"

"Some," his daughter said quickly. "It's not as bad, though, as everyone says. I mean, the way people talk about it, everybody at school is a druggie. That's not true."

"But the stuff's there," he said.

"Sure . . . grass . . . Tylox . . . even some coke."

It sounded strange to hear his daughter using words

from the streets and the courtrooms. "You've never tried it, I hope."

"Daddy!"

"Well, I'm your father, and you know fathers. We worry a lot."

"You should trust me more than that."

"I do," he said, "but everyone's curious . . . if you know what I mean."

"I told you, Pops. I've never used that stuff, not even the grass."

"I believe you."

"Do you think Anna's all right?" Tressa asked.

"Sure, but she's up to something. I can sense it."

He heard his former wife's angry voice in the background. "What's she fussing about?"

"Anna," Tressa said in a whisper. "She heard me mention her name."

Whit grinned. "I should have known. I'll let you get to bed, and I'll see you Friday night."

By the time he got into the living room, the eleven o'clock news was on. A network reporter was standing in front of a barricaded federal building in Miami where a kingpin in a Colombian drug operation was scheduled to go on trial. The reporter was talking about official concerns that some type of terrorist activity might take place in an effort to disrupt the proceedings.

But Whit's mind wasn't on the story. He was worried about Anna. Maybe she was trying to worry him, her way of punishing him for having her arrested.

Anna had managed to stay away from both the bar and the drugs. The crowd at the party was becoming more and more rowdy as it decreased in size. By 11:15 only a dozen couples remained, and about three of them had filtered upstairs, doing God knows what, Anna thought.

The surgeon had spirited Barbie Fields upstairs not long after Anna had recognized her. So far they hadn't returned. As far as Anna was concerned, Doctor Good Hands could keep the *Journal* employee busy all night.

Several times, some of the men at the party had attempted to approach Anna. Sometimes they wanted to dance; other times they had tried to make casual conversation. Each time, Anna had finessed her way out of the situation before it reached a level beyond "casual."

She was looking for Bobby so that they could slip away when someone put a hand on her shoulder.

She turned.

"We haven't met," Dr. Cletus Wilson said.

Anna's body froze, her eyes darting about in search of Barbie Fields.

Like his wife, he wore jeans. He had changed his shirt and was wearing one of those safari jacket styles, gaping open almost to his stomach. Thick curls of graying hair covered his chest.

"Annie Tyson," she said.

"Clete Wilson, Annie. It doesn't look to me like you're having much fun."

"Oh, no. I am. Actually, Clete . . . it is Clete?"

"Yes, Clete."

"I've been feeling a little under the weather tonight, so I've tried to slow down a little."

"I'm a doctor—" He brought his hand up to examine her eyes.

Damn . . . damn . . . damn. What a stupid thing for me to say. She had forgotten that he was a doctor. "It's nothing like that. I'm okay."

He tried to place his palm on her forehead. In the process it knocked against her wig, which she felt shift a little. "Maybe I can give you something to make you feel better."

"Please don't," she said, leaning back from his touch. "It's nothing, the usual women's problems."

Where the hell was Bobby? She wanted out of here!

"There's some grass over on the table. It's potent but very mild in flavor. I can't speak from experience, but, according to my wife, it does wonders for her PMS. I have read research—"

"I just need some sleep," Anna said.

Bobby still wasn't anywhere to be seen, but the corpulent silhouette of Princess appeared at the foot of the steps. Her dark hair was mussed and she was adjusting her clothing.

"Have you seen Bobby?" Anna asked.

Princess giggled. "Actually, he's upstairs. I think he sniffed something that didn't agree with him."

"Oh, dear. I'd best go check on him."

"Auntie's takin' care of him, Annie. He's in good hands."

Clete Wilson approached from Anna's blind side and dared to caress her face with his hand. "The poor child doesn't feel well either, Princess."

He exchanged a wicked grin with his niece.

"Would you like to go up and lay down?" Princess said, again daring to put a fleshy arm around Anna's waist.

"No, I really must be going."

"But the evening's young," Clete said.

"No . . . No," Anna said, pulling away.

She moved toward the steps. "I'll go find Bobby—"

Someone walked right into her. The blow almost put Anna on her back. She felt her wig shift, and she reached up to steady it.

"Slorry," a female voice said, the word coming out in a drawling slur.

Anna looked into the flushed face of Barbie Fields.

"I'm fine."

"Hey, don't I . . . I know . . . you," the blonde said, her eyes bloodshot.

"I don't think so." Anna brushed past her and started up the steps.

"I'm sure I know you, honey."

Anna stumbled midway up the narrow steps. She scrambled the rest of the way on all fours. She heard footsteps behind her, pounding on the steps.

"Wait . . . I know you." It was Barbie Fields.

"Who is she?" the doctor asked.

Anna didn't stop to look for Bobby Harrington. She ran through the living room and to the front door. She could hear them behind her, shouting at her.

"Stop! You're just having a bad trip." It was the doctor.

"I know you—"

Anna bounded off the front porch of the house. The gusting wind threatened to rip away her wig. She held it with one hand as she made a quick turn toward the rear of the house—toward some kind of cover, she hoped.

Kathy Binder answered her door with a fireplace poker in her hand. "What do you want?" she demanded to know.

Her employer's reaction stunned Anna. "For God's sakes, Kathy, it's me. They're chasing me."

"Get away from my house!"

Terror made Kathy Binder's voice shrill and biting. Anna started to back away from the door. "It's me, Kathy. Anna."

"Anna?" Kathy's eyes narrowed. "Anna!"

"I forgot how I looked."

"What in God's name have you done to yourself?"

She hurried into the safety of the publisher's home and slammed the door. "Don't even ask."

Her friend's fear had turned first to astonishment and now to hilarity. "My God, you should see yourself."

Anna followed Kathy into the living room, where she caught sight of herself in a full-length mirror. The wig sat askew on her head. Her face was white, except where it was painted with rouge or eye shadow. The tight skirt was hiked up just above her knees.

She started to laugh, too.

Kathy was giggling. "I thought you were some kind of freak. Jimminy, Anna. What a start you gave me. Whit's called here looking for you."

Anna went to a chair and fell into it. "Serves him right," she said, yanking off the silly wig.

"Where have you been?"

"Bobby Harrington took me to a drug party."

"A what?"

"I'll tell you about it later. Right now, I just want to straighten myself up. God, I ran right out of the place and forgot my jacket."

"What about Bobby?"

"He's still there, I guess."

"Maybe he'll remember your jacket."

Anna shook her head. "I don't think there's any danger of that. If he sampled any of the goodies they were serving, he won't even remember I was with him. Do you know what kind of people you have for neighbors?"

Tory Appleton found Jimmy Carr drinking a beer in Chilly's Tavern, a country-and-western joint on the outskirts of Milbrook. He'd phoned Carr earlier—from the office of the prosecutor—to arrange for the meeting.

Appleton took a seat on a bar stool beside Carr. "I need some dope, Jimmy."

"So what's new?" Carr asked.

"I mean it, Jimmy. I need a heavy load this time. I

got a chance to make some awesome bread. It might even become a regular thing, too."

Carr glanced around the establishment. On weekends the establishment hired country bands and hosted dances. A stage and dance floor filled one end. The bar and the closely packed tables occupied the other. On that night, the sound of country music—a slow beer-drinking ballad—came from a jukebox. It was near to closing time, and most of the night's revelers had already left. Other than Carr and Appleton and another man at the other end of the bar, the remaining patrons were couples, huddled with each other in the bar's booths.

"You're actin' nervous, Appleton. I don't like dealing with guys who act nervous."

"I'm just excited, man. We both could make a lotta bread on this one."

Carr's face hardened. "I don't like the sound of that, Appleton—like maybe you're gonna do me some favors if I do you some . . . like extend you a little credit? Surely you don't have any notions that you're gonna get anything on credit, do you?"

"Fuck, no! Cash, man! Cash up front."

Carr's hand locked onto Appleton's thigh. "Keep it down, asshole! Folks in this joint got big ears and mouths to match."

The other man flinched in pain. "Jesus Christ, man. Take it easy."

Carr glanced to the other end of the bar—to the big man who was finishing a beer. He eased his grip on the muscle in Appleton's leg. "How much you want? And, remember, it's cash up front."

"Two ounces."

Carr laughed aloud. "You're shittin' me, Appleton."

"That's how much I need, man. I thought I'd buy local this time."

"That's four grand worth. Where the hell's a piss ant like you gonna come up with that kinda green?"

"I got it, Jimmy. I've done deals this big before."

"So let's see it then."

Appleton started shaking his head. "No, no. I ain't got it now. I mean I can get it. Tomorrow . . . sometime tomorrow, man."

"Tomorrow, huh?" The fingers on Appleton's thigh grabbed another fist full of muscle. "So help me, asshole, if this is some kinda scam—"

"God, Jimmy, you're killin' me. I swear . . . I'm being straight."

"So why do I think you're full of shit?" Carr said.

"Come on, Jimmy. We've dealed before."

"That's a lot of stuff. You ain't never bought that much before. I'd still like to know where you gonna come up with four grand."

"I swear to God, Jimmy. I've got it."

"Stay put," Carr said. His hand let loose of Appleton's leg.

"Jeez, I think you bruised it or something."

But Carr had swiveled off the stool and was on his way to a pay phone on the far side of the establishment. Appleton looked down at Curtis Felty, the big man at the other end of the bar. A couple of minutes later Carr returned. He came up behind Appleton, wrapped his arms around him, and dug his fingers into Appleton's chest.

Appleton tried to jerk away. "What the fuck you doin'?"

"Checking you, pal. For a gun or maybe a wire."

"Whatsa matter, Jimmy? You don't trust me?"

Carr's rough hands searched Appleton's chest. "Sure, I do, Appleton." He finished the search.

"You satisfied?"

Carr remounted the bar stool. "You know where the old Four Leaf Clover used to be?"

"That old beer joint near Tipple Town?"

"West of Tipple Town on Black Lick Road."

"Sure, I know it."

"Be there in the parking lot tomorrow night, say around ten-thirty P.M."

"Christ, Jimmy, that's awful far out."

Carr grinned. "Yeah, but it's nice and quiet. You want the stuff, that's where you come. Tomorrow night."

"Sure, Jimmy."

Appleton started to leave. Carr's hand wrapped around his upper arm, the one that had been grazed by the bullet earlier that day. Appleton yelped, drawing the attention of several of the couples still in the club.

"One thing, Appleton. You show up without enough dough, or if anything else goes wrong, you're gonna be dead—flat, fucking dead."

SEVENTEEN

As Tony Danton stepped from his two-story frame home in North Milbrook, a blast of icy wind took hold of his storm door and threatened to dislocate his shoulder as it catapulted him into the yard. He looked up to the sky. Clouds the color of gunmetal raced toward the northeast, their dark bellies so heavy with moisture that they struggled to maintain their altitude.

A snowstorm rarely crept up on the mid-Appalachians that time of year. Strong and comparatively warm winds from the southwest, racing along the approaching cold front, usually heralded its arrival. With the winds came the moist air from the Gulf of Mexico. As the air cooled, the moisture condensed; the clouds thickened and lowered. In November, those conditions foreshadowed several possible scenarios—a cold rain, occasionally an ice storm, and sometimes heavy thick snow. It all depended on how cold the air mass was behind the front and whether the atmospheric moisture escaped the region ahead of the front or was trapped and overrun by it.

Snow often fell in November, but seldom did it accumulate. The ground was generally too warm. This time Tony wasn't so sure. He remembered a Thanksgiving several years before when two feet of the frozen precip smothered Raven County and made the long Thanksgiving weekend a time for hibernation rather than celebration. It wasn't quite Thanksgiving yet, but the clouds probably didn't care. They looked quite capable of dumping a prodigious amount of moisture. He hadn't yet exchanged the regular tires on his car for the studded snow tires that gave him some degree of mobility on winter-slick roads.

He buttoned his overcoat against the wind and hurried toward the sanctuary of the Chrysler Le Baron that was parked in his drive. He had tossed his briefcase over the passenger side and had slid under the wheel before he saw the piece of paper. Even then he might not have noticed it had he not heard the tick-tick-tick. The blade of the passenger-side wiper trapped the small square of paper against the windshield. In the strong wind, its edge flicked against the Le Baron's rich maroon finish.

"What the hell—" Tony studied the paper for several seconds, trying to see if it was just a piece of trash that had somehow lodged itself on his car. That possibility didn't seem likely. It was held down too firmly by the rubber blade.

He exited the car and went around to the passenger side. The wind tussled his dark hair as he fought to extricate the white piece of paper.

Clearly, it was a note, folded over to conceal its contents. He hurried back inside the car before he opened it.

His jaw set as he read the printed words. COOL THE OUT-OF-TOWN COP. BE WISE OR BEWARE.

It was a warning—a threat. Somebody, during the dark of the night, had dared to tamper with his vehicle. He jammed the warning in his coat pocket and backed out of the drive, leaving a double track of rubber as he sped toward the courthouse.

Whit hadn't really been asleep when Anna finally arrived home, but he had pretended to be. She had slipped quietly into the bedroom they shared, retrieved his frayed old shirt that she sometimes used as a pajama top, and had gone into the bathroom to change. It had been one-twenty-eight A.M. according to the digital clock on the nightstand. Several minutes later she had emerged from the bedroom and gingerly eased herself into the bed. Whit continued to pretend that he was asleep. They each had stayed awake for an hour or so thereafter. For his part, Whit could tell that she hadn't gone to sleep by the silent tension in her body. Her breathing, too, was irregular and restless, not the rhythmic cadence that signaled when she was asleep. Eventually, Whit had drifted off. Since she was sleeping soundly when he awakened that morning, he assumed that she, too, had done the same thing, some time after he did.

What the hell had she been up to? As he sipped his coffee and listened to the wind rattling the windows of his house, he couldn't help the thoughts that played hide-and-seek in his mind. For all of their arguments and their professional rancor, he loved her deeply—a fact he didn't often share with her. He knew just how insufferable he could be sometimes. It had amazed him that she had fallen in love with him, and deep in the recesses of his ego he often wondered how long it would last. Worse, if it didn't last, he knew it would be his own damned fault. On the other hand, he was what he was . . . and entertained little optimism that he could change. How many times had he vowed to himself that he would try?

"A penny for your thoughts."

She stood in the kitchen doorway, her hair mussed, wearing the old shirt of his, looking like one of those movie stars who woke up in the morning looking better than everyone in the theater knew was plausible. She was smiling.

''What time did you get home last night?'' He tried not to sound angry, but the question itself bore an accusatory edge.

She went to the coffeepot and poured herself a cup. ''You know what time, you sly devil. You were wide-awake.''

''I was worried about you. I mean, your car was here.''

That simple admission made Anna turn away from the sink and look back at him. It was so un-Whit-like.

''At one point,'' he said, elaborating, ''I actually had the phone in hand, ready to call the state police detachment and the sheriff's department to see if there had been any traffic accidents . . . to see if one of their units was on the way here to deliver the bad news.''

''I was working on a story.'' She sat down beside him and put a hand on his shoulder.

''I thought you had reporters to do that now.'' Whit struggled to keep his voice flat.

She reached up to stroke the gray hair on his temples. ''I need to keep in touch with that aspect of the paper, Whit. I love reporting. I suspect I'll always do a little of it.''

''You might have called me.''

''In case you don't recall, I phoned you yesterday afternoon to tell you that I'd be late. In fact, you said you would be late, too.''

He hadn't forgotten about the call. ''But I thought you meant that you would be working late at the paper.''

''In a sense I was. I just wasn't at the paper.''

''I know that, Anna.''

She leaned away from him, a shocked smile on her face. ''Whit Pynchon! You're jealous.''

"I am not."

"Yes, you are. I'm flattered."

For the first time, he looked her in the face. "Flattered?"

"Most of the time, you act as though you could care less whether I'm here or not."

He dropped his eyes. "That's not true."

She placed a warm, soft hand on his cheek. "I'm glad to hear you say it."

"I love you, Anna. You know that. Like I said, I was just worried."

She leaned over and pecked him on the cheeks with her lips. "I'm sorry. I should have told you I wouldn't be at the paper. Tell me, are you in a hurry to go to work?"

"I'm never in a hurry to go to work."

"Give me a chance to apologize." Her hand stroked his thigh.

"Ummm, sounds like a good idea. Finish your coffee first—and tell me what kind of story it was?"

She grinned. "I hate to do this to you, Whit, but no comment."

For an instant, his face clouded. But when he saw the humor on her face, he started to laugh. "I guess I had that one coming."

"And it doesn't even come close to evening the score," she said.

Whit arrived over an hour late at the office and found Tony in a state of unhappy anxiety. "Where the hell have you been?" the prosecutor asked.

"What's got you riled up?"

Tony brandished his watch. "It's almost nine-thirty. You're just a little late."

"So, do me a favor and fire me, Tony." For most of the many years Whit had worked for Tony Danton, their relationship had been something of a partnership. He wasn't accustomed to Tony playing the part of a clock-watching boss. Whit headed into his office.

"Go to hell," Tony said, following him inside, "but first take a look at this." The note fluttered down to the top of Whit's desk and was almost at once lost in the clutter of papers that covered it.

Whit picked it out and read it. "So this is why you're so stirred up."

"Hell, yes. Obviously, that Appleton kid spilled the beans to somebody. I don't like being threatened—not one damned bit."

"I don't know anyone who does," Whit said, examining the printed handwriting. "Christ, given your tone of voice, you'd think I was the guilty party."

"Don't be silly. I'm just irked. I'm the goddamned prosecutor. Who do these bastards think they are anyway?"

"Remember what Ed Leslie said, Tony. Felty, too. These guys are a different breed of scum, especially for this area. They play rough, and the best defense is a good offense."

Tony slumped into a chair in Whit's office. "They're trying to scare us off this case. You know the thing bothering me the most."

Whit looked at the prosecutor. "Yeah, Tony."

"You do know?" The lawyer's question had been rhetorical. He hadn't expected Whit to respond as he had.

"They succeeded. That's what bothers you. You are scared."

"Let's just say I'm a little apprehensive."

Even above the incessant roar of the wind, Willie Mack heard the car coming up his unpaved driveway. The surface of the road was covered with red dog, a chunky lavalike waste produced by the coal processing that had once flourished in the hollows in and around Tipple Town. The fresh load of the stuff that covered the approach to his house cracked and popped as the tires of the car rode over them. Willie Mack hurried to the window to see who was coming to call.

The battered old GMC truck belonged to Jimmy Carr. Willie Mack stepped outside to greet him. Out in the country, the wind made even more noise than it did in the city as it rustled the thick boughs of the pines and set the denuded limbs of the deciduous trees to clicking against each other. To make it worse, the wind was blowing out of the southwest toward the northeast, which was the geographical orientation of the hollow. The valley became something of a wind tunnel.

Carr held on to his greasy baseball cap as he mounted the front porch of the Smith home.

"We got us some little trouble," Carr told Willie Mack.

"Got a snowstorm comin', too. Let's get inside."

Once they were in the house, Willie Mack called out to his wife for some coffee for him and Carr. They settled down into chairs in front of the fireplace.

"What's up?" Willie Mack asked.

"I made that delivery to Poo this morning. There's this reporter that's wanting to buy some stuff from him."

"A reporter? A local one?"

"Yeah."

Willie Mack shrugged. "So what? He sells to doctors and even lawyers. What's so strange about a reporter wanting to snort a little?"

"Poo invited the guy to some party last night, and he brings along this flaky broad. Turns out she's wearing a wig kinda like a disguise. One of the chicks at the party knew her. She's the editor of the newspaper."

Willie Mack grinned. "Damn, Jimmy. We're gettin' a little par'noid here, ain't we? So maybe she didn't wanna be recognized. From what I hear about them parties, I can't say I fault her none."

Jimmy leaned forward. "I ain't finished. According to this splittail that works at the paper, this female editor lives with the investigator for the prosecutor."

Willie Mack whistled just as his wife, Jerilyn, appeared with two cups of steaming coffee.

"Don't sound good, huh?" Jimmy said.

"Sounds to me like it's time we really threw the fear of God in a few of these folks."

EIGHTEEN

"GATHER ROUND," TONY SAID. Whit was already in his seat beside Tony as the other four officers settled down at the conference table. Together they represented the brain trust of Raven County law enforcement. Corporal Al Downing of the state police took a seat beside Whit. On the other side of the table were Sheriff Ted Early, Chief Tom Wampler of the Milbrook Police, and Sinclair. All of them except Whit nursed white foam cups of coffee and a doughnut courtesy of the jail's kitchen.

"How's the wife?" Tony asked of Sinclair as the others settled down for the meeting.

The captain rubbed his weary eyes. "She had a pretty bad night. It's getting to the point that the pain medication has very little effect. I don't think this last chemotherapy session did any damned good at all."

"It's gotta be tough on you," Al Downing said.

"It's tougher on her," Sinclair said, his voice devoid of emotion.

"Felty's not here yet," Tony said, "but we might as well get started."

At that moment, they heard footsteps coming down the hallway that halved the suite of offices belonging to the prosecuting attorney.

"I bet that's him now." Whit went to meet the North Carolina officer.

Instead of Felty, he found Lenny Barker, the chief of the Tipple Town Police. "Hope I'm not too late," Barker said, his ruddy face glowing from his obvious exertion to be on time.

"Late for what?" Whit said, stunned to see the man in the hall.

"For this pow wow you guys are havin'. Sheriff Early called me about it."

Whit refrained from his customary sarcasm and guided Barker into the conference room. The corrupt aura of slept-off booze hung about the small-town chief. When Barker stepped into the room, Whit was a pace or two behind him, his face twisted into a mask of disgust in the wake of the stench. Tony's face reflected his shock as the man began shaking hands with the other cops around the table. Tony exchanged a handshake and slipped out into the hall to join Whit. Ross Sinclair exited behind Tony. They eased down the hall away from the conference room.

"What the hell's he doin' here?" Tony demanded to know.

Whit was shaking his head in frustration. "He said Early invited him."

Sinclair had joined them. "I meant to tell you about it, but when I saw he wasn't already here, I figured he wasn't coming. I let it slide. The sheriff told me he invited him. Lenny's wanting to run for mayor of Tipple Town next election. Early figured it might boost the guy's image a little if he was involved in a drug operation."

Tony threw up his hands. "Politics, goddammit! I should have known it."

"Barker carries some weight in the eastern end of the county," Sinclair said. "Early owes him."

Whit was leaning against the wall, his arms folded over each other. "I say we don't even mention the Appleton operation. We can make plans later. I don't trust Barker. He's a lush.''

The prosecutor had an odd look on his face. Whit saw it. "What's up, Tony? You look like you just got caught with your hand in your mother's cookie jar.''

"I was planning to cancel the operation.''

Whit's jaw dropped. "You what?''

"Why?'' Sinclair asked.

"We're calling it off. I've got reason to believe that our informant's playing both ends against the middle, Ross.''

"Then why have the meeting?'' Whit asked.

Sinclair was even more perplexed. "I don't understand, Tony. What's going on?''

Tony waved off both questions. "I've been pondering another plan of action. I'll go over it in the meeting.'' He turned back toward the conference room.

Whit reached out and grabbed his employer's arm. "Hold up a sec. Let's talk about this.''

"There's nothing to talk about.''

"The hell there's not. Felty's been all over this town. We don't know how many damn people he's rousted. Any of them could have planted that note on your car. Christ, Tony, he's got every damned drug indictment for the past year. That threat could have come from anywhere.''

"What threat?'' Sinclair asked, increasingly agitated by what he didn't know.

"Dammit, Whit. I can't take the risk—''

"What risk? We're big boys. We can handle ourselves.''

"I'm sorry, Whit. We forget using Appleton.''

The voice of Curtis Felty boomed down the hall. "Why the fuck are you gonna do that?''

The three men turned to see the North Wilkesboro detective marching straight toward them. "I've got the damn buy set up for tonight. What's this shit about not using Appleton?''

Kathy Binder had made a decision, and she entered Anna's office with a solemn face that underscored her grim determination. She closed the door behind her.

''After last night's little incident, Anna, we're going to stop messing around with this drug investigation. You could very easily get yourself in over your head.''

Anna had been reading the *Charleston Gazette*. ''I can't believe this,'' she said, pointing to a front page article. ''The state of West Virginia is on the verge of bankruptcy, and the damned governor is too ignorant or too stubborn to admit it.''

Kathy settled into a chair. ''I don't want to talk about the financial condition of the state of West Virginia, Anna.''

The editor offered Kathy a wry smile. ''Believe it or not, Kathy, I agree with you about the drug story. I couldn't believe what I saw last night—where I saw it. That asshole Wilson is a surgeon. For all I know he's cutting away on somebody this morning. Last night his eyeballs were aglow from booze and dope. He's a pig, Kathy.''

''Did you tell Whit?''

Anna shook her head. ''I started to, but I held off. I just didn't want him thinking that he had anything to do with the decision. That's one satisfaction I'll deny him.''

Kathy laughed. It released her anxiety. ''I didn't sleep at all after you left, Anna . . . worrying about the situation, I guess. You knew all along I had a lot of reservations. On the other hand, I didn't want to pull rank. I have all the faith in the world in your abilities, except when you're trying to get the better of Whit. That's when your judgment suffers. Sometime around dawn I think I decided to do what a friend should do, but I was afraid you wouldn't see it that way.''

"Last night opened my eyes. There must be an awful lot of it circulating in this area," Anna said. "I don't think Whit or Tony, or the cops for that matter, have the slightest idea.''

"Then we can enlighten them a little," Kathy said.

But Anna was grinning and shaking her head. "Whit will absolutely chew me a new one over this.''

Someone knocked lightly on the door.

"Come in," Anna shouted.

The door opened. Bobby Harrington's head peeked inside.

"It's about damned time," Anna said. "You left me in a fine mess last night.''

Bobby pushed the door the rest of the way open and came sheepishly into the office. A typical redhead, his complexion was fair to start with, but that morning it had become doughboy white. His eyes were bloodshot. Lifelessly, he slumped down into a chair beside the publisher.

"I'm sorry, Anna. I think they drugged me last night.''

Kathy sat straight up in her chair. "Drugged you?''

"I drank a beer," he explained. "One little beer. That's all I remember until I woke up—''

He stopped. "Well, never mind. What happened to you?'' His question was directed, of course, to Anna.

"I escaped—barely. You didn't finish your sentence a minute ago. Where did you wake up, Bobby?''

"I'd rather not get into it." He held a hand to his stomach. "I'm not feeling so well.''

"Then go to the bathroom," Anna snapped. "I don't want you messing up the carpet.''

The young reporter's face turned an even more colorless shade of white as he made a dash for the private toilet in Anna's office. Both Kathy and Anna could hear him retching.

"Drugged, my behind! I bet he just got drunk," the publisher said, revolted by the sounds from the bathroom.

But Anna came to his defense. "Maybe not. That crowd last night would have been perfectly capable of doing something like that. As I told you, you live in an exemplary neighborhood, Kathy. Most of the people who were at that party looked as if they could buy me ten times over. I bet you've even had some of them over for tea."

"Surely not," Kathy said.

Several minutes later, Bobby emerged from the bathroom. His color had turned from white to a putrid shade of green.

"Maybe you oughta see a doctor," Anna said.

"I think it was a doctor that made me this way."

"He won't be a doctor for long," Kathy said.

Bobby's brow knitted. "What do you mean?"

Anna tendered the explanation. "She means that you and I are going to the prosecutor this morning and tell him what we know. Based upon our information, they should be able to get a search warrant for that friend's house of yours and for Dr. Wilson's residence."

Bobby had been easing down into the chair, but Anna's words brought him back to his feet. "We can't do that!" he exclaimed.

Anna was stunned. "Just why not?"

"My sources are supposed to remain confidential. Christ, Anna, we can't go to the cops—"

"Oh yes, we can," Anna said. "As for that business about the confidentiality of a source, you didn't go to your friend to obtain information per se. You went to him to get dope, and you got dope. We saw a lot more dope last night."

"Jesus, Anna, Poo's a friend of—"

"Poo's a drug-dealing son of a bitch," Anna said. "The matter isn't up for a debate. Come hell or high water, we're going to see Tony Danton."

"There's no goddamn way he tipped anybody off," Felty declared after Danton finished telling him about the note on his car.

"How do you know that?" Whit asked.

"He's been with me since yesterday. He made a call and met this guy at a beer joint—Chilly's or something like that. I was inside the bar for the meeting."

They were in Tony's office—Felty, Whit, Tony, and Sinclair. The other cops were still waiting in the conference room.

"You were with him?" Tony asked.

"No, but I was close enough that he wouldn't pull nothing like that. After that, I took him back to the motel room. He slept in the same goddamn room with me, only I didn't do much sleepin'. That slimy bastard snored like a senile old bull."

"He coulda tipped whoever it was he was talking to in Chilly's," Sinclair said.

"I said he didn't, goddammit!"

Sinclair's face flushed. "Don't get uppity with me, Felty. You don't know what the hell they said."

"Where is he now?" Whit asked.

"Back at the motel."

"You hope," Tony said.

"I don't hope a gawdamn thing, Mr. Prosecutor. The bastard's back there chained to the pipes in the friggin' bathroom."

"Jesus," Tony mumbled.

"What's the setup?" Whit asked.

"Appleton arranged for a buy tonight at someplace called the Four Leaf Clover. Appleton says it used to be a beer joint—"

"Just on the other side of Tipple Town," Sinclair said.

Whit nodded. He vaguely remembered the rickety old building.

"He arranged to buy two ounces."

"Who was the guy he talked to?" Tony asked.

"Some slimeball name of Jimmy Carr, but the main supplier is somebody called Willie Smith."

Sinclair was slowly shaking his head. "I don't think we can put much stock at all in what Appleton tells us. I've never heard of either one of those guys."

Felty's angry eyes met Sinclair's. "I suspect there's a lotta damn people in this world you never heard of."

"I say we abort this thing," Sinclair said. "I don't like the sound of this."

But Whit said, "I like it. Let's do it."

The weight of the decision fell upon Tony Danton.

NINETEEN

THE BUSINESS DISTRICT of downtown Milbrook had developed in a straightforward fashion—without any geographical complexity. Main Street bisected the town. The core of the town's commercial presence occupied the buildings on either side of the street. Drivers of vehicles turning off Main Street, either to their left or right, immediately found themselves in residential areas. On each end of the town, Main Street became Route 12. To the east the highway began its ascent of Tabernacle Mountain. To the west it meandered toward the coalfields in western Raven County.

Twenty years before, when the coal industry still enjoyed the breath of life, Milbrook's downtown had thrived. Its single greatest problem at the time had been parking along Main Street. The city fathers had devised a plan to sell bonds that culminated in the construction of a three-tiered parking garage squarely in the center of the business district, just across the street from the offices of the *Milbrook Daily Journal*. With the death of the coalfields, business in Milbrook lessened. So, too, did the need for parking. The town had just barely managed to pay off the bonds. In prosperous times, city employees had manned tollbooths at the three entrances to the garage. As the bustle of business waned, the tollbooths were closed, and parking meters were installed.

Seldom was it necessary for a customer of the garage

to drive up the oil-slick ramps to the second floor to
find a parking place. In fact, rarely were all the parking
spaces on the first floor filled. The top two floors of the
building became lonely places, populated by pigeons
and the occasional wino looking for some place to escape the cold winds of winter.

On that day, though, as the wind was compressed
beneath the third floor roof and the second floor parking
area, a single truck—its muffler loud and throaty—eased
into a position at the edge of the second floor tier. Pigeons, agitated by the rare intrusion into what had come
to be their exclusive domain, chortled and clucked as
Jimmy Carr reached behind the seat of the old GMC
and withdrew a long, dark brown case. He grunted as
he rolled down the stiff window and gazed down at the
front door of the Milbrook newspaper.

"This oughta do jus' fine," he said to the other person in the car.

Poo Kerns wasn't in the mood for small talk.
"C'mon, man. There ain't no reason to do this. You
don't know for sure Bobby was tryin' to mess over us."

"That chick he was with shacks up with one of the
top cops around here. You fucked up, Poo. Now you
gotta help us straighten the situation out. It's the price
you gotta pay."

Poo dug into the pocket of the leather jacket he wore
and pulled out a vial of pills. He opened it and popped
one into his mouth. "Christ, Jimmy. I might not even
recognize the bitch. I was pretty strung out last night."

"You best recognize her, asshole. I'm gonna kill
somebody today. If it ain't her, then you're the only
other choice I got. Besides, we know she's there."

Not ten minutes before he had gone inside the door
and asked to buy a copy of that day's paper. The receptionist had pointed to the front door.

"There's a rack just outside," she had said.

Jimmy had feigned shock. "Gawd! I guess I missed it. Is the editor in today?"

"Miss Tyree?"

"Oh, it's a female."

"Yes, sir. She's here. Do you have an appointment?"

Jimmy Carr had made a face and looked at his watch. "Naw. I was just gonna complain about not getting my paper."

The receptionist had smiled. "You should talk to the circulation manager about that—not the editor. Does your carrier miss you often?"

"First time in five years," he'd said, making it all up as he went along.

The receptionist had reached beneath her desk and brought out a paper. "Here—with our apologies."

Jimmy had accepted the paper. "Why, thanks."

After he had left the *Journal*, he walked around the corner, climbed into his GMC, and circled the block so that he could drive into the garage. Poo had been silent throughout, wishing to God he hadn't been home when Jimmy Carr had come to visit.

The wind whistling through the parking area was turning much colder—so cold that Jimmy rolled the window back up. No telling how long he would have to wait for her to walk out, but he was reasonably certain she would use the front door. Before he had gone into the *Journal*, he had driven through the first floor of the garage and saw a parking space reserved for A. TYREE. It was occupied. He had also checked out the side entrance to the garage, which he planned to use as his escape route.

As he watched the door, Jimmy opened the brown case and began to extract the various parts of the weapon. He gingerly lifted what appeared to be a bulky scope from its padded crevice inside the box.

"This is a real trick, Poo. According to Willie Mack,

it's what cop sharpshooters use. Willie Mack's an expert on guns.''

His reluctant accomplice eyed the gizmo. ''Looks like a scope to me.''

''Not quite.'' Jimmy flipped a switch on the black tube. A bright red dot of intense red light appeared on the dash. ''It's a laser scope. You just put this dot out there on your target and whap! Neat, huh?''

Poo Kerns shivered.

Of the five other men in the conference room, only one had heard of Willie Mack Smith and Jimmy Carr.

''They live down my way,'' Lenny Barker said. ''I sure can't believe those boys are dealing drugs.''

''What do they do?'' Whit asked.

Barker shrugged. ''I always figgered they drew welfare like most other folks down my way. Willie Mack lives on his old home place just outside of Tipple Town. Now, when he was a youngster, he was into a lot of crap—fighting, mostly . . . drunk on Saturday nights. Married Jerilyn Cisco—Jeri, we called her. He had a kid and settled down. Never heard anything out of him until now.''

''What about Carr?'' Whit asked.

''He and Willie Mack ran together. So did Didimus. That's Willie Mack's baby brother. Didimus, now, he's partial to the bottle. Ever' now and again I gotta run him home, but he's got a shoulder-wide yellow streak down his back. I cain't imagine him gettin' into nothing too dangerous. As for Jimmy, he used to get into the same kinda shit that Willie Mack did, but he's settled down, too.''

Sinclair came back into the room with two file folders in his hands. ''We had a record on Smith and Carr. Smith's about thirty-three now. Last time he was in jail was ten years ago on a Drunk in Public charge. Looks like he was arrested twice before that on minor assault charges and five or six other times for intoxication. I see you got him once or twice, Lenny.''

"That's what I was telling the guys.''

Sinclair opened the other folder. "Carr's records seem almost identical, even to the arrest dates. I say these guys used to stick together.''

"They pretty much still do,'' Lenny said. "I think they're cousins. Come to think of it, old man Smith used to be one hell of a moonshiner. He made it and run it, too. That was kinda unusual. You didn't see too many fellas involved in both cooking and distribution.''

Felty had been listening to the exchange. "That's the same type of folks that are now dealing drugs in North Carolina and Tennessee—the ones that used to run 'shine.''

Whit looked to Tony. "Whadaya say, boss? Do we go ahead with it or not?''

The prosecutor eyed the chief of the Tipple Town Police. "Lenny, you haven't been involved in any big-scale drug operations. I can't impress on you enough the need to keep quiet about this.''

Barker's face contorted in offended surprise. "God, Danton, I know that! I'm no damned fool.''

"I didn't say you were,'' Tony responded. "For right now, I'd appreciate it if you wouldn't even share this information with the rest of your department.''

Barker laughed. "Hell, I just got one other man, and he wouldn't do us much good anyway.''

"I'm glad we understand each other,'' Tony said. "Okay, fellas, we'll go ahead with a drug buy we have arranged for tonight. I'm gonna let Felty here outline it to us. I guess most of you know his interest in the case.''

They all nodded that they did.

"Go ahead, Felty.''

"Our informant is one of your local slimeballs known as Tory Appleton," Felty said.

Al Downing shook his head. "Good old Tory. We nailed him last year."

"That's how I found him," Felty said. "I started checking on your recent drug indictments. Appleton is to meet this guy Carr or maybe Smith at an empty beer joint somewhere near Chief Barker's town."

"The Four Leaf Clover," Sinclair said. "I know you guys know it."

"We know it," Downing said.

Barker belly-laughed. "Shit, when I was just a kid, I about got my liver sliced out in that place. That was before I turned respectable."

The Milbrook police chief, Tom Wampler, was beginning to fidget. "If this isn't going to involve us, I have a meeting at city hall—"

"I'd appreciate it if you would hang around," Tony told Wampler.

The chief threw up his hands. "I don't see why, but if that's what you want—"

"It's what I want," Tony said.

Felty continued. "Appleton's made arrangements to buy two ounces of coke for four thousand dollars."

At that point, Tony jumped into the explanation. "And we've got to have the money. It's got to change hands. We'll put a wire on Appleton. As soon as the transaction takes place, we take them down. The area around that place has to be secure."

"That'll be easy," Barker said. "You can close off the Black Lick Road at both ends, above and below the Four Leaf Clover. There's no other way outa that holler."

Downing's doubt was showing on his face. "Is there any other cover for us?"

"How about the building?" Barker said. "I know the guy who owns it. He's clean. I can get us in there."

Downing remained skeptical. "I've seen that place, Lenny. It looks like it's about ready to collapse. I don't much relish the idea of going inside it."

"Aw, it ain't that bad," Barker said.

"The one thing I don't want to happen," Tony said, "is to lose the money and the drugs. I don't like these kind of operations. I've seen too many of them go awry."

"Shit, Mr. Danton, like I said, this'll be a snap," Barker said.

Ted Early had been uncommonly silent throughout the meeting. "I've got one question," he finally said. "What makes you think these guys had anything to do with the River Road deal?"

"What difference does it make?" Whit asked. "They're major drug dealers in this county. Isn't that reason enough to try to bust them?"

"So how many of my men are you gonna need?" Early asked. "My overtime budget is already blown all to hell."

Whit's eyes settled on the sheriff. "As few as possible, Early. We don't want this thing screwed up."

The sheriff's body tensed. "Dammit, Pynchon, why don't you get off my department's back? I've had it—"

"We may have a problem," Felty said. He was standing at the window, gazing outside.

"What are you talking about?" Tony asked.

Felty nodded toward the window. "It's snowing like a son of a bitch outside."

Bobby Harrington was staring idly at the blank screen of his word processor when Anna came for him. "I just called the prosecutor's office. He's in a meeting, but he's there. Let's go."

"I don't like this," the reporter said, without offering to get up.

"That's too bad, Bobby. You don't really have a choice."

He looked up at her, and she saw the fear in his dark brown eyes.

"These guys are bad," he said. "It's not so much that I care about Poo Kerns. I just don't wanna to get on their bad side, Ms. Tyree."

"You should have thought about all that. You do remember that this little episode was your idea—and mine, too. We've both got to suffer the consequences. Besides, I think you're just psyching yourself out. This is Milbrook, not Chicago or Miami."

He was shaking his head. "I just have a bad, bad feeling."

"Come on, Bobby. Let's go. It's starting to snow, and the roads are going to get bad."

"The snow's the last thing I'm worrying about." But he got to his feet and pulled his jacket from a coat tree.

"I promise," she said as they headed toward the door. "The next good story that comes along, you can give it a try."

Bobby's head was bowed. "If I live that long."

TWENTY

"WE'D BEST GET the hell outa here," Poo said. The third floor of the parking building provided a ceiling that protected them from the snow, but it was falling so heavily that it formed a virtual curtain between them and the building occupied by the *Daily Journal.*

"We'll give it a few more minutes," Jimmy Carr said. He again reached behind the rear seat of the GMC and withdrew a pair of field glasses. "Here. Use these."

Poo brought them to his eyes and aimed them down at the front entrance to the newspaper. The wind had died just as soon as the snow had started to fall, and the driver's window had been rolled down again. The truck continued to idle, its heater pumping exhaust-tainted warm air into the cab.

"Better?" Jimmy asked.

"Not a whole goddamned lot." He lowered the glasses. "Christ, man, even if she does walk out, how are we gonna make our getaway? The roads are gonna be slicker than shit, Jimmy. This ain't worth the risk."

"You're a fuckin' whiner, Kerns. Like I said, we'll give it a few more minutes. I know what I'm doing. This little baby"—he patted the shabby dash of the aging GMC—"goes in snow like a tank."

"So do some of them cop cars," Poo said.

Jimmy was looking back at the front door of the

newspaper. It was made of glass, and he could see into the reception area. He saw movement.

"Give me them binoculars."

He focused them on the front door and the reception area beyond. The snow seemed to have eased a little, enough for him to see a man and a woman standing just inside the door. The man had his hands in his pockets. The woman was adjusting a muffler around her neck.

He jammed the field glasses back at Poo. "Take a look."

Poo inched across the seat and did as he was told. He leaned across Jimmy as he tried to focus on their faces.

"Well, is that her?"

"Gimme a sec. I can't tell."

Jimmy popped the flat of his palm against Poo Kerns's ear. The younger man wailed in pain and fell back toward the passenger side of the truck.

"Jesus, Jimmy—"

"I could see her fuckin' face and his, too, asshole! So could you. Is it her, goddammit!"

Poo was holding his hand to his ear. "Jesus, man! Hell, yes! It's her. It's him, too."

"Him?"

"Bobby Harrington."

"I just knew this was gonna be a good day," Jimmy said. He brought the laser scope to his eye and directed it toward the front door of the newspaper.

"I think it's lovely," Anna said as she tucked the ends of the muffler down into the front of her coat.

"Look how it's sticking to the road," Bobby said. "I hope you have snow tires."

"We'll make it."

At that point, she heard the low rumble on the street. Moments later, a huge snow plow passed, its blade scraping the pavement while a spreader attached to the rear tossed a mixture of salt and gravel out on the street.

"The city's on the ball this time," Anna said. "It's not too cold outside. Once they treat the streets, it should keep them pretty clear. You ready, Bobby?"

"No."

"Let's go anyway. After you."

She opened the door for him, and he moved out into the short protected entry way. Anna was behind him. He paused before he stepped out into the snow that was already covering the sidewalk. It gave Anna a chance to come up beside him.

"What are you—"

The small dot of red light was centered squarely on his forehead. She frowned when she saw. Before she could say anything else, the dot—and his head—vanished in a starburst of wet crimson mush. It inundated her face and splattered into her mouth as she screamed. She tasted blood and could feel small particles of bone on her tongue. The glass door behind her exploded almost simultaneously. In her shock and nausea, she stumbled backward toward the door.

The meeting had ended in the prosecutor's conference room, but Whit and Tony remained seated at the long table. They were conducting a postmortem of the meeting. "I've still got a bad feeling about this," the prosecutor said.

"You're prejudiced against undercover operations," Whit said.

Tony studied the confident face of his investigator. "You used to be prejudiced against them."

"As a rule, I still am, but in this case I don't know of any other way to try to solve it. We know Clark and the rookie interrupted a major drug deal—"

"Not quite," Tony said. "We don't *know* it. We suspect it, and it certainly seems like a valid assumption. But we don't know it, not for sure."

"No other theory fits as well," Whit countered. "Since they were so far off the beaten path, it makes sense that those on the other side of the buy were from Raven County."

Tony leaned back in his chair and started to massage his temples. "I know all that, Whit. We've gone over it a dozen times. I don't fault the logic a damned bit. I've just seen too damned many of these things blow up in our faces. And what about the goddamned weather?"

Whit looked to the window. White light, the kind that was reflected from lots of snow, poured through the glass and the blinds.

"We've got to be able to keep control of that situation," Tony said. "Can we do it with two feet of snow on the ground?"

"It'll be tough," Whit said, "but it'll be just as tough on the suspects. As soon as they reach the beer joint, we close off the road east and west of it. If we can manage that, we've got 'em. The situation is just about as ideal as we could hope for—except for the snow, of course."

Ross Sinclair—breathless . . . his face pale and damp with sweat—rushed into the conference room. "Whit, there's been some kind of shooting down at the newspaper. There are injuries."

Whit's stomach tightened. A knot of helpless fear rose into this throat. "Anna?"

"We don't know. We monitored the call that went to a city unit. I'll run you down there."

Whit was on his feet, rushing toward the door.

"I'm going, too," Tony said.

Whit saw the shrouded body resting in the entryway to the *Milbrook Daily Journal.* Blood had seeped down the slight incline and into the mushy snow of the sidewalk. Bits of flesh and bone and spongy globs of brains flecked the gory sidewalk and the aluminum supports that had held the huge sheets of glass. The ambulance was double-parked in front of the building. Whit hesitated over the body.

A paramedic reached down to grasp the bloodstained sheet.

"Hold on a second," Tony Danton said. He bent down and peeked first. "Jesus, is it a man?"

"Yeah," the paramedic said. "Leastways, the body's got a coat and tie and pants on. Kinda hard to tell when the head's blown away like that."

Whit sagged with relief. "Is he the only fatality?"

"Yeah, we got some other injuries, but nothing serious."

Whit started into the decimated front lobby, but he stopped and turned to the paramedic. "Leave him be until we tell you to move him."

"One of the city detectives said we could go ahead and transport—"

"Dammit! I said leave him there!" Whit snapped.

Glass littered the newspaper's front lobby. Inside, a paramedic was treating the receptionist's face. It had been sliced by a shard from the shattered front window. Apparently, the glass had been the only victim of a second shot. The same kinds of gore had been blasted into the lobby. Everything appeared to be covered with a sheen of crimson.

The receptionist saw Whit. "She's in Mrs. Binder's office, Mr. Pynchon."

Whit didn't even bother knocking on the publisher's door. He swung it open and was surprised to see Anna stretched out on a couch. Another member of the ambulance crew was checking her over. Kathy sat at the head of the couch, dabbing at Anna's face with a bloody washrag. A city cop stood over her, a notebook in his hand.

The cop nodded to Whit.

"She's okay," Kathy said quickly. "She's got a few minor cuts where she fell in the glass, and she's very upset . . . but she's okay."

The paramedic mounted his feet and headed out of the room. The Milbrook officer had his pen on the notebook. "Now, Miss Tyree, if you can just tell me—"

"Out!" Whit bellowed.

The cop gaped. "Whatsa matter, Whit? I'm just—"

"Get out, goddammit. I'll handle this. She's in no shape to answer questions."

Tony had come in behind Whit. He put a gentle arm on the cop's shoulder. "We can handle it from here."

The cop was baffled. "I didn't mean—"

"It's okay," Tony said. "Go on outside and wrap the scene down tight. Have some of your guys check with some of the neighboring businesses. See if we've got any witnesses."

The Milbrook officer shrugged. "Okay, Mr. Danton, whatever you say."

Whit was kneeling down by the couch. He had Anna's hand in his. Her arm was heavily bandaged. He could still see the drying remnants of blood in her hair and on her face. Kathy was trying to wipe off as much of it as she could, but it was going to take a hard shower to rinse away all the gore.

"I'm here, Anna."

Her face was devoid of color, and her eyes were closed. She turned slowly, trying to open her eyes. "Whit?"

"Yes, Anna. I'm here."

"The little red light . . ."

"The what?"

"The red spot . . ."

Her head rolled to the side.

"Anna!"

Kathy wiped the wet rag over Anna's forehead. "They gave her a shot, Whit. She was on the verge of going into shock. She's mentioned that several times . . . about some little red light."

"But she's not hurt?"

"Just like I said, some minor cuts from the glass. That's all. That bandage makes it look a lot worse than it is. It doesn't even need stitches."

Anna had slipped back into a drugged stupor.

"She just needs to rest," Kathy said.

Whit squeezed her hand. "What the hell happened?"

"She was on her way to see you," Kathy explained. "She and Bobby. He's the boy out there in the entryway. They killed him."

"Who?" Whit asked.

Someone put a hand on his shoulder. It was the paramedic who had left as Whit entered. "Here's a clean towel. It's moistened with cold water if you want to finish wiping her face."

Kathy reached over to take it. "I'll do it."

"Who killed him?" Whit asked, trying to draw Kathy back to what she had been saying.

"I don't know for sure, Whit. Anna and Bobby Harrington—the dead young man—had been working on a story about drugs in Milbrook. Well, they had just started working on it. Last night they went to a party at the home of a local doctor. It must have gotten pretty hairy from what Anna told me. There were drugs everywhere, mostly cocaine and marijuana. At least that's all Anna saw. She and Bobby were on their way to your office when—" Her voice faltered.

"Did you know about the party?" Whit asked. "When I talked to you last night, I mean?"

"No, she didn't tell me."

"Go on," Whit said.

"She and Bobby stepped out the door. At least that's what the receptionist says. Bobby was in front, sort of. The receptionist doesn't even remember hearing the first shot. She heard the glass shattering. When she looked up, Bobby was falling down, his head—"

Kathy started to weep.

Tony leaned down and put his arm around her. "You can tell this later."

"No," Kathy snapped. "I want to tell it now. I want you to get those bastards!"

Tony glanced back at Whit. Kathy took a breath and then went on. "Anna fell back through the broken door. That's when the big window exploded. Glass covered Anna and the receptionist."

"There must have been two shots," Whit said. "You say Anna went to a party at a doctor's house last night?"

"Yes, she was coming to give you all the information. We decided we had no business trying to investigate that kind of thing."

Tony was still standing behind Whit. "What was the doctor's name?"

"Wilson," Kathy said.

"Clete Wilson?" Tony asked.

Kathy nodded.

"Mother of God," the prosecutor said.

"He's a surgeon, isn't he?" Whit asked.

Tony nodded. "I've played golf with him."

TWENTY-ONE

"I HAD THE BITCH," Jimmy Carr said through clinched teeth. "I had that nice red dot right on her tits, and this yellow-bellied asshole knocked off my aim."

Poo Kerns whimpered as the rough surface of the hemp cut into his wrists. The white glare from the snow spilled but a short distance into the moist mine shaft, not nearly as far into the mine as they had taken Poo. The illumination on their faces came from the glow of a half-dozen kerosene lanterns hung around the wet walls.

Willie Mack Smith was leaning against one of the coal-blackened timbers that supported the roof. "What got into you, Poo?"

"I was scared, Willie Mack."

"Scared?" As Willie Mack stepped away from the timber, it creaked. Coal dust sifted down from the crevices in the huge slab of slate that formed the natural roof for that section of the shaft.

"Honest," Poo said, his voice liquid with emotion. "I was just scared."

"Of what?" Willie Mack asked, circling the chair in which Poo was bound.

"I dunno. The cops, I guess."

"You were scared of the wrong fellas then. You oughta been a hell of a lot more scared of us. The cops, all they can do to you is put you in jail."

"Please, Willie Mack, I panicked. God, please, just give me another chance. I'll go take care of her myself. You'll see. I'll do it. Honest."

Willie Mack went to another timber. A rusty railroad spike had been driven into it from which one of the kerosene lanterns was suspended. He lifted the lantern off the spike.

"Lemme show you this, Poo." Willie Mack circled the area around Poo. Boxes lined the walls. "These are guns and ammo. There's plenty of dope here, too. It's down in the next section where it's a little drier. You ever seen so much killin' power?"

"Please . . ." Poo begged.

"After this shaft played out, my daddy, he made his 'shine in here. Never did get caught makin' the stuff. Just like we ain't gonna get caught. He learned me to be real careful."

"I won't tell nobody about this place. I swear to God, Willie Mack. Just let me go."

"I know you ain't gonna tell nobody, Poo. I just wanted to show you all this stuff. Not too often I get visitors here to the mine shaft. I'm kinda proud of all this hardware."

The man's voice was soft and friendly, but that frightened Poo all the more. Willie Mack was many things, but he'd never been soft and rarely friendly.

He circled the chair to which Poo was bound. "Problem is, Poo, you went against me. I can't have that. See, if the word gets around that Poo got by with somethin' on Willie Mack, well, other folks might think they can do the same thing. The kind of business I'm in, I just can't have that. You can see that, can't ya?"

"Word won't get around," Poo whined. "I swear I won't say nothin'. I swear it on my mother's grave."

Willie Mack held the old railroad lantern in Poo's stricken face. Sweat had oozed from the captive's forehead and had created a series of black stripes as it streaked through the film of coal dust on his face. His jaws and lips quivered in fear.

"Boy, I wouldn't be swearin' on nobody's grave right now. You don't wanna meet your maker with that kind of blasphemy on your lips."

The tears flowed from his eyes as his face twisted in a pleading mask. "Don't kill me, man. Dear God, don't kill me. I don't wanna die, man."

"We all gotta die, Poo . . . some just sooner than others."

But Poo was starting to gag as the fear turned into a belly-twisting nausea. His vomit erupted from his mouth. With his hands tied behind him and his body lashed to the chair, all he could to was tip his head to the front. Willie Mack barely managed to jerk his booted foot out of the way of the first splash. It soaked into the dank floor of the mine shaft.

"Jesus Christ," Willie Mack cried. "You're like a goddamn pig about to be butchered."

Jimmy Carr had been standing in the shadowy recesses as his cousin toyed with the prisoner. He chuckled. "I bet he's pissed his pants, Willie Mack."

"Pissy-assed punk," the leader mumbled.

Poo was coughing, trying to clear the burning effluvium from his throat and nose. Quietly, Willie Mack circled behind the wooden chair.

"God," Poo was murmuring. "I'm gonna be sick—"

Willie Mack planted his huge hands on each side of Poo's face.

The captive tried to turn. "What the—"

Willie Mack wrenched.

The sharp crack of Poo's neck echoed down into the depths of the old Smith mine.

* * *

Tony slid Anna's handwritten affidavit across the desk to Magistrate Felix Harman. "I think you'll find more than enough probable cause to support the issuance of a search warrant," the prosecutor said.

Whit sat in a chair beside Tony, watching the aging face of the lower court judge. Harman accepted the documents without any obvious emotion, but when he saw the name on the first of the applications his slack face tensed and his eyes swiveled up to Tony, then over to Whit.

Harman didn't even read the detailed description of the home to be searched, or the items for which they wanted to search, or even that all-important few sentences of the application for a search warrant in which Whit, as the applicant, established his reasons for believing that evidence of a crime was concealed in the house to be searched.

"Is this Dr. Wilson?" Harman asked.

Tony nodded. "Dr. Clete Wilson."

Harman was already shaking his head. "For heaven's sakes, Tony, you can't believe that he's involved in some kind of illegal drug operation?"

"With all due respect, Judge, you haven't read the probable cause. I think you'll find it impeccable."

Harman started to say something else, but he thought better of it and returned his attention to the application for the search warrant.

"Before you do that," Tony said, "may I ask that you note on our application the time we started this hearing?"

"Why?" Harman asked.

"I just want to establish a record that a hearing on the application was held and that you spent a reasonable amount of time inquiring into the basis for our request to search Dr. Wilson's home. I'm not suggesting that you would rubber-stamp any search warrant, but you know what they say. If it isn't on paper, it didn't happen. The good doctor will probably hire the best defense attorney in the state."

"You can bet on it," Harman said. The judge checked his watch and noted the time on the application. "This still doesn't mean I'm going to issue a search warrant, Tony. I find your allegation incredible."

"Please, Felix . . . just read the probable cause statement now. It speaks for itself."

As the magistrate turned his attention to the document, Whit glanced at his own watch. It was almost 4:00 P.M. They didn't have a lot of time. The buy was to be made by Appleton later that night, and they still needed to scout the scene for that transaction. To make matters worse, the snow was continuing to fall. It threatened to turn into a major winter storm, coming more than a month ahead of the actual calendar date for the beginning of winter.

"I dunno," the judge said as he finished reading the application.

Tony sighed. "C'mon, Felix. You're skittish because of who it is. You know that's one of the best statements of probable cause you've seen in a long time. For once we don't even have to depend on a confidential informant. Anna Tyree was in that house. She saw the contraband. She's offered a detailed affidavit. She enjoys a good standing in the community."

The jurist tossed the affidavit back to Tony. "Christ, Clete Wilson operated on my wife five months ago. He saved her life. Maybe I'd best disqualify myself in this matter."

"There isn't time for that," Whit snapped.

Harman slammed his fist on the desk. "Dammit, Pynchon! You don't tell me how to do my job, and I won't interfere with yours."

Before Whit could respond, Tony said, "Seriously, your honor, if Clete's clean and we don't find anything, no harm done to him. He can sue our ass off. If we do discover contraband, well, then that's how it is."

Felix Harman massaged his temples with his fingers. "I just feel uncomfortable about this, Tony."

Whit was seething. Tony eased a hand over to Whit's knee in a gesture that the magistrate couldn't see. Its purpose was to hold the investigator's temper in check.

"Jeez, Felix. I play golf with the man. How do you think I feel? I know Anna Tyree very well, and she's not going to invent this kind of thing. Besides, you do recognize her name, don't you?"

The magistrate's brows knitted. "No, not really."

"She's the editor of the newspaper," Tony said.

"Then what the hell was she doing at his house?" Harman asked, his dilemma obviously deepened by Tony's information.

Tony made a face. "You know reporter types. She was working on a story about the extent of the drug problem in Milbrook. We've always suspected that some rather prominent members of our community were snorting a little, but her information hit us like a freight train. She expects us to do something, Felix. If we don't, she'll probably blow the story wide open. It won't look good on any of us, your honor."

"Damn," the magistrate sighed. He glanced at Whit. "I don't keep up with all the social news, but I heard somewhere that you were engaged or something to the editor of the newspaper. Is this the woman?"

Whit, in spite of his mood, had to smile. "I wouldn't use the word 'engaged,' but we are involved."

"Can't you cool her down?"

Whit's smile evaporated. "My God, Judge, some-body tried to kill her this afternoon. They blew away the head of one of her reporters as he and she walked out of the newspaper. This has mushroomed into more than just a drug case.''

''Surely Wilson didn't have anything to do with that?'' the magistrate asked.

''No,'' Tony said. ''As far as I know, his only involvement is in the drug matter.''

''Why didn't you tell me about a shooting?'' Harman asked.

''We assumed you knew,'' Tony said. ''That kind of news travels fast in Milbrook.''

''I've been in a jury trial all day.''

He picked up a pen and told Whit to raise his right hand.

''Do you swear the information contained in this affidavit is true based upon information and belief, so help you God?'' the magistrate said.

''I do, your honor.''

With a flourish, the judicial officer put his signature to the complaint and stood. ''I'll have my secretary prepare the search warrant.''

''There's a second one,'' Tony said.

He slipped the second affidavit from Anna across to the magistrate, who reluctantly accepted it, saying, ''Who now? The mayor? Or maybe my minister?''

Tony smiled. ''No, this one's a little less controversial. The residence of Paul Kerns. He's just a two-bit dope dealer, but he's Clete Wilson's supplier.''

Harman barely glanced at the second complaint before again administering the oath to Whit Pynchon. ''I'll be back in a few minutes,'' he said as he carried out the two complaints to his secretary.

''Amazing,'' Tony mumbled once the magistrate was out of the office.

Whit was shaking his head in disbelief. In truth, the probable cause on which they depended for the second search warrant—the authorization to enter Paul Kerns's residence—was marginal at best. Although Anna had signed the affidavit used in support of the complaint, her information about the Kernses' residence had been based upon hearsay from a dead man . . . Bobby Harrington.

"Harman was so shaken over the Wilson warrant that he never even read the other one," Tony said.

But Whit had the night's drug buy on his mind. "You should have let me handle the arrangements for tonight."

"Sinclair can take care of it. I want to complete these two searches as soon as possible. I'll work with Sinclair once we get the warrants. You and Downing handle the two searches. Let Downing take someone and go to Kerns's house. I want you to search Wilson's place. Do it by the book."

"If I find drugs, do you want me to go ahead and make the arrests?"

Tony shook his head. "No, I'll wait and indict at a special grand jury. That way we can avoid a preliminary hearing."

Under West Virginia law, a suspect arrested by warrant was entitled to a preliminary hearing before a magistrate no later than twenty days after the arrest. Either waiting for a special grand jury or calling a special grand jury to indict Wilson eliminated the need for a preliminary hearing.

"It might put more pressure on the good doctor if we arrest him," Whit said.

"It also might give another gutless magistrate a chance to toss the case out on us at a preliminary hearing. We'll wait on the grand jury."

"Same thing on Kerns?" Whit asked.

"Hell, no. Bust the little asshole. I wanna talk to this Kerns kid. We just might get him to talk."

"You're gonna deal with him?"

"If he can lead us to the bastards that gunned down those two troopers, you bet your ass I am."

TWENTY-TWO

THIRTY MINUTES AFTER the search warrants had been issued for the two residences, Whit—accompanied by a state trooper—stood in the deepening snow that covered the front porch of the Wilson residence. A second trooper was wading his way through the heavy wet snow to the back of the house . . . just in case. Whit tested the doorknob, found it locked, and then hammered on the front door.

The trooper's name was Fred Winslow. "Is this an Announce Then Bust In situation?" he asked. He was one of the younger officers assigned to the local detachment, having just recently completed his probation period.

"It meets the standards," Whit said as he waited.

"Well, what the hell are we waiting for?"

Whit pointed to the heavy door. "You think you can kick it in?"

Winslow studied the door. "You got a point."

The door opened to reveal a puffy middle-aged woman whose bleary eyes and unstable stance spoke volumes.

"Ohmigod," she said as her eyes focused on the green uniform of the state trooper.

Whit brandished the warrant. "Police, ma'am. We have a warrant to search your house."

Both he and the trooper brushed right by her.

"Jest a gawdamn minute—"

Whit noted the smell of booze as the woman staggered away from them.

"Go to the back and let your buddy in," Whit said.

"You can't do this," the woman was saying.

"Are you Mrs. Cletus Wilson?" Whit asked.

"Yesh, but—"

"Is anyone else home?"

"No, but I'm gonna go phone my husband. You know who he ish?" She had moved toward him, her harsh alcoholic breath threatening to push him back.

"You're free to call whomever you want, ma'am, but I'm only going to caution you once about interfering with the search. My name's Pynchon. I'm an investigator with the office of the prosecuting attorney. Here's a copy of the warrant."

He handed the paper to her. She snatched it and ripped it apart. "You best git outa my house," she screamed.

Winslow and his fellow officer came into the living room.

"One of you stay with her," Whit said. "We'll take it a room at a time."

"By God," the woman screamed, "you're not gonna—"

She started toward Whit, but Winslow grabbed her and set her down in a chair. "Stay with her," he told the other trooper. "If she causes any more trouble, cuff her and take her to the car."

"You motherfuckers!" she shrieked. "You got no right to arrest me."

Whit had started toward the back of the house, but he stopped and turned on the woman. "Mrs. Wilson, we've got a lawful court order. If you interfere, you'll be charged with obstructing an officer. Let's go, Winslow."

As Whit and the trooper entered the kitchen, the odor of recently smoked marijuana was overpowering. An open bottle of gin sat on the kitchen table. There was also a small plastic baggie full of grass.

"Bingo!" Winslow said, pointing to the grass.

Whit ignored it. "I think we can do better than that."

Winslow started rummaging through the kitchen cabinets. Whit opened the refrigerator. It had become one of the most popular places for stashing drugs. The top shelf was loaded with beer. Whit pulled each one of the cans out and measured its weight in his hands. He found what he was looking for near the back of the refrigerator. By all appearances, it looked like a can of Budweiser, just like the other six or seven cans, but he knew by its weight that it contained something other than beer. He tested the rim of the top of the can. The entire lid came off in his hand to reveal small ounce baggies containing a white powder.

"You got that field test kit?" Whit asked.

Winslow had moved to the area under the sink. He looked up. "You find something already?"

Whit showed him the beer can.

"Christ," Winslow said. "I'd have never even thought to check the beer cans." He pulled the small plastic bag containing the field test kit from his pocket and handed it to Whit.

The investigator pulled one of the small packets from its place of concealment and opened it. "About a year ago," he was saying, "the wife of one of the small-time dealers brought a can like this to the office. She and her husband had just had one hell of a fight, and she figured she could get even with him by turning him in. She told me that these fake beer cans were the most popular way of hiding a stash these days."

"I'll be damned," the trooper was saying.

He had put a small pinch of the powder into the test

kit and snapped the vials. The liquid inside formed two separate layers, one pink and the other blue. "It looks like she was right," Whit said.

Winslow was counting the small sealed baggies. "Must be about twenty of them here."

"Enough to indict the son of a bitch for possession with intent to deliver," Whit said.

That's when they heard the commotion, preceded by the loud squawking of another female voice. Whit and Winslow exchanged momentary glances and dashed toward the front of the house. Before they could reach the living room, a gunshot rocked the walls of the spacious home.

"God, I wish it would stop," Tony said as Sinclair's car fishtailed on the slick roads. The prosecutor and the sheriff's department captain were in the front seat. Curtis Felty and Tory Appleton were in the back seat.

"I ain't gonna do this," Appleton said. "I'll call Carr and put it off. He won't suspect nothin', not with this shit going on. Man, my car ain't gonna go in this kinda stuff. I got no roof on my car!"

"We'll find you a car," Felty said.

But Tony, too, was beginning to entertain some very serious second thoughts. It was 4:30 P.M., and the storm showed no sign of letting up. Six to seven inches covered the roads, and it was piled up even deeper off the roads. The highway crews were tied up on the county's main arteries and wouldn't treat the back roads around Tipple Town until the next day.

"Perhaps we really should try to arrange this for some other night," Tony said.

Sinclair was hunched over the steering wheel, trying to decide where the curvy road actually was in the mass of white in front of his eyes. "The Four Leaf Clover's just ahead,'' he said. ''As for the buy, you know I never did like the idea.''

''You want these bastards?'' Felty said from the backseat.

Tony turned. ''You know damn good and well I do, but I don't want to blow it either.''

''Then this is your best chance. It's gonna affect them just as much as it is us. Once we secure them in the parking area, then they'll be stuck. The weather's on our side.''

''What the hell makes you think the other side will show?'' Tony said. ''Dammit, Felty, I want these people as bad as you do, but we're just gonna have to try to set it up for another night.''

''Like I said, I can call Carr,'' Appleton said. ''He'll buy the story about the weather.''

In the front seat, Tony and Sinclair had their eyes riveted to the road. They didn't see Felty's huge hand move across the backseat. His fingers locked on Appleton's knee and squeezed. The young man tensed in immediate pain. He started to scream, but Felty released his threatening grip.

''How much goddamn farther?'' the North Carolina cop quickly asked, his hard eyes on his informant.

''There's the place,'' Sinclair announced.

In the waning daylight, the abandoned building looked as if it were sagging under its load of thick snow.

Sinclair slowed the car.

''Don't pull in!'' Felty cried. ''Let's not mess up the gawdamned snow!''

Sinclair's foot went to the brake. The car began a stomach-turning glide that ended squarely in the middle of the parking area in front of the Four Leaf Clover.

''Great!'' Felty said.

Tony was shaking his head. ''No damn way are we

going through with this. We're aborting. Let's get back
to Milbrook.''

In the Wilsons' living room, Whit saw the trooper
grappling with Mrs. Wilson. She had what looked to
be his service revolver in her hand. Another woman,
much younger and obese—she had to weigh well over
two hundred pounds—kicked at the trooper.

"Get the gun!" Mrs. Wilson was screaming. "Kill
the pigs!"

Winslow lowered his head and charged toward the
mountain of a female that was assaulting his partner.
Whit cautiously approached the wildly waving gun.

"I'm gonna kill you all!" Mrs. Wilson cried.

Winslow's shoulder drove into the soft mass of flesh
around the unidentified woman's midsection. The breath
exploded from her as her fleshy body went careening
toward a china cabinet that occupied a wall of the living
room. She crashed into it, causing its doors to fly open.
Pieces of china inside the cabinet were launched into
the air, shattering as they landed on the hardwood floors
of the living room.

"I'm gonna sue!" Mrs. Wilson shrieked.

Whit managed to get his hand on the warm gun just
as the trooper lost his grip. The hammer on the weapon
was back, and Mrs. Wilson's finger was going toward
the trigger. The barrel swiveled around toward Winslow, who was subduing the stunned young woman.

"Look out," Whit cried.

He jammed the palm of his hand at the hammer just
as he heard it click.

TWENTY-THREE

THE FOUR MEN in Ross Sinclair's cruiser rode back toward Milbrook in tense silence. The narrow two-lane road from the western coalfields of the county made, for the most part, a lazy ascent toward the county seat. The town itself occupied a flat plateau at the base of Tabernacle Mountain, which—now heavily snow-covered—stood like an intimidating, ghostly specter to the east of the plateau. The entire geologic width of Raven County itself was little more than an apron to the towering double summit of the mountain. The eastern county line ran along its uppermost ridges. From that point the county descended first to the plateau on which the county seat had developed and then on down to the stumpy ridges and tight hollows that represented the beginning of the state's western coalfields.

Just to the west of the Milbrook city limits, the road's ascent toward Milbrook and Tabernacle Mountain became more severe as it climbed a natural lip to the plateau.

The windshield wipers struggled to overcome the intensity of the falling snow. Even when they managed to sweep the snow from the windshield, Sinclair found it hard to see through the densely packed precipitation itself.

"We haven't passed a car in five minutes," Sinclair noted.

"There aren't too many fools like us," Tony said, his body urged forward in the seat by the strain.

Several minutes earlier, Sinclair had radioed the courthouse and had been warned that road conditions throughout the county were treacherous. He had asked if the Department of Highways crews had started to treat the roads and had been told that the local supervisor had a crew working on the twisting highway up Tabernacle Mountain, but that the rest of the crews were waiting for the snowfall to let up.

Tony was examining the dash of the cruiser. "You have a regular radio in here?"

"Sure," Sinclair said.

"Turn it on. Let's get a weather report on the hour." It was almost 5:00 P.M.

Sinclair slowed the vehicle even more as he removed a hand from the wheel and flipped on the radio. The twangy sound of bluegrass was coming to an end. Moments later, a series of high-tech beeps announced the news on the hour. The snowstorm garnered the headlines.

"Forecasters are predicting that the snow itself should start to taper off just after dusk," the announcer said.

Tony studied the golfball-size white flakes that cascaded down upon the windshield. "If it's gonna slow down, it's going to have to hurry."

"If it stops," Felty said from the backseat, "I see no reason why we can't go on with the buy."

The prosecutor threw up his hands. "Jesus, Felty. Let it rest. There's no way I'm going back down toward Tipple Town on a night like this. You don't know our weather. The goddamned road crews probably won't even touch that road until tomorrow . . . if then."

"It might be our only chance," Felty countered.

"I ain't doing it!" Appleton cried.

The back of Felty's hand caught Appleton at eye level,

the main impact concentrated on the bridge of the nose. The drug dealer's head snapped back. Blood gushed from his nose.

"Damn you, Felty!" Tony shouted back at the officer from North Carolina. "I can indict you just as well as I can anyone else! You gave me your word."

The disruption also caused Sinclair to glance back. He saw the dark red fluid dripping down on the upholstery of his cruiser. "Jesus Christ—"

But when he had turned, he had also pulled the steering wheel of the cruiser just a little bit toward the right. In the deep wet snow, the tires lost their grip. Sinclair felt the car begin to glide again, just like it had back at the Four Leaf Clover.

"Oh shit!"

Tony wheeled around. His hands lunged forward to grab the dash as the cruiser did a gentle doughnut on the road. In the backseat, Felty was lowering his head into the seat. Tory Appleton had his hand to his nose. His pain-glazed eyes became fixed on the dark, cylindrical object that appeared to be on a collision course with his door.

The blanket of snow insulated the sound of the metal yielding as the cruiser slammed into the power pole. It was over very quickly. Within seconds, the only sound coming from the bent vehicle was the gentle clicking of the stalled motor as it started its immediate cooldown.

Whit stood at the unattended nurses' station on the second floor of the Milbrook hospital.

"Anybody home?" he shouted.

A hallway opened just behind the station into what looked to be a room filled with a stock of bedpans and towels and floor scales. A pudgy face appeared around a distant corner. "I'll be with you in a few minutes," the woman said.

Whit could hear the sound of laughter from the supply room. Quietly, he moved behind the nurses' station and down the hallway to the point that he could actually hear the soft voices.

"Anyway," a female voice was saying, "I hear that Dr. Petrozani asked her out and she—"

Whit stepped into the supply room itself.

Three nurses—all of them in white—gaped. The pudgy one appeared to be the oldest of the three. She charged toward him. "You have no right to be back here. You'll have to leave—"

But Whit didn't offer to step back from her offended anger. "I didn't mean to interrupt your tale about the amorous adventures of Dr. whatsisname, but I thought you should know. Anna Tyree's going home."

The two younger nurses appeared stricken that their conversation had been overheard.

The head nurse didn't seem the least concerned. "The doctor hasn't released her. Now I must ask—"

"The doctor doesn't need to release her. She's perfectly capable of releasing herself. I've just been with her, and she says she's fine. I think she is, too. She's going home."

"Where did you get your medical degree?" she snapped.

But Whit turned to leave.

"I'll have to call the doctor," the nurse said, waddling after Whit.

"Fine. Call whomever you want."

"And Miss Tyree will have to sign a statement that she's leaving this facility against medical advice."

Whit stopped and slowly turned. "Miss Tyree doesn't *have* to sign anything. You're operating a hospital here, not a jailhouse. I just wanted to show you the courtesy of informing you that she's leaving. Now, you call whomever you need to call . . . make whatever report you need to make, but you aren't going to tell Miss Tyree or me what we *have* to do.''

Anna was waiting at the door to the four-bed ward she had been placed in for what the emergency room doctor had called ''observation.'' She remained shaken by the ordeal at the front door of the *Daily Journal.* Her thoughts were still a little muddled by the sedative they had administered, but no way was she going to spend any more time in a cramped ward with three women, one of whom was retching every five minutes or so.

''We're ready,'' Whit said.

''You should stop by the emergency room and let them look at your hand,'' Anna said.

A blood-crusted puncture was centered on the soft web of skin between his forefinger and his thumb. A purplish bruise darkened a sizable area of skin surrounding the thumb. The hammer of the revolver had been separated from the gun's firing pin by the width of Whit's flesh.

''It's fine,'' Whit said. ''I cleaned it out with peroxide after we got those two women booked.''

Anna staggered a little as she started out of the room. Whit walked down the hallway and appropriated a wheelchair, which he rolled back to Anna. The nurse was coming toward them with a clipboard.

''I don't need that,'' Anna said as Whit positioned the wheelchair behind her.

''Sit down,'' he said.

At that point, the nurse reached them. ''Miss Tyree, I must insist—''

Whit's temper began to slip. ''Lady, I've told you—''

Anna eased down into the chair and put a restraining

hand on Whit's arm. "I'm fine, nurse," she said. "I'm just a little shaky from the medicine."

"But the doctor hasn't released you," the nurse said.

Whit struggled with his temper, but he allowed Anna to respond. She nodded back toward the ward. "I can't get any rest in there," she said. "I'm going home."

The nurse looked up at Whit. He saw the fury in her eyes. He couldn't help himself. He smiled at her. "You can't win them all," he said.

"Then I must ask that you sign this release of liability!" The nurse jammed the clipboard under Anna's face.

Anna gently pushed it away. "I just want to go home."

The nurse pivoted and marched back down the hall.

"Maybe she's going to call a security guard or something," Anna said.

Whit started the wheelchair toward the elevators across from the nurses' station. "That would top off a fine day."

They reached the elevators. Whit pushed the button to call it to the second floor. The head nurse stood behind the protection of the station glaring at him. The elevator was on its way when the hospital public-address system came alive.

"Whit Pynchon. Call 201 stat."

The elevator door opened for them.

"Did you hear that?" Anna asked.

Whit glanced back at the nurse as the public-address announcer repeated the message. "Whit Pynchon. Call 201 stat."

"What the hell does stat mean?" Whit mumbled.

"At once, I think," Anna said.

The elevator door closed in their faces.

"You'd better check on it," Anna said.

Reluctantly, Whit turned back to the nurse.

There was the hint of a smile on her face. "Have you changed your mind?" she asked.

Whit approached her. "No way, lady. That message was for me. I'm Whit Pynchon."

She looked baffled. "Why would they want you?"

"I dunno, but how do I call 201?"

She pointed down to a telephone. "Just pick it up and dial 201."

"What is 201?"

"The emergency room, Mr. Pynchon."

"What the fuck do we do?" Didimus Smith asked.

His brother sat in a sagging recliner in front of a roaring fire. In one hand he held a can of Rolling Rock beer. In the other, he had a dull black, fully automated Mac 11, equipped with a thirty-shot clip for the 9-mm ammo. He sighted the modified automatic into the core of the fireplace. Above him, he could hear his ten-year-old bouncing across the floor of his bedroom.

"Little Willie hates it when they call off school," Willie Mack said. " 'Fraid he ain't gonna get to play with those godless computers. I always loved it when we got out because of the snow. 'Course that wasn't too often. They didn't hardly ever call it off when you and I was in school. Didn't make no difference how fuckin' much it snowed. We had to go to school . . . leastways, we were s'posed to go to school."

"Dammit, Willie Mack, what are we gonna do?"

"We're gonna wait, you dumb fuck. I'll get a call if it's still on."

The front door opened in a flurry of snow. Jimmy Carr stepped into the living room and began stomping the snow off his feet on a soiled carpet in front of the door.

"Have any trouble?" Willie Mack asked.

Carr grinned. ''Shit, that damned GMC will go anywhere.''

''So where'd you put Poo?''

''Someplace where they'll get the message—loud and
clear.''

TWENTY-FOUR

WHIT WHEELED ANNA toward the emergency room of the hospital.

"Did they say how Tony was?" she asked.

"They didn't say shit. They just said he'd been in an accident. He and Sinclair were scouting—" He stopped in midsentence, realizing he was about to let the proverbial cat out of the bag.

Instead, he changed the subject. "I can't believe you were trying to play cop again. You're damned lucky to be alive."

While in the ward with the three other women, Whit hadn't said a word about the incident—about her stupidity. He had been gentle and concerned, just the way you wanted someone to behave in front of other people. She knew the lecture was coming, sooner or later. The worst part of it was that she deserved it. The death of Bobby Harrington was a guilt Anna was going to carry for a long time. Even in the depths of sedation, she hadn't been able to escape the image of his head exploding.

The wheelchair stopped.

Anna looked up.

"Tony!"

The prosecutor stood just outside the door of the emergency room. There was a small white bandage on the right side of his face. His right arm was in a sling.

"I'm fine," he said.

"The way the nurse talked," Whit said, "I thought it was serious."

Tony lowered his head. "Serious enough. Appleton's got a concussion."

"Appleton?"

Tony slowly nodded. "You can blame that damned asshole from North Carolina."

Ross Sinclair stepped out of the emergency room. He showed no signs of injury whatsoever. "Hi, Whit." He nodded to Anna.

"What the hell happened?" Whit asked.

There was a small lobby area adjacent to the emergency room. Tony went over and sat down. Whit started to roll Anna over to him, but she stopped him. "I'm okay, Whit. I'll walk."

"We all look like we've been through a meat grinder." It was true. Anna's arm remained bandaged. The wound on Whit's hand was visible and ugly, and now Tony had an arm in a sling and was limping.

Whit helped her out of the chair, and they joined Tony. Sinclair followed. Once they were all seated, Tony started to tell the story.

"Uh, what about Anna?" Whit asked.

Tony looked at her. "This is one time I think we can forget about her job. We had finished scouting that building down near Tipple Town. We were coming up the grade into Milbrook. I had already decided to call off the operation for the night—"

Tony glanced at Anna. "I do hope none of this will end up in your paper. It might cost somebody's life."

Anna closed her eyes. "You know it won't, Tony. Besides, I still haven't the foggiest idea what you're talking about."

"I think she's learned a very hard lesson," Whit said.

"I'm sorry about your reporter," Tony said. "We're

dealing with terrorists here. I don't think any of us realized just how vicious these drug dealers are becoming.''

"We were warned," Whit said.

Tony went on with his story. "Anyway, Felty was still pushing. He wanted to go ahead with the operation.''

"You've got to be kidding," Whit said.

Tony shook his head. "He's carrying a lot of hate, Whit—too much for us to tolerate. I don't really remember what all was said, but Appleton said he wasn't going through with it tonight. Hell, we were all petrified. You know how treacherous the roads are.''

"Almost impassable," Sinclair said. "I lost control—"

Tony stopped Sinclair. "It wasn't Ross's fault. As I said, Appleton announced he wasn't going through with it tonight, and Felty busted him in the face. It startled us all. The car started sliding. We wrapped it around a telephone pole.''

Sinclair's face was colorless. "I couldn't help it. I looked around to see what the commotion was and that was it. The car started sliding. I lost it . . . pure and simple.''

"The point of impact," Tony explained, "was smack against the right rear door where Appleton was sitting. His head struck the window. He's got a mild concussion.''

Anna kept silent, trying to correlate the information she was hearing into some semblance of logic.

Whit sighed. "So much for our informer.''

His comment made Sinclair tense. "Dammit, Whit, I couldn't help it!''

"I didn't mean anything toward you," Whit said quickly. "It was a thoughtless comment. At least it resolves the issue about tonight.''

The voice came from behind them. "The hell it does."

They all turned and saw Al Downing, the state trooper. It had been his voice. He was with Curtis Felty, who was wearing a neck brace. Lenny Barker was also with them. He'd driven up from Tipple Town in anticipation of the operation.

"C'mon, Al," Whit said. "Give it up—for tonight at least."

The trooper shook his head. "No way. Felty and I have been talking. According to the doc in there, Appleton's not hurt that bad. He can still handle his part of it, and we've still got time to set it up."

"I forbid it!" Tony cried.

Downing stepped into the waiting area. "Felty told me you were getting cold feet—"

Whit stood and put a friendly hand on the trooper's shoulder. "It's not cold feet, Al. There's no sense risking lives. We'll nail the bastards. It's just gonna take a little longer. I was as much in favor of this operation as you were. You know that. But this weather—" He left the sentence unfinished. The word "weather" said it all.

But Downing wasn't going to be sidetracked. "I can understand, Whit. Miss Tyree's had a rough day, and I'm sure you want to take her home."

Whit's face reddened. "That's not the goddamn point, Al."

But the trooper's eyes settled on the prosecutor. "You've been down on this since the start, Tony. More than likely, the bastards that killed Clark and Mahoney are gonna be out at that beer joint tonight at ten-thirty. We're gonna be there waiting for them—either with or without you."

Tony mounted his feet. "You seem to forget, Al, that

I'm the chief law enforcement officer in this county. There's no way I'm going to approve of this.''

Several other state troopers had arrived at the hospital and were gathered with Felty and the chief of the Tipple Town department. They all were held rapt by the confrontation.

Downing looked over to Felty before he spoke. When he did finally speak, his voice carried a reluctant timbre of defiance. ''You're not the only game in town, Tony. I just got off the phone with an assistant U.S. attorney. She said they would prosecute the cases if we busted these assholes with two ounces of cocaine.''

Whit's anger was overwhelmed by his astonished amusement. ''Damn, Al, you're getting awful ballsy in your old age.''

Tony was taken aback. ''I can't believe you did that, Al.''

''I'm sorry, Tony. I just about lost another officer this afternoon in that raid on the doctor's house. It's time we stopped farting around with these assholes.''

''What makes you even think these guys will show tonight?'' Whit asked. ''Maybe they've got more sense than we do.''

''Maybe they won't show,'' the trooper said, ''but if they do, my men are gonna be there. I'd like some help from you, Sinclair.''

The captain had been listening to the conversation. Luckily, the waiting area was otherwise empty. Given the weather outside, even the hospital emergency room was likely to remain quiet that night.

Sinclair was shaking his head. ''I've already caught hell from the sheriff for wrecking a cruiser. I don't think he's gonna be too anxious to risk any more. I agree with Whit and Tony. The weather's just too damned bad.''

The trooper's eyes narrowed. "We'll remember that, Sinclair."

For the first time, Tony saw the ugly wound on Whit's hand. "What happened to you?"

"Nothing important," Whit said.

"Like hell nothing happened," Downing said. "Whit jammed his hand between the hammer of a .357 and the firing pin."

"It's nothing," Whit said. "We've got Mrs. Cletus Wilson and her young niece in custody."

"Before we get too embroiled in our differences," Tony said, "maybe you'd best fill me in on what happened with the search warrants."

Whit told of the incidents at the home of the surgeon.

Downing announced the conclusion to that aspect of it. "I just got word that Winslow now has the doctor himself in custody and is on his way to the courthouse."

Tony glanced at Whit. "I thought I told you to hold off on Wilson's arrest."

"Since we had to jail his wife," Whit said, "I figured we might as well go all the way."

Tony made a face, but then said, "I guess it really doesn't matter."

Anna had remained silent throughout the conversation, but she had tensed when she heard that Mrs. Wilson's niece was also under arrest. "They call her Princess . . . Mrs. Wilson's niece, I mean. She's Poo Kerns's girlfriend."

"What about the search of Kerns's home?" Tony asked.

Downing fished into the pocket of his uniform jacket and pulled out several Polaroids. He handed them to Tony. "There's about a kilo of coke there. Those two big trash bags are full of nickel-and-dime bags of marijuana. Those bottles in the photo are filled mainly with

Tylox. I suspect a check with area pharmacies will reveal that most of them were obtained by prescriptions issued by Dr. Cletus Wilson.''

"Quite a haul," Tony said. "What about Kerns?"

Downing returned the photos to his pocket. "No one was home. We have no idea where Kerns is.''

"Oh, you might wanna know," Downing added, "that Wilson phoned a lawyer in Charleston from his office.''

"Which lawyer?" Tony asked.

"Ben Trautman.''

The prosecutor shrugged. "As we suspected, he can afford the very best.''

Downing took a seat across from Raven County's prosecuting attorney. "So what's the decision, Tony? Do we have your blessing? Or do we depend on the Feds?''

"I've already told you my opinion, Al. If you want to go ahead with this, you do it on your own authority. I'm opposed to it.''

The trooper nodded. "So be it.''

Sinclair stood. "I'll phone the sheriff, Al. Maybe we can give you a little help.''

"Don't put yourself out," Downing said.

As the officers moved away from the lobby, Whit moved to a chair beside Tony. "Maybe I'd best go along with them.''

Tony looked over at his friend. "I didn't want to ask.''

Whit smiled. "I know you didn't. Can you see that Anna gets home?''

"I can call Kathy Binder," Anna said. "What's all this about anyway? This has something to do with the River Road thing, doesn't it?''

"No comment," Whit said, a warm smile on his face.

The kindness in his voice, though, wasn't enough to

buffer Anna's anger. "Dammit, Whit. I'm not asking as a reporter. I want to know what kind of danger you're putting yourself in."

"I'll be careful," he said. "Tony can fill you in. I'd better catch up with those guys."

"Don't give them the impression that I've changed my mind," the prosecutor said.

"I won't. I'll just do my best to see that they don't screw it up."

TWENTY-FIVE

THE CONTINGENT of law enforcement officers convened in the Tipple Town city hall. It provided the most convenient point to coordinate the operation at the Four Leaf Clover. Most of the officers were from the local state police detachment, but none of them were distinguishable by their uniforms. It was a plain clothes operation, and given the weather, that meant heavy down-filled parkas, wool caps, gloves, and boots.

The snow had stopped almost as suddenly as it had started, but not before it had accumulated to a solid eight inches. The temperature hovered around twenty-five degrees, and the forecasters were now saying that an approaching warm front would bring warmer temperatures and rain. In the mountains of Appalachia, a heavy snow followed by rain and warming temperatures meant one thing—flooding. Even small branches, once the grounds were saturated, turned into raging rivers as they were compressed by the narrow mountain ravines.

Ross Sinclair was the last to arrive at the staging point. He came alone. "Sheriff Early said he was sorry, but he—"

Corporal Al Downing shrugged it off. "Forget it, Ross. At least you're here. With Whit and Felty, we've got enough men."

"Where's Appleton?" Sinclair asked.

"He's lyin' down in Barker's office. Says he's got a headache." There was a wry smile on the trooper's face.

Sinclair chuckled. "I expect he does. His head cracked that windshield pretty solidly."

"Felty's keeping him company," Downing said.

Whit stood at the head of the room with Barker. They were studying a detailed relief map from the Department of Highways that was mounted on the wall. Sinclair and Downing joined them.

Whit tapped a point on the map. "Barker tells me there's a road that leads to a strip mine site located on the ridge behind the beer joint. He thinks we can get a four-wheel drive up to a point a hundred feet or so behind the place. Maybe we can then come down the slope on foot and go in the beer joint from behind. I'd hate to have that parking lot full of tracks."

Downing scratched his chin. "Christ, Whit. Even if we could get up behind the place, coming down that slope in that snow at night—"

"It ain't that steep a slope," Barker said.

"Besides," Whit added, "It's just about the only way we can get into the place. You know they might be watching it already."

"Wouldn't they see the front-wheel drive?" Sinclair asked.

Barker traced his finger along a feint line on the map. "You can keep the lights on until you get about here. The strip road runs behind a little ridge that'll give you cover to that point. Once you get here, though, you sure oughta kill the lights. But if you looked outside, the moon's done out. You won't have no trouble seeing. Glaring off all that snow, it'll be like daylight out there."

"Which might be as much a disadvantage as it is a help," Downing said.

"If we're gonna commit this insanity, we best get

ourselves in position in that building,'' Whit said. ''The longer we put it off, the more risk we run of being seen.''

''What's this 'we' stuff?'' the corporal asked.

''I'm going with you into that building,'' Whit said.

''I thought you were against this.''

''Just because of the snow, Al. That doesn't mean I want to see it fail. By the way, I want Felty with us.''

Downing pulled Whit off to the side. ''Let's leave Felty here. He's got no authority in this state, and he's already just about screwed this whole deal up.''

''That's why I want him with us. We can keep an eye on him.''

''Good point,'' the trooper said, yielding to Whit's logic. ''Every now and then, you're worth having around.''

''One thing, Al. If we make any busts in this case, we go to state court. I'm not fuckin' around with the Feds.''

Downing laughed. ''Don't tell me you bought that bluff.''

Whit's mouth dropped. ''That was a bluff?''

''Hell, I tried to call the Feds, but all I got was a mother-fucking recording.''

''I'll do you a favor, Al. I won't tell Tony.''

''I appreciate it. I figured it this way. If we didn't turn up any shit on this deal, then it didn't matter. On the other hand, if we do luck up, I knew Tony wouldn't turn his back on the case.''

''So where did you get the money?''

The trooper brandished two stacks of what appeared to be a lot of cash. ''Several of us chipped in. Besides, it just looks like four thousand dollars. If the sellers look too close, they'll know right away it's blank sheets of paper. That's why we've got to be ready to move quickly.''

Whit cringed. "That's gonna put the kid in there in one hell of a dangerous position."

"Do you really care?"

"Yeah, as a matter of fact, I do. Let's get this thing going."

Downing organized the rest of his men. There were a total of five additional troopers plus Barker and Sinclair. He assigned Sinclair to watch over Tory Appleton. The units would divide into two groups, one to secure a point to the west of the site and the other to secure a point to the east. Sinclair was to dispatch Appleton toward the abandoned building from his location on the eastern side. Appleton would be wearing a wire that could be monitored by Whit, Curtis Felty, and Al Downing from their position inside the building. If the dealer or dealers did get away, the units east and west of the building would close off the road.

Sinclair replaced Felty in the room with Appleton. The burly Carolina cop joined them as Downing went over the plan one last time. When the trooper was finished, Whit turned to Barker. "You're flat sure that there's no other avenue they can use to escape?"

Barker shook his head. "No good way. They can abandon their cars and take off into the woods, but there ain't no danger of losing them, not with the snow this goddamned deep."

"Okay," Whit said. "Let's roll then."

Tony had offered to arrange a ride for Anna, but she had declined and called Kathy Binder at the newspaper. "Maybe you should let Kathy take you home, too," she told the prosecutor.

Even to the most casual observer, Tony's discomfort was obvious. He flinched with even the most insignificant movement. "It's my shoulder, Anna. It aches like a bad tooth, but I couldn't rest if I went home. Maybe

Kathy wouldn't mind dropping me off at the courthouse. I can monitor the operation on the jail's radio.''

They were still in the small lobby adjacent to the
hospital ER. Anna nodded toward the ER entrance.
"Didn't they give you something for pain?"

Tony fished into his shirt pocket and pulled out a red
and white pill. "Tylox," he said, managing a smile.

Anna laughed. "So take it. It does have a legitimate
use."

Tony turned the small pill over in his fingers. "You
know the kids around here snort this stuff just like coke.
We've even heard of them mainlining—shooting it
straight in their veins. I can't help but feel like a lot of
this is my fault, Anna. I just never believed the problem
was so . . . so pervasive.''

"None of us did."

While they waited for the publisher of the newspaper,
Tony briefed Anna about the operation that was getting
under way as they talked.

Anna listened without comment until he was finished. "I have one question," she then said. "What on
earth makes you think that these guys are the same ones
that killed all those people on the River Road?"

"That's the crux of it, Anna. We don't know—not
for sure. We have reason to believe these guys are the
biggest dealers in the county. We think the River Road
killings were drug-related. Because the killings happened in such an obscure part of the county, it makes
sense that the killers are local people. We're betting it
all on a hunch. Nothing more. For the record, but off
your record, I was opposed to it from the start.''

Anna shrugged. "Why? It makes sense to me. Even
if they aren't the killers, you might manage to arrest
some dope dealers.''

"As you discovered, undercover operations have a

way of turning to baby poop, m'dear. You've heard of Murphy's law.''

"Whatever can go wrong, will,'' Anna said, repeating her version of the old saying.

"I think Murphy must have been a narc.''

Kathy Binder came through the door and hurried over to them. She was surprised to see Tony's injuries. "What happened to you?''

"I went sleigh riding in a car.''

"Could you take Tony by the courthouse, too?'' Anna asked.

"Sure,'' Kathy said. "Do you think you got the people that killed Bobby?''

"Not yet,'' Tony said, "but maybe by tomorrow.'' He went to stand up. A stab of pain—from his elbow to his neck and on into his temples—drove him back down in the seat.

"You should go home, Tony,'' Anna said.

"I will. Just as soon as I know everyone's safe.''

Barker had been right. The heavy shroud of snow caught the light from the nearly full moon and turned night into a silvery replica of day. He had been right, too, about the steepness of the slope. It wasn't gentle by any means, but it certainly wasn't so sheer that they couldn't make the descent. Each one of the three men had fallen once or twice as they made their way down toward the dark shadow of the Four Leaf Clover. Barker, though, had omitted one detail. Under better circumstances, it wouldn't have mattered. He had neglected to mention the small stream that ran behind the abandoned structure.

"Looks like we wade,'' Whit said.

"I'm freezing already,'' Downing said. "These damn boots are about as waterproof as my basement.''

"Want me to carry you?" Felty asked, his tone laced with derision.

"Fuck you, Felty."

Whit edged downstream several yards. He called back to them. "I think we can get across here on some rocks."

Downing and Felty moved down to join him. The trooper remained unimpressed with Whit's solution. "There's no way I can go rock hopping. My feet are too damned numb."

Felty didn't wait for the debate to end. In a quick and agile move, he tiptoed over the rocks and reached the other side. "It's a piece of cake."

"After you," Whit said.

Downing had been right. He made it halfway before he lost his footing. Whit reached to catch him, but it was too late. His fingers snatched at thin air. By the time Downing finished falling, he was knee-deep in the icy branch.

"Jesus fucking Christ! I'll fuckin' freeze."

Whit eased over the rocks and helped Downing out. "Come on. let's get you inside. Maybe it's a little warmer in there."

They stepped onto the rear porch. Whit tested the door and found it locked.

"Stand back," Felty said.

With one blow of his foot, the door flew open. The noise sounded like an explosion in the velvet silence of the snowy night. As the three men vanished into the darkened interior of the building, a fourth figure emerged from the dark moon shadow thrown by the building. From inside the building came the sound of the men's feet on the wooden floors. Outside, there was a low, evil laughter, ripe with satisfied contempt.

TWENTY-SIX

KATHY EASED THE LONG BLACK LINCOLN to a stop in front of Anna's house. "Come inside for some coffee," Anna said.

"I had better go on home, Anna. I'm exhausted."

"Just for a little while, Kathy. I dread the idea of going into that empty house all alone."

Kathy nodded her consent. "What am I thinking about? Of course you do. In fact, why don't you come home with me and stay the night? No telling how late Whit will be, and you really shouldn't be alone tonight."

"I want to be home when he gets here," Anna said.

Kathy turned off the car. "I understand. These days, loneliness is my specialty."

They exited her car and trudged their way up the snow-covered sidewalk toward the house. "You should start leaving some lights on," Kathy said as they approached the darkened house.

"Normally we do. I can't even remember who left the house last today. It seems like an eternity since this morning."

Anna fished in her purse for her house key and unlocked the door. As she stepped into the house, the atmosphere was at once odd. Her mind, still slowed by the residual effects of the sedative, didn't immediately seize upon the nature of the abnormality.

Kathy's mind, though weary, recognized the problem at once. "Your heat's off, Anna. It's icy in here."

That was it! If anything, it felt colder inside than outside.

"That's never happened before." She reached for the light switch and flicked it. Nothing happened. She flicked it off and on again.

"The power's off, Kathy." She turned back toward the door and glanced at the house across the street. Its windows were ablaze with light. "Scratch that. They've got lights."

"Maybe a fuse blew," Kathy said. "Perhaps that knocks out the heat."

"If so, I haven't the foggiest idea where the fuse box is. It's never happened before. I've got a flashlight in the kitchen. You wait here."

With a sense that comes only from living in a particular house, Anna threaded her way across the dark living room and toward the kitchen. Gradually, her eyes were adjusting to the interior darkness. Outside, the light bouncing off the snow made the night unusually bright, but that reflected light had a difficult time finding any receptive material inside the home. There were glimmers of light off the trinkets in the living room and even a bright splash of light around a wall mirror, but the room was otherwise pitch black.

As she neared the entry into the kitchen, she felt the movement of air on her face. It stopped her in her tracks. "Kathy? Are you all right?"

"I'm fine, Anna. What's wrong?"

"I don't know." She turned the corner that led into the kitchen and saw the back door standing wide open. Snow from the expansive rear deck of the house had spilled into the room. With such a wide portal to enter, moonlight filled the kitchen. She emitted a sharp cry of shock.

"Anna! What's wrong?"

Back at the front door, Kathy started into the dark interior of the room. She didn't cross the room with nearly as much grace as Anna had. She walked with her hands held low in front of her. Her knee knocked into a coffee table, which she remembered was there only after the painful collision.

"Anna?"

In the kitchen, Anna heard her friend, but she kept still. Her heart pounded. Her eyes were locked on the footprints that marred the deep snow on the deck. As far as she was concerned, someone had entered the home she shared with Whit Pynchon. At that moment, she believed the intruder was still there.

She heard Kathy cry out as she bumped into a piece of furniture.

"Stay there!" Anna cried.

But Kathy had started to move again, more slowly this time, her hands running interference for her. They touched the corner of an upholstered chair. She used the chair as a guide and started around it. It was unusually stable—as if someone was sitting on it. In the eerie darkness, she probed with her hand and touched a cold shoulder.

The receiver was about the size of a pack of cigarettes. Attached to it were a pair of earphones, which, at that moment, were on Curtis Felty's head. He turned the small receiver over in his hands. "What's its range?"

Al Downing was huddled on the dusty floor, trembling with the moist chill. "Three hundred feet."

Felty peeked out the dirty window at the parking lot. "That shouldn't be a problem."

"We tested it this afternoon at the detachment,"

Downing said through chattering teeth. "It works just fine."

Whit stripped away his parka. "Here, Al. Put this over your legs. Maybe that'll help some."

"But you'll freeze then," Downing said.

"Naw. I got a sweater on, a shirt, and some long johns. I'll be fine. When winter comes, I overdress. I hate the damn cold."

The trooper accepted the offer and draped the thick coat over his wet pants. "You still planning on moving south before long?"

Whit slipped down beside the trooper and pulled a cigarette lighter from his pants pocket.

He was fishing beneath the sweater in search of his shirt pocket and the pack of cigarettes it contained when Felty said, "Watch the damned glow."

Whit's eyes flared. "Mind your own goddamn business, Felty. If anybody screws this up, it'll probably be you—or that damned toy in your hand."

Downing managed a grin. "You work so damned hard at being an asshole, Whit."

Whit leaned down close to the floor to light the cigarette. "I'll forget you said that. To answer your other question, just as soon as Anna gets tired of playing editor, I'm heading south. One way or the other, I swear this is the last winter I'll spend in this no-man's-land. Of course, I've said that before, but this time I mean it."

"It's not that bad," Downing said.

"Tell it to the Indians. Even they didn't have much use for this part of the country."

"What'll you do at the beach? Do you plan to try to get a job with the local police?"

Whit savored the flavor of the cigarette. "Hell, no. I plan to walk the beaches . . . collect shells and sharks' teeth."

Both Downing and Felty laughed.

"Is there good money in that?" Al asked, knowing better.

"I've got a little bit put away. I don't need a whole lot to get by, and with any luck Anna will come with me and support me."

"You got no pride," Al said.

Whit laughed. "If I have to, I'll get a private investigator's license," Whit said, "but that will be a last resort."

The trooper suddenly tensed. "Did you hear that?"

Felty jerked the earphones from his head. "Hear what?"

"I dunno. I thought I heard something."

Whit was listening, too. "It's probably this building. The wood's rotten."

But Downing wasn't satisfied. "It sounded more like it was outside."

Felty started toward the back. "I'll go see."

"No!" Whit hissed. "We stay put. If you go wandering around out there now, they might make you—a hell of a lot quicker than they'll see my cigarette."

Downing was nodding. "Whit's right, Felty. It's probably just my imagination. Hand Whit the receiver."

"You handle it," Whit said. "I despise those things. I've never seen one yet that didn't foul up when you needed it most."

Felty offered the small piece of equipment to the trooper, but he pushed it toward Whit. "No, you take it, Whit. I might short the thing out I'm shiverin' so hard."

"So what do we do?" Felty asked.

"You do nothing," Whit said. "I'll monitor the conversation. Just as soon as we have an exchange, I'll radio Sinclair and the units can move in. If Appleton blows it or the sellers somehow get wise, then I guess we'll have to move outside and try to take them down. Otherwise, we wait for the units to arrive.''

There was a sudden snap of static on the walkie-talkie attached to Whit's belt. He struggled to free it so he could turn down the volume. Sinclair's voice exploded in the silence of the ramshackle building.

''Are you in place?''

Whit finally got the walkie-talkie in his hand and switched down the volume. ''Dammit, Sinclair. Yes, we're in position.''

''What's wrong?'' Sinclair responded, his voice now barely audible.

''Nothing. We're in place.''

Downing checked the luminescent dial on his watch. ''Thirty minutes to go.''

Kathy's shrill scream brought Anna charging into the living room. She was fumbling with the switch on the flashlight that she had retrieved from atop the refrigerator.

''He's there,'' Kathy was crying. ''There in the chair. A man!''

The flashlight came on. Anna aimed the beam at the chair.

''Dear God!''

The circle of light illuminated a face. The head lolled back against the back of the chair. Stains of thick blood formed a double path down both sides of the mouth, which was open. So, too, were the eyes—bulging and lifeless, staring without seeing at the ceiling.

Kathy stumbled over the furniture as she rushed back toward the door. Anna, though, kept the light on the stricken face. To her, it resembled the handiwork of one of the makeup artists in those ''road kill'' movies Whit's daughter loved to watch—a display so horrible that she couldn't even associate it with reality, not until she was wrenched by recognition. The face belonged to Poo Kerns!

Only then did she begin to scream.

"It's time," Sinclair said.

Tory Appleton's face was slick with sweat. The perspiration dribbled out from under the swath of bandages that covered the top of his head. "Not yet it ain't," he said. "We got fifteen minutes."

Sinclair jammed the two stacks of money into the young man's lap. "I'm not in the mood for any of your shit, boy. Remember, goddammit. Give them the right stack of cash first."

"You think those wads of paper are gonna fool anybody?" Barker asked from the backseat where he sat with Fred Winslow, the trooper who had assisted Whit in the search of the Wilson residence.

The sheriff's captain shrugged. "It'll have to do. Unless you got a wad of money on you, it's all we could come up with."

Barker belly-laughed. "You gotta be kidding me."

Sinclair reached over and opened the door of the cruiser. "Get your ass out, Appleton. You drive that old Buick there down to the Four Leaf Clover, and you wait."

"Jesus! C'mon, man. I don't wanna do this."

"Don't make us jerk your ass out," Barker said.

But Sinclair was already in action. He lifted his boot from the accelerator and swiveled. He drove the informant out of the car with one swift blow with his heel. "Get in the goddamned car, Appleton."

The car he referred to wasn't Appleton's ragged rag top. Lenny Barker had volunteered the use of a decrepit Buick LeSabre that he had impounded several months earlier. The car had run off the road and into a ditch just inside Tipple Town's municipal limits. Its owner had never returned for it. Tipple Town's only service station had kept the car in storage for Barker. Earlier in the evening, a mechanic at the station had put chains on its bald tires.

"What if I wreck?" Appleton asked.

Sinclair shrugged. "Then Felty gets his way with you."

"And so will I," Barker volunteered. "That's town property you're driving."

"This ain't right, man." Moonlight glistened on the boy's face.

"Move it, asshole."

Trooper Winslow was laughing. "He's sweating like a stuck pig."

Sinclair had a more realistic concern. "I just hope he doesn't sweat so fuckin' much he shorts the wire."

Both of the vehicles were parked in the shadow of a large barn belonging to a retired coal miner, who had been more than willing to cooperate with "the law." The sheltered area behind his barn became the eastern checkpoint for the operation.

"And don't fuck up the wire," Sinclair shouted just as Appleton got into the car.

The engine turned several times before it caught. Appleton eased the car out from behind the barn and down toward the road that led down to the Four Leaf Clover. Sinclair picked up his transmitter and keyed the mike. "Whit, he's on the way. He should make it to your 'ten-twenty' in three minutes."

The response was a whispered "Ten four."

"I'll sneak up to the corner of the barn and watch the road for our suspects," Sinclair said. "You guys monitor the radio."

* * *

By all rights, Tory Appleton should have been freezing. The heater in the old Buick hadn't warmed up even during the drive down from Tipple Town. The sweat continued to roll down his face. He could feel it seeping underneath his arms, too. His head still throbbed. The least the bastards could have done was to give him some pain pills.

The car's interior reeked of must and mildew. Its brakes were so loose that the pedal almost touched the floor. The lousy excuse for buy-money rested beside him on the seat. He had no idea how much was there, but from what the cops said he doubted it came anywhere near to the four grand he was supposed to deliver. What the hell was going to happen to him when Carr or one of the Smith brothers started to count the green?

With the chains on the tires, the Buick drifted easily down the slight grade toward the Four Leaf Clover. Appleton started braking even before the building was in sight. The chains grabbed against the wet snow, and the car slowed.

His stomach started to cramp, very low down . . . just above his cock. The pounding in his head intensified. Worse, the wire on his chest . . . or maybe the tape that secured it to his flesh . . . started to itch. He didn't dare scratch. He eased the car into the parking lot and stopped it squarely in front of the building. In his headlights, he caught sight of a figure as it ducked around the corner of the building.

"Stupid assholes!" Tory mumbled, thinking it had been a cop that he'd seen.

TWENTY-SEVEN

"I THINK IT'S APPLETON," Whit said, easing his head up so he could peek out the dusty window at the parking lot. As the car had pulled into the parking area, its headlights had filled the Four Leaf Clover with light. They were still on.

"The dumb son of a bitch oughta douse the headlights," Felty said.

Downing's teeth chattered. "Christ, I'm freezing. I'm numb from the knees down."

Whit had slipped back down and was adjusting the receiver. The earphones were on his head. "I can hear Appleton's heart beating. It sounds like a horse galloping. I bet it's going two hundred beats a minute. The kid's petrified."

Downing rubbed his legs fiercely and then eased up to sneak his own look through the window. The Buick just sat there, its headlights still burning and the thick exhaust rolling out the rear. "I bet the bastards don't show."

"Goddamn snow," Felty mumbled, his words punctuated by the fog from his mouth. "If we had this much down in Carolina, they'd roll up the fuckin' sidewalks."

Whit was beginning to feel the damp cold, too. He was starting to tremble. "I swear it. Not another winter in this damned state." He wrapped his arms over his chest in a futile effort to retain his body heat.

Downing was replacing Whit's coat around his legs. The lower portion of his pants were frozen stiff. "Damn, this is ridiculous. We shoulda used a little common sense. I shoulda listened to you, Whit. No way are they gonna come out on a night like this."

From behind them, the floor creaked. In a simultaneous reaction, all three of them snapped their heads toward the sound. An immense form, silhouetted in the glare from the Buick's headlights, took a single step toward them.

"Wrong," the shadow said. "We're here."

"What the hell—" Downing's hand dropped to his side.

"No!" Whit shrieked.

Too late. A bluish-orange flash squirted from the hand of the intruder, followed immediately by the muffled puff of a silenced gun. Downing's other hand reached to his throat. His sharp cry withered into an ominous gurgling as hot blood jetted through his fingers from a wound just below his Adam's apple. He slumped to the side.

Appleton saw the lights of the car first, even before it rounded the curve located just to the west of the parking area. The beam from the headlights played across the white forested slope behind the beer joint. Then the vehicle—a truck—came into view. It rolled slowly to a stop beside Appleton's vehicle, and the door opened.

"Here they are," Appleton whispered as he watched a small figure exit the truck. It circled around behind the Buick.

The driver's door to his car was opened. Didimus Smith jammed a small weapon against Appleton's temple. "Slide over."

Appleton obeyed. "Where's Carr?"

"He's around," Didimus said. "You remember me, don't you?"

"Yeah, you're Willie Mack's brother." As he spoke, his stare remained fixed on the weapon, which he now recognized as a two-shot derringer.

"This snow sucks," Didimus said.

Appleton smelled the fresh booze on Smith's breath. "Let's get this over with. Do you have the stuff?"

Didimus smiled and waved the small handgun. "This is all I brought."

Appleton's mouth was dry. Even his sweat had dried up. He could feel his heart hammering away in his chest. "C'mon, man. Me and Jimmy had a deal."

"Know what this is?" Didimus asked, still moving the barrel of the gun back and forth in front of Appleton's face.

"A derringer, man. But you got no need for it. I'm not packing a gun."

Didimus snickered. It was a sickening sound, accompanied by an even stronger stench of boozy bad breath.

"It's a special kind of gun, asshole. It belongs to Willie Mack. It's loaded with a shotgun shell—a .410 gauge."

"Look, Smith. All I wanna do is buy some dope. I got the bread right here." He patted the two stacks of bills.

Didimus didn't even look at the money.

"You know, I figured this little thing would kick like a son of a bitchin' mule. It don't. Know why?"

Appleton didn't answer.

"I'll tell you why. It's the short barrel. That's what Willie Mack says. He says, too, that the pellets start to spread just as soon as they leave the barrel. So you gotta be real close to use it . . . like we are now."

* * *

Inside the building, Whit was stripping the clothing away from Downing's neck. The blood, steaming in the icy night air, continued to pump from the small wound in copious amounts. It gushed down the front of the trooper's shirt. Whit could smell it, sharp and coppery, but so long as it was flowing the trooper was alive. Felty was on the other side of the wounded man, waiting to do anything Whit asked.

"We gotta stop it," Whit said, trying to cover the wound with the palm of his hand.

"Forget him," the intruder said.

"Fuck you." Whit kept working.

The trooper's eyes were open. They were seeing. Whit read the fear in them. "C'mon Al. Hang on. You can make it."

Felty was gauging Downing's assailant. He was a Goliath of a man, bigger even than Felty himself, and dressed in grimy coveralls. On his feet he sported heavy black engineer boots. He wore no coat, and his broad face was concealed behind a red-and-white ski mask.

"Dammit, I said to forget the son of a bitch!"

"Look out!" Felty cried as the man made his move.

A booted foot rocketed forward, catching Whit just under his arm. The force of the blow lifted him off the floor and slammed him against the wall. Felty braced to launch an attack from his position by Downing, but the masked man quickly leveled the gun at the brow of the out-of-state cop.

"Do it." The man sneered. "Do it, motherfucker! I'll put a friggin' slug right into your gawdamned brain."

Whit was holding his side, trying to right himself, when he saw the blood cease to pump from Downing's neck. A bubbling rattle issued from the trooper's mouth; his body relaxed.

Whit had heard the voices over the earphones as he

had been struggling frantically to stay Downing's loss
of blood. Now, with the life gone from Downing's body,
he was actually hearing the words. Beneath the words,
he could still hear the agitated throbbing of Tory Appleton's heart.

Downing's killer shifted the large pistol from one
hand to the other. "Can we all hear on that damned
thing?"

Arrows of pain shot through Whit's chest as he pulled
himself to a sitting position.

"Answer me!" He pulled back his foot as if to un-
leash another kick.

"Sure," Whit said, grimacing with a pain produced
by the simple act of speaking. He pulled the earphone
jack from the receiver.

"I'll blow your double-crossin' face away, asshole."
The voice coming over the receiver was vicious, high
pitched—like something from a child's scary fantasy,
distorted to an even greater degree by the cheap ampli-
fier in the receiving unit.

Their captor laughed as he listened. "Kill him," he
said to the receiver.

The walkie-talkie was beside Whit's thigh. Slowly,
he inched his leg over to a point where the flesh of his
thigh pressed down on the mike key to the walkie-talkie.

"Please don't." The second voice, weak and whining, belonged to Tory Appleton.

"Gawdammit! Kill him!" the man in the building
shouted.

Whit's eyes narrowed as he studied the imposing
frame of the man. "He can't hear you. This thing just
works one way."

Then, as if to mock Whit, the sharp crack of a blast
rattled the receiver, followed by deep moaning, the
whisper of something rustling, and finally the erratic
rhythm of Tory Appleton's dying heart.

* * *

Sinclair had returned to the cruiser. "A truck just drove by, heading down toward the beer joint. I'd say that's them."

"How do you know?" Barker had asked.

Sinclair had shrugged. "Who the hell else would be out on a night like this?"

The answer hadn't satisfied Tipple Town's chief. "Hell, it coulda been a lot of people."

Sinclair shook his head at the chief's doubt. "Fine, Barker. Then you go out there and stand guard for a while. My damned hands are frozen solid."

Barker momentarily considered it. He decided to stay in the warm car. "I don't guess it'll matter. They'll radio us when they show."

Moments later, they heard the crack of static from the walkie-talkie. "Here it goes," Sinclair said.

They had expected to hear the voice of Al Downing or Whit Pynchon. Instead they heard the flat crack of a gunshot.

"Oh, shit!" Barker said.

"Damn!" Sinclair said. "It must be falling apart. Let's get down there."

"In one piece," Winslow said from the backseat.

Police officers—especially when panicked—are anything but subtle. The two police cruisers arrived at the Four Leaf Clover simultaneously, their red and blue lights wildly whirling in their holders and their whooping sirens rupturing the tranquillity of the wintry night. Tory Appleton's Buick loaner was scissored in the bright beams of their headlights. On the passenger side, the door slowly opened and Appleton himself spilled out into the snow.

It was Sinclair's headlights that were illuminating that

side of the vehicle. He inched the car closer as the body came to a rest.

· Barker was leaning forward. "His goddamn face is gone."

On the other side of Appleton's car, three troopers were pouring out of the state police cruiser that had been assigned to the other end of the road.

Sinclair snatched up the radio mike and switched over to the public-address system. "Surround the building."

Barker and Winslow were already out of the car. The chief was checking Appleton. "He's still breathing, but—"

Sinclair was out of the car then, moving toward Barker, when the mountainside several hundred feet above the Four Leaf Clover exploded in a blinding cataclysm of fire and smoke. The concussion battered his eardrums. He dove face first into the cushion of the snow.

Barker, still kneeling over Appleton, rolled away from the scalding shock wave.

"What the fuck was that?" someone shouted.

"Look!" another voice cried. "It's the four-wheel drive. It's burning!"

At that point, flames reached the gas tank of the vehicle. The second explosion, this one not nearly as sharp as the first but far more dramatic, sent a liquid blaze boiling high into the night sky. Pine trees erupted into flame. It rained fire on the rear portion of the Four Leaf Clover.

"Oh, God, the building's gonna burn," Barker cried.

At that moment, the front door of the beer joint was flung open. "Hold your fire! This is Pynchon. I'm stepping out." He had to shout to be heard over the roar from the blaze behind the building.

Sinclair lifted his face from the snow. The burning car and pines cast a flickering light over the parking lot.

Dancing fingers of flame ran along the roof of the building.

"Don't fire," Sinclair shouted. "It's Whit!"

Several .357 magnums as well as a couple of .12 gauge shotguns were aimed at Whit as he stepped out on the sagging porch of the old beer joint.

"Put your weapons down," Whit told them.

Winslow looked over to the captain for instruction. Sinclair motioned for him to comply. "Hell, yes. Do as he says."

"Like hell I will," another trooper shouted.

Whit heard him. "Dammit, man. You wanna die? That was a frigging antitank missile, or something like it. There's a couple of guys on the bank behind you."

All of them looked back over their shoulders. The flat crack of a rifle shot was followed immediately by the hissing deflation of a tire on Sinclair's vehicle. It proved Whit's point. The men, most of them prone in the snow, relinquished their weapons. One by one, they got to their feet.

The man wearing the ski mask shoved Felty out the door first and then stepped into view. The fire on the roof had already burned through the dry wood, and flames could be seen through the front door.

"Where's Downing?" Winslow asked.

"Inside," Whit said. "He's dead."

"Mother of God," a voice shouted, "we oughta get him outa there."

Winslow took a step toward the building. The snow at his feet puffed up to the sound of another rifle shot.

Twenty-Eight

"HAVE YOU GOT HIM OUT OF HERE YET?" Anna asked of the city officer who had just stepped into her kitchen.

"Not yet, ma'am. We don't wanna move him until the photographer gets here. One of our units is on the way with him."

"I just want him out," Anna said.

Kathy, her face still pale, sat at the table with Anna. "Give them time. You know they have things to do."

The publisher of the *Daily Journal* turned her attention to the baby-faced officer. "Have you reached Whit Pynchon yet?"

"No, ma'am. Mr. Danton said to hold off on that."

"Where is he?" Anna asked.

"Mr. Danton? He's in the living room. He'll be in here—"

"No dammit! Where's Whit?"

"I'm afraid I don't know. I just wanted to tell you that it was just a fuse . . . I mean, whoever was in here had thrown the switch on the circuit breaker. That's all."

But Anna wasn't interested. "Please, try to reach Whit for me."

Tony Danton came limping into the kitchen. He went straight to Anna, who rose as soon as she saw him. His good arm went around her.

"I want him out of my house," Anna said as the prosecutor pulled her to him.

"Just as soon as we can, Anna. The officer said you identified him."

Anna started to weep again. "It's Paul Kerns. Why here, Tony? Was it because of me? Or Whit?"

"Who knows?"

A plainclothes city detective stuck his head into the kitchen. "Mr. Danton, can I see you a minute?"

"Sure, I'm on my way out." He eased Anna away from him. "We'll move the body just as soon as we can. I prefer to have Whit check out a scene in a case like this. He has an eye for evidence, developed no doubt from all that time he spends beachcombing when he's at the beach."

The comment, an inside joke in a way, brought a trace of a smile to Anna's face. "Yeah, he can find fossilized shark's teeth no bigger than a pinhead. I don't know why he wastes the effort to bend down for them."

Tony took her hand. "Since this happens to be his home—and yours, too—well, I don't think I'll wait on him this time. He doesn't need this on top of everything else."

Anna patted Tony's hand, released it, and then slumped down into the chair. "I know the poor boy's dead. I'm sorry he's dead, but it makes me feel so vulnerable, so helpless. They brought him right into our house."

"I know," Tony said. "I promise . . . I'll get things squared away and cleaned up just as soon as I can."

Tony went out into the living room. The body of Paul Kerns was still seated in the chair, but the ambulance crew had covered it with a sheet. The detective knelt down at the dead man's feet.

"Take a look at the bottom of the shoes."

Tony flinched in pain as he knelt down. "What is

it?'' he asked, scrutinizing the black residue on the soles
of the tennis shoes.

"Coal dust," the cop said.

"Coal dust?"

"That's sure what it looks like."

A cop's nightmare come true.

That's how Whit thought of the hellish scene on the
parking lot of the Four Leaf Clover. The masked man
had ordered them off the porch as fire spread through
the decaying building. In a wide circle around the structure, the heat was melting the snow.

The cops themselves stood in the snow, the flames
flickering in their slack faces. They had been defeated,
and that did something to their masculinity. Whit saw
it in their eyes—a mixture of disbelief, anger, and even
fear. Many of them expected to die. So, too, did Whit.

The gunman moved to a position beside Whit. He
lifted his hand and waved it. A second masked figure,
this one not nearly so large, darted from a place of
concealment on the other side of the road. He lugged
an oversized shotgun that sported an ammo drum.

As the second man approached, Whit knew at once
that it was the same weapon that had been responsible
for the River Road killings.

"Blast the radios," the larger of the two said.

The second giggled, at least that's what it sounded
like to Whit, and went to Sinclair's cruiser first. He
jammed the gun in the open driver's door and fired. The
inside of the car filled with smoke and sparks.

"Jesus," Sinclair mumbled.

The man with the shotgun then dashed around to the
second cruiser and opened the driver's door. He unleashed a second barrage. The other man was signaling
again, this time to someone high on the bank on the
opposite side of the road. Almost immediately, a shot

rang out. Most of the officers started ducking as a tire on the other cruiser was ruptured.

That's when Frank Winslow made the last mistake of his young life. Whit, who was standing about twelve feet away from Winslow, saw the young officer's gaze shift quickly from the big man to the other. The trooper then glanced down at his revolver.

"For God's sakes, don't try—" Whit didn't get to complete the warning.

Winslow dove for his magnum and managed to get it in his hands. He rose to his knees and was lifting it toward the big man as he catapulted himself to his feet. Just as he started to level the sites, the gunman on the bank fired. The large-caliber bullet struck him squarely between his shoulder blades. The impact exploded the trooper's heart. As the fragmented projectile exited, it took most of his rib cage with it. He flopped to the ground. The warm blood and gore quickly dissolved into the blanket of snow.

"Anybody else wanna die?" the big man said. "We wouldn't mind a damn bit making your wish come true."

Whit had rushed over to the fallen officer. The others stood rock still.

"Show 'em how easy it is!" the big man shouted. "C'mon, show 'em."

The smaller figure was moving among the cops. He started to laugh as he passed by Barker. "You're marked for death," he said.

Barker frowned. "What the fuck does that mean?"

"Turn around."

"Go to hell," Barker said.

The big man moved closer. "Do as he says."

Barker turned. He saw the small red light centered on his chest. "What is that?"

Whit abandoned Winslow's body. The cop had been

dead before he even hit the ground. He moved to where he could see Barker's chest. Anna's red light . . . a laser directed rifle.

"It's a laser scope," Whit said.

"Get it away!" Barker smacked at it as if it were a pesky wasp. It hung to his chest. "Dammit! Get it off me!"

Whit put a hand on the chief's shoulder. "Take it easy. You're fine until they pull the trigger."

The dot shifted to Whit's chest. Suddenly he knew how Barker felt. It was just a light. By itself, it had no power to injure. Whit knew all that, but he couldn't help himself. He reached out to block it. The light vanished.

The big man laughed first. Then the smaller of the two giggled.

"Kinda gets ya, don't it?" the man said.

Whit didn't answer.

The leader gave yet another hand signal and then jammed the silencer into Curtis Felty's back. "Get your ass into that car."

Felty turned. "Which car?"

"The one in the middle, goddammit."

He was talking about Appleton's car—the Buick on loan from Tipple Town.

Felty moved slowly toward the car. The smaller of the two gunmen stepped over Appleton's body and climbed into the backseat. Felty was guided to the passenger side and ordered inside. As soon as he sagged down into the worn seat, the icy barrel of the shotgun came from the shadows of the rear seat and was placed against the back of his neck.

The bigger of the two men moved around the front of the vehicle and stopped before he climbed inside. He motioned to Whit. "C'mere."

Whit crossed his arms and stood his ground.

The leader lifted the barrel of the pistol he carried. "I said, come over here."

Sinclair eased over to him. "For crissakes, do as he says! We've lost enough guys tonight."

Whit took three steps closer to the man. He fully expected to be ordered into the car.

Instead, the man said, "You've got a present waitin' for you when you get home. Just remember. It might have been that meddlin' newspaperwoman you've been shacking up with."

Whit started forward, but Sinclair grabbed him from behind. "Don't *you* do anything stupid."

The man slid into the car. His eyes settled upon the stack of money in the front seat. "This oughta just about pay for our gas."

He fired up the battered Buick.

Whit watched as the car fishtailed out of the parking lot and headed back toward Tipple Town. Sinclair eased over to him, his attention riveted on the wooded bank on the other side of the road. "Jesus, Whit. We screwed up royally."

Whit's gaze dropped down to the body of the slain trooper. "We didn't screw up at all, Ross. Somebody tipped the bastards, and it wasn't Appleton. We've got a dirty cop on our hands."

TWENTY-NINE

AT ONE A.M. Thursday morning, Anna still sat at the kitchen table. She was slumped over, her head resting on her crossed forearms. Kathy Binder occupied the chair across the table from her.

"You really ought to go to bed," Kathy said. "I'll stay until Whit comes."

Anna lifted her head. Anxiety and fatigue were etched into her face. Her usually tan skin appeared beige, and the puffy skin beneath her eyes was dark. "As soon as I talk to Whit, Kathy."

The publisher of the *Daily Journal* shook her head. "But Tony called. Whit's fine."

"I just want to hear his voice, Kathy."

"Well, let's at least go into the living room. They cleaned it up—"

But Anna was shaking her head. "I can't. I know the chair's gone, but every time I walk into that room I still see him sitting there, his face . . ." Her voice trailed off.

Kathy understood. In a way, she felt the same aversion to the living room, but her reaction was slightly different. Whenever she entered the room, she smelled the coppery odor of blood. Not that there had been all that much. The city detective who had supervised the team of cops had commented on the lack of blood.

Tony had said, "He was killed somewhere else."

Small comfort, Kathy had thought.

A few drops had tainted the worn upholstery of the chair in which the body had been placed. Even after a good fifteen minutes of scrubbing with a cold rag, the telltale stains had remained. At Anna's request, the cops had lugged the chair out into the snow that covered the rear deck of the house she and Whit shared.

"Then go rest on your bed, Anna. You're about to pass out from exhaustion."

"I'll be fine." Immediately after she spoke those words, she sat straight up in the chair. "What's that? Do you hear it?"

Kathy listened. "Yes, I hear it."

For Kathy, though, the sound became familiar. "It's water dripping . . . outside."

Anna stared at the back door, her eyes shocked open by her sudden panic. "Why is water dripping?"

Kathy stood up. "I'll go see."

"No!" wailed Anna, jumping to her feet, too.

Kathy rushed around the table and put an arm around her friend. "Easy, Anna. C'mon, girl, get hold of yourself."

The frightened woman slumped back down into the kitchen chair. "I don't know what's wrong with me. It's just the idea that they brought it—him, I mean—into my house. It makes me sick to my stomach."

"I'll see what's dripping." Kathy went to the back door. As brave as she had pretended to be, and as certain as she was that it was only the sound of dripping water, her heart still climbed into her throat as she opened the back door. In her mind, which was almost as fatigued as that of her friend, she had visions of another body, hung upside down in some irrational fashion, with its blood dripping into the trampled snow that covered the deck.

But what she saw was a multitude of sparkling rivulets of water cascading from the eaves of the house. "The snow's melting," she said, somewhat astonished. "It must be warming up."

Anna came to see.

In working the scene, the cops had swept a small path through the snow on the deck. The overhang of the roof extended several feet beyond the back door. So Anna stepped out onto the wet deck and inhaled. She averted her eyes from the wingback chair sitting at the closed end of the deck. "I can't believe it's warming up in the middle of the night."

But there wasn't much doubt about it, given the volume of water that poured from the roof.

"It feels good," Kathy said, inhaling the crisp night air.

The phone rang.

Anna started back into the house to answer it.

"You wait," Kathy said. "I'll get it."

It was Whit.

"Are you all right?" Kathy asked.

"I guess. How's Anna?"

The newspaper publisher looked back over her shoulder. Anna was in the house, closing the door behind her. "Well, she's a nervous wreck, and she looks like death warmed over, but she's okay."

"I appreciate you staying. Tony told me what the bastards did."

"It was terrible, Whit."

Anna was beside her by then, nudging her, reaching for the phone.

"Here's Anna, Whit."

She snatched the phone from Kathy.

"Whit? Are you really all right?"

"I'm fine, hon. How about you?"

"They came into our house, Whit. They left that—"

"Easy, hon. Tony told me."

Tears were rolling down Anna's face. "I feel so stupid, Whit. I thought I was stronger."

"It's over, Anna. Tony told me they cleaned the place up. Is it okay? I mean, did they really—"

"There wasn't much of a mess that way. There were some stains on that wingback chair, and I made them set it outside."

"In the snow?"

"I want to get rid of it, Whit. I'll never be able to look at it without remembering—"

"That's fine, Anna. We'll get rid of it."

A tremor of emotion returned to Anna's voice. "I kept thinking, Whit . . . what if Tressa had come here? What if she had found him? Worse, what if she had come here while they were here?"

"I'm sorry you had to see it."

"It was meant for me, Whit."

"For both of us, Anna."

Kathy had settled back down at the table. Whit and Anna talked for a few more minutes, and then Anna called Kathy back to the phone. "He wants to talk to you a second."

Kathy took the phone. "I understand you people had a rough night."

She didn't need to see him. Even over the phone, she could hear him tense.

"Darn you, Whit Pynchon. I'm not asking for a news story. That's not really my department."

He managed a weary laugh. "Sorry, Kathy. Old habits die hard. Yeah, we did. We lost some good men. What's worse is why it happened."

"What on earth do you mean?"

"Nothing. I'll fill you in later. I was going to ask if you might stay with Anna. I'm going to be tied up for a while . . . maybe the rest of the night—"

"She wants to see you."

Anna was standing beside her. "I'm better now, Kathy. I really am."

Kathy nodded to her and said to Whit, "Of course, I will."

"See if you can get her into bed," Whit said.

"I'll try."

Kathy hung up the phone and smiled at Anna. "There are times, m'dear, when he actually sounds human."

The comment brought a weary smile to Anna's face. "He wanted you to tuck me in bed," she said.

"He ordered me to."

The precipitation began to fall again about 4:00 A.M. that morning, but it wasn't snow. This time the sky released a moderate but steady rainfall. The weather system that had brought the deep, wet snow had been rushed northeastward by warm southerly winds. The relatively humid air from the south was overrunning the cooler air left by the front from the north, and now rain beat down on the snow. The warm rain would hasten the demise of the heavy snow, and the runoff promised to swell the mountain streams. In the dismal gloom of the morning, a weather service official in Charleston had already issued a flash flood warning for small stream flooding in southern West Virginia.

Whit, standing in the control room of the Raven County Sheriff's Department, watched the teletype as the warning was hammered out on the thin paper. A dark stubble shadowed his face. His eyes were angry and impatient as he waited for Tony Danton to finish his conversation with Ross Sinclair. The old Buick provided by Barker had been found abandoned on the outskirts of Tipple Town, and Tony was telling Sinclair to have it towed to Charleston for examination by the state police lab.

"It's a waste of time," Whit said. "We know where to go."

Tony turned to his investigator. "Dammit, Whit, what evidence have we got that it was the Smiths?"

"Enough to satisfy me," Whit said.

The prosecutor and Sinclair traded frustrated looks. Tony went to Whit and placed a hand on his shoulder. "We've got the word of a dopehead who says it was the Smiths. He's dead, Whit. If he were alive, I'd use him to get a search warrant, but I can't. I've talked to the state police superintendent. He's talking to the governor—"

Whit continued to stare at the teletype, which was now silent. "The hell with the governor. Screw search warrants, too, Tony. The bastards sure as fuck didn't bother with warrants when they left their dead trash in my house. We oughta go in after Felty, Tony. These assholes will kill him without giving it a second thought."

"And blow the whole case? Is that what you want me to do, Whit? Christ, man! Besides, there's a good chance Felty's dead already. If not, then they're keeping him alive for a reason, and that means we have some time. Think about it. I don't have any admissible evidence against the Smiths. They'd walk, Whit."

"From what I've seen of this crew, you won't have to worry about your case. The only way we're gonna be able to take them is dead."

Sinclair joined the conversation. "The trouble is, Whit, our own casualties might be too high. If Felty's not dead by now, we just might end up getting him killed, and a hell of a lot of other officers, too. Those bastards have some high-powered weapons in their hands. From what Barker tells us, they could see us coming from a mile away. They have a convenient killing ground."

Whit whirled on the captain. "I wouldn't believe Barker on a stack of Bibles. I've got to get out of here."

The investigator started for the door. Tony hurried to catch him. "Where are you going, Whit?"

"Home," Whit shouted back. Under his breath, he mumbled, ". . . to get more firepower."

Anna was sleeping when Whit got home. Kathy herself was dozing on the couch in the living room and was startled awake by the sound of Whit opening a door to a closet in the entryway of the home. He pulled a long, black case from the dark depths of the closet. A low-wattage bulb in a table lamp provided the only illumination.

"You frightened me," she said, still reclining on the couch.

"I was trying not to wake you."

"What are you doing?" she asked.

"I've got to leave again, Kathy,"

She pulled herself up to a sitting position, trying to rub away the sleep from her eyes. "How long have you been here?"

"I just got home. Can you stay with her?"

Kathy glanced around the living room. "What time is it?"

"Almost 5:00 A.M."

"What are you going to do this early?" She mounted her feet and moved closer to him. As unenlightened as she was about such things, she finally recognized the case he held in his hands. "Is that a gun?"

"It's a rifle, Kathy."

"I think you should go tell Anna where you're going. If she wakes up and finds that you've been here—"

Whit placed the gun case beside the front door and returned to the closet. He knelt and began rummaging in the rear. "I don't have time, Kathy. Besides, you and

I both know Anna. I'd play hell getting away without some kind of explanation. This isn't the time or the place. Ah, there they are!''

He jerked a pair of knee-high rubber boots from the closet and tucked them under his arm. He turned to Kathy. "Can you stay?"

"Of course, I can stay! But I want to know what's going on. I want to be able to tell her something. She has a right to know, Whit. Put yourself in her shoes. How would you feel?"

"She's a tough lady, Kathy." He started toward the door, but she stepped in front of him to block his way.

"Yeah, she is tough, Whit, but everyone has their limits. Jesus, man! She was standing beside a young man when his head was blown off. She comes home and finds a dead man, his neck broken and blood all over him, sitting in her living room easy chair. Sure, she's tough, Whit, but she's about ready to break."

Whit lowered his head. "Okay . . . you're right. For now, though, it'll have to be brief. She deserves an explanation. We had a drug buy set for last night. I'd say she knows about all that . . . you, too, probably. We think the sellers were the ones who killed those two troopers on River Road. I'm certain they had something to do with the killing of that reporter of yours. Anyway, the drug deal went bad—very bad. Several officers died, and one was taken as a hostage."

"And?"

"He needs help."

"So you know where he is?" Kathy asked.

"I have a pretty good idea."

"How many of you are going?"

Whit hesitated before he answered, just long enough that Kathy Binder divined the answer herself. "You're going after him by yourself?"

"Don't tell her that," Whit said, taking advantage of

her dismay to step around her. He picked up the rifle
case.

"Dammit, Whit. I can't lie to her."

"If she's as tired as she sounded, she'll probably
sleep late. By that time, it should be over."

Whit started to open the door.

"What should be over?"

It was a feminine voice, but it wasn't Kathy's. Whit
wheeled around and saw Anna standing in the doorway
of their bedroom.

THIRTY

THE LAST THING CURTIS FELTY remembered was the careening ride away from the Four Leaf Clover. The smelly Buick hadn't gone a mile when it stopped in the middle of the snow-covered road. He could remember a dark shape emerging from the wintry wooded landscape. He could also remember a face as the figure approached the stopped vehicle. That's when his memory ceased. The way his head throbbed, he figured he had been knocked out. When he came to, he found himself lashed to a chair, his eyes covered by a thick blindfold. Even without the blindfold, he probably wouldn't have been able to see anything. There was no light at all, not even a hint of one, at the lower edge of the blindfold. In the inky darkness, he had to depend upon his senses of hearing, touch, and smell to forge some sense of reality. The most telling sensation was the musty dampness. The atmosphere around him reeked of the grave—of moist earth never consecrated by the touch of the purifying sun. There was a secondary odor, a trace of something pungent and man-made. He knew the odor; he just couldn't put a name to it.

The rhythmic dripping of water, too.

The trickling of water, as if the chair in which he was strapped sat over some very small brook.

Felty inhaled. The air moved with a gravid sluggish-

ness, so damp it was. It resisted his efforts to draw it
into his lungs.

"Anyone here?" he said aloud.

His voice echoed forever.

"Hello!"

The noises remained constant; the dripping, the
trickling, an occasional creak from . . . a creak from
what? It sounded like wood.

A basement!

He was being concealed in somebody's basement.

He tried to move his feet, but they were lashed to the
legs of the chair in which he sat. His arms were bound
behind him and were also tied to the wooden back slats
of the chair. He tried to rock the chair. The back of his
head struck something hard. The pain behind his eyes
mushroomed as the blow aggravated the misery his
brain had already suffered.

A hint of nausea formed deep in his gut. He swal-
lowed and started to breathe deeply, trying to avert the
discomfort. He didn't want to vomit.

That's when he heard the chirping . . .

Birds? Felty again listened.

It wasn't really chirping, more like a curious squealing. The sound was familiar.

What the hell is it?

Rats!

The realization turned him ice cold.

Anna was livid. "You weren't even going to wake
me?"

She stood with Whit in the living room. Kathy had
gone to the kitchen, not anxious to be a part of the
scene that was playing itself out between Whit and
Anna.

"You need to sleep," he said—a pitiful excuse, but
the best he could do under the circumstances.

Her rage had returned most of the color to her face. "I swear to God, Whit Pynchon. Sometimes I wonder about you."

"I'm sorry, Anna. I just didn't want you to worry."

She circled him. "I love you, dammit. I have a right to worry. Where were you going?"

Outside, the intensity of the rain had increased. He could hear it hammering the small aluminum awning that provided shelter over the front door. With a futile shrug, he allowed the rubber boots to drop to the floor. He leaned the gun case against the door facing. "If we're going to have this discussion, let's at least go sit down."

Anna had stopped her angry pacing. She was staring into his face. As soon as his arms were empty, she rushed to him and threw her arms around him. "Damn you, Whit. I don't think you'll ever understand."

He kissed her. "I understand," he whispered. "Really, I do. I was telling you the truth. I was hoping you'd sleep until noon, and I could come in and wake you and tell you it was all over . . . that the scum were in jail . . . or dead."

He guided her into the main area of the living room, where they sat down beside each other on the couch. Kathy exited the kitchen with two steaming cups of coffee in her hand. "Can I fix you breakfast?"

Anna shook her head, but Whit smiled. "Now that you mention it, I'm starving. Just a couple of pieces of toast."

"You need more than that," Kathy said. "I can whip up some eggs and bacon in no time. It's about the only thing I can cook."

The image appealed to Whit. "Yeah, do it. I don't think a few more minutes are going to matter. It sounds good. Fix enough for us all. Anna will eat."

Kathy looked down at her friend. Anna's eyes were filled with tears. "If I fix it, will you eat it?"

Anna smiled. "Why not? If I survived yesterday, your cooking shouldn't kill me."

They all laughed. Kathy started toward the kitchen, but a thought stopped her. She turned. "You know something, Anna. You became angry at Whit, and you seemed to heal right before our eyes. I don't think I'll ever figure you two out."

Anna gave Whit a firm but playful punch on the arm. "Well, I guess I'm just glad I still have him around to make me mad, but"—she turned to Whit—"I still can't believe you were sneaking out of here."

"I wouldn't call it sneaking."

"Just what would you call it?"

"A discreet exit."

"You were being sneaky!"

He sipped the steaming coffee that Kathy had brought. Already, the aroma of frying bacon was drifting from the kitchen. He leaned back. "This feels good."

She snuggled against him. "I'm glad you stayed."

"As soon as I eat, though, I have to go. You know that."

"I know it," she said, some of the joy gone from her voice. "Where are you going? You never did say."

"Is this off the record?"

"Whit!" She sat up, her eyes blazing. Then she saw the mischievous twinkle in his chocolate eyes. "You bastard."

He told her what had happened . . . what he had to do . . . why he had to do it.

"You're going by yourself?"

"Pretty much so."

"What the hell does that mean, Whit? Pretty much so?"

"I'm going to take one person with me . . . the one that tipped off those bastards."

"Don't do it, Whit. Do like Tony says and wait."

Whit finished the coffee. "Tony's going to do the right thing, Anna. He's going to play it by the book. Usually that's the best way, but this time it won't work. This isn't just cops and robbers this time. It's something else. It's a war, and you know what they say about war."

She was looking at him, the concern heavy on her face. "They say it's hell . . . remember."

"Yeah, but they also say that all is fair . . . in love and war."

Voices, distant but sharp, had silenced the rats. The vermin hadn't bothered Felty, if that's what had been making the squealing noises, but Felty had a thing about rats. He despised them . . . had ever since he had been bitten by one when he was a kid. Not that the little bastard hadn't had good cause. He'd been trying to kill it with a broom, convinced that the five foot length of the broomstick was a sufficient buffer between his hand and the squealing little bundle of furious fur. He had been wrong. The rat had charged up the broomstick with a speed that had paralyzed young Curtis. Before he could even drop it, the teeth of the rat were buried in the skin on the back of his hand. Since then, he had more than a healthy respect for the revolting creatures.

So, in an odd way, the sound of the men's voices was a kind of rescue. Their words, just as his had, echoed in whatever kind of chamber he was captive. They reverberated so much, in fact, that Felty couldn't understand what they were saying. He only picked up bits of the conversation.

". . . powder . . ."

". . . on the shelves . . ."

". . . fuckin' water . . ."

The voices became louder. He heard the sound of feet. Moments later, a yellow flickering light was barely visible at the bottom edge of the blindfold. Felty's heart started to race.

"You sure he's tied good," one said.

Another snickered . . . sort of giggled. "He's hog-tied, Willie."

They were on top of him. He could smell them . . . body odor mingled with the aroma of pork sausage. A rough hand fumbled behind his head. The blindfold was ripped away, and Felty squenched his eyes against the blinding glow of fire that danced in front of his eyes.

"Mornin'," a man said.

Felty eased his eyes open so they could adjust to the sudden assault of light. He saw that he was in a cave. No, it was more than a cave. It was a mine. Its walls glistened with a sparkling blackness. He was in a coal mine.

He looked up at his captor. The man towered above him.

"My name's Willie Mack Smith."

Felty kept silent, somewhat awed by the size of the man. As tall as he was, his girth made him seem even larger . . . big-boned with a bulging gut and a head made to look several sizes too large for his body by the wild beard that covered much of his face. This was the same man that had trapped them in the building, the same man that had killed Al Downing, but now he looked even more colossal. There was someone else, too, but he was concealed behind the bulk of the man who said he was Willie Mack Smith.

"This is my brother Didimus."

A young man, tiny by comparison, stuck his head around his brother's shoulder and smiled. "You comfy?"

The one that had carried the automatic shotgun!

I'm a dead man, Felty thought. *I've seen their faces.*

"How do you like it here?" the big man asked.

"I can think of places I'd rather be."

Willie Mack stepped back. The light came from a kerosene lamp that he carried. He held it up high. "Look around. We've been collecting this stuff for years. This is the second time this week I've got to show it off."

Felty's vision had quickly returned to normal, but for an instant he thought that his imagination was still playing tricks on him. Several metal shelves were set against the mine walls. They were loaded with what appeared to be weapons and ammunition.

"You expecting a war?" Felty asked.

Willie Mack laughed. Didimus giggled.

"We're in one," Willie Mack said.

THIRTY-ONE

THE DOORS to Tipple Town's municipal hall were locked tight when Whit got there. He had expected as much since it was just a little after seven. The business district of the town itself appeared uninhabited. If Whit had been a stranger to the small community, he would have pegged it as a ghost town. The short three blocks that comprised the town's business district amounted to little more than a string of empty storefronts. Bits of papers and cans littered the rain-wet street. Other refuse collected in the chipped depressions in the deteriorating sidewalks. Several of the stores—a pharmacy, a ma and pa grocery, and three beer joints—still operated, but anyone unfamiliar with the small town wouldn't have known it at that time of the morning. Even that early, most small communities had their share of activity—folks going to work if nothing else. There wasn't any work to go to in or around Tipple Town, not since the last layoffs at the mines. So the few folks remaining in town stayed in bed late on most days. The only exception came the first of the month when the welfare and social security checks arrived at the post office, which itself was located in the pharmacy.

The rainfall remained constant, not really a downpour but steady enough to soak Whit's raincoat during the short walk to the front door of the town hall and then back to his car. He was backing out when a rusted black police cruiser turned a corner. Whit stopped his car. The cruiser pulled in beside him. A pudgy kid, hardly more than an adolescent, lifted himself from the car. Dark blue work clothes, decorated by a tarnished badge pinned to the right pocket, constituted his uniform. He wore a long-barreled sidearm, the general species of which was known in the police business as a hog leg. It was that big.

Whit rolled down his window.

"Help ya, buddy?" the cop asked.

Whit brought out his identification. "I'm Whit Pynchon with the prosecutor's office. Where can I find Chief Barker?"

The kid of a cop eyed Whit's shiny badge. "Home, I guess. But he probably don't want to be disturbed."

"Where does he live?"

"Like I said, mister, I kinda doubt the chief much wants to be woke up this time of the mornin'."

Unlike most police uniforms, the one the kid wore sported no name tag.

"What's your name?" Whit asked.

For a moment, Whit thought the kid wasn't going to tell him, but the boy finally said, "Tilden . . . Tilden Jones."

He had dark hair that looked as if it had been soaked several times that night. It was a mass of dark curls on top of his head. Streams of water were starting to emerge from his thick hairline and trickle down his face.

"Officer Jones . . . Tilden, I don't really give a damn about what the chief wants. I need to see him on official business. Now, do you want to tell me?"

To Whit's surprise, the kid cop seemed to want to think about that question, too. "Look, Jones, you may work for the town here, but the authority that lets you carry that hog leg comes from the county. I suggest you answer my damned question."

As with most cops, the kid's weapon represented the center of his being. The uniform may have been unimpressive, the badge dulled by oxidation, but like Sampson's long hair, once the sidearm was gone, so, too, was the power.

The cop glanced over his shoulder and pointed. "He lives in that apartment over there."

Whit squinted. "Above the storefront?"

"Yeah, the town owns it. They let 'im live there free. It makes him handy."

At what, Whit thought to himself.

"I'll just leave the car here," Whit said, rolling up the window. The rifle case, containing a .44 caliber lever-action carbine, was in the trunk, but still Whit took the time to lock all four doors.

The cop stood by his own cruiser, seemingly unbothered by the icy rain that peppered down.

"Don't they supply you a rain slicker?" Whit asked.

"It's in the car. It gets in my way."

Whit took that to mean that the kid couldn't get to his weapon beneath the rain gear. In a miserable place like Tipple Town, he assumed it made sense. Several years before, the small community had been the scene of a series of homicides. Several of the families who lived in and near the town had found themselves in a feud. The killing ended when most of the young men were either dead, maimed, or doing time. Family feuds had been a fact of life in the southern coalfields of West Virginia long before the Hatfields and McCoys made them famous. They continued to be a tradition of the culture, so much so that coalfielders didn't give such episodes of violence much more than a passing thought. Not too often did they culminate in the kind of carnage that had beset Tipple Town a few years back, but it was only because so very few people could shoot straight.

"I'm s'posed to go off duty in twenty minutes or so,"

the kid said. "Reckon I oughta stick 'round, Mr. Pynchon?"

Whit smiled at the not-too-subtle curiosity behind the question. "No, kid. Barker and I can handle this little situation just fine. You'd best go home and get into some dry clothes."

"Maybe I'd best stick here at town hall just the same."

"Suit yourself," Whit said. "Is he the only one living up there?"

"Yep. Just go to the top of the steps and you'll run smack into a door with his name on it."

"Handy," Whit quipped. "Just like you said."

Most of the snow had already melted from the sidewalks and the street. The water ran along the curbs in black muddy rivers. If the rain continued, most of the river bottom land in Raven County would be underwater. Floods, like feuds, weren't unusual, but they usually came with spring's winter thaw. Whit jumped the curb flow and crossed the street.

The odor of rancid grease greeted him as he stepped inside the building. A worn set of steps climbed to the second floor, where Whit could actually see the door. A yellowed piece of paper was taped to it—with Barker's name, Whit guessed. He climbed the squeaky risers, the odor becoming more pungent with each step.

He hammered for several minutes before he heard a slurred voice shout, "Jest a gawdamn minute!"

When Lenny Barker opened the door, he looked more like one of Tipple Town's many street bums than the town's chief of police. His thinning gray hair stuck high in the air. A gray stubble covered his red face. Apparently, he wore dentures—except at home. His lips shrank back into a toothless mouth. A ragged plaid robe, stiff with grime, hung on his wasted frame.

"Pynchon! What the fuck do you want?"

"I need your help, chief."

"My help?"

"I want you to take me to the Smith place."

The chief's eyes narrowed. "Just you?"

"Just you and me."

"No fuckin' way. My momma didn't raise no fool."

"C'mon, Chief. Get dressed. We don't have a lot of time."

"I got all the friggin' time in the world, Pynchon. I don't work for you. 'Sides, the Smiths don't live in Tipple Town. I got no business out there. It's outside my jurisdiction."

"You didn't have any business at the Four Leaf Clover last night, but you sure were Johnny-on-the-spot. Why was that, Chief?"

"The sheriff asked me."

"Oh, yeah. I forgot. You wanna be mayor of this graveyard. Well, maybe I can add a little more glory to your record."

"Go screw yourself, Pynchon."

Barker started to close the door, but Whit's body slammed against it before it could latch. The door panel swung back into Barker's face, knocking him off his feet. He tumbled back onto a dirt-blackened floor.

"Gawdamn you, Pynchon!" Without his teeth, Barker was spitting as much as he was talking. His anger faded, though, as he saw Whit's small revolver aimed at him.

"What the hell's gotten into you?" the chief said as Whit stepped into the apartment.

"I don't have time for your bullshit, Lenny. Get dressed. You're taking me to the Smiths' place."

Barker got to his knees. "Pynchon, you're making one damned big mistake. I don't give a shit if you are Danton's pet. I'll sign a warrant on you for this."

''They'll be plenty of time for that after you and I do what we have to do. Now get dressed, Barker.''

The chief got to his feet. His right palm massaged his back. ''Damn, I think I pulled a muscle or something.''

Whit laughed. ''No, you didn't. If you're thinking about doing something cute, don't try it. I'm in no mood for any bullshit. Just get dressed.

Tony was heading for the shower when his phone rang. His wife was downstairs. ''Dammit to hell. Get that, will you? If it's for me, take a message.''

Tony paused at the door to his upstairs bathroom. At the foot of the steps, he heard his wife talking. When she said, ''Just a minute,'' he closed his eyes.

''Dammit! Dammit! Dammit!''

The face of his wife appeared halfway up the steps. ''Tony, it's Anna. I think you'd better take it.''

''Anna?'' He looked at his watch. It wasn't even 8:00 A.M. yet. ''I'll get it in the bedroom.''

He went to the phone. ''Anna, what's wrong?''

''It's Whit, Tony. He left here an hour or so ago. He made me promise not to call you, but the more I thought about it, the more concerned I became. He took a rifle with him, Tony. He's going to wherever he thinks they're holding that North Carolina policeman.''

''Oh, hell. I wish you had called me just as soon as he left.''

''I should have. I know.''

''Damn him! The state police are sending a S.W.A.T. team and hostage negotiations officer in here. Why couldn't he have waited? They're due here early today.''

''You know Whit. He's got a low patience level. Besides, he thinks he's the only one that knows how to deal with these things.''

"Okay, Anna. I'll try to get some help out there to him."

"I don't think he was going alone. He said something about taking the person with him that double-crossed you all."

"What?"

"That's what he said. I couldn't get anything else out of him. Who double-crossed you?"

"I dunno for sure. He thinks it was Lenny Barker."

"Who's that?"

"Tipple Town's chief of police."

Barker was at the sink of his kitchen putting his dentures in his mouth. Whit stood at a window that looked down on Tipple Town's main street. Barker's lone patrolman waited in his car, which remained parked beside Whit's. He cursed himself for not moving his car in front of Barker's apartment.

Barker finished at the sink. He hadn't put on his uniform. Instead, he wore faded old jeans and a corduroy shirt. What remained of his hair had been pushed down into place. With his teeth providing some support to the lower half of his face, he at least looked a little better than a street derelict.

"I swear to God, Pynchon, I'll have your job for this."

Whit laughed. "Hell, Barker, if either of us lives beyond this morning, it'll be a miracle. You'll be welcome to the job."

"Why are you doing this?"

"C'mon, let's move. I don't have time for twenty questions."

"Jesus, Pynchon! I got a right to know—"

Whit jammed the gun in his ribs. "Now listen and listen good. That kiddie cop of yours is down there in the car. I'm gonna slip the gun in my pocket. We're

gonna walk out of the building and straight across to
my car. We're gonna both go to the passenger side door.
You open it and slip inside . . . all the way across the
driver's side. I'll get in the passenger side. Don't say a
word to the kid. Just smile and wave goodbye.''

"Kidnapping's pretty fuckin' serious, Whit.''

"So's aiding and abetting murder, Barker.''

"What the hell are you talking about?''

"Down the steps, Barker. As far as the kidnapping
goes, just think of yourself as under arrest. You are,
you know.''

"For what?'' Barker started to turn.

"For being stupid in a no-stupid zone. Best take your
coat, Chief. We wouldn't want you catching a cold.''

Whit kept tightly behind Barker as they descended
the steps, so tight he could smell the fermenting odor
of the accumulated B.O. The chief started to open the
door, but Whit put a hand on his shoulder. "Remember, Barker, just act natural. I know the kid's wondering
what's going on. If he stops us, just tell him that you'll
be back shortly.''

"I don't think you'll shoot me, Pynchon.''

Whit cocked the gun. "I'd try not to kill you, but I'd
sure as hell shoot you. Now move out the door and walk
slow and easy.''

The rain was still falling, and Whit wished that he
had put on the rubber boots that were in his car. In his
effort to get around Barker's sidekick, he'd forgotten
about the boots. Barker waded right through the stream
running down the curb. Whit had no choice but to follow. The filthy street water filled his shoes and squished
out of them as they crossed the center portion of the
street. He kept his eyes on the young officer. As far as
Whit could tell, the kid hadn't even noticed them yet.

He was right. Not until the chief was already in Whit's

car and Whit himself was sliding in did the kid turn his head. He threw up a hand at the chief.

"Just wave back," Whit said.

"He's getting out."

Quickly, Whit shifted the weapon to the pocket closest to Barker. "Fine, roll down the window, and play it cool."

Tilden Jones leaned down to the chief. "Can I help, Chief?"

"Go on home, kid. You know the town can't afford no overtime."

"Ah, hell, Lenny. I won't charge no overtime."

"Go on home," Barker snapped.

"Yes, sir." Jones leaned down a little further so that he could see Whit. "Nice to meetcha," he said.

Whit smiled. "Likewise."

"See ya t'night, Chief."

"Sure thing, boy."

Barker rolled up the window.

"That's some gun the kid's wearing," Whit said.

"Yeah, but he can't hit the broad side of a barn."

Whit relaxed. "Okay, Chief. You're driving. I'd like to sneak up on them without being seen. What are the chances?"

Barker shook his head. "Slim to none, Pynchon. Unless you wanna walk a mile or so through this glop."

Whit shrugged. "If that's what it takes, Chief, then that's what we're gonna do."

THIRTY-TWO

WITH THE COMING OF DAWN, a significant amount of sunlight filtered back into the mine. The Smiths had left the blindfold off Felty as they went about the business of lifting the bulk of their arsenal off the floor of the mine. Eventually, enough light reached into the shaft to allow Willie Mack to turn off the kerosene lamp. He constantly chatted with his brother and with his prisoner as he worked.

"Makes me nervous having this thing in here," he had said as he turned off the lamp. "We got enough ammo in here to take off the top of this here hill."

He held up a tube of green metal. "This here's what took out that four-wheel drive ya'll had last night. It's an M79 antitank missile . . . a LAW, they call 'em, though I don't know why. You shoot it once and throw it away. Gawdamned amazin', huh? No fuckin' wonder the government's busted. I bought half a dozen . . . cheap. And that—" He pointed to a device that looked like a tear gas gun. "That's a blooper . . . a grenade launcher. It ain't disposable. It cost me a lot, too."

"Fascinating," Felty said. He had noticed an increase in the flow of water from the mouth of the mine. "Where's the water coming from?"

"It's raining outside. On top of all that snow, it's gonna make a real mess. No danger of the shaft filling

281

up. It's too deep for that, but we gotta get some stuff up out of the muck—just in case.''

"They know it's you,'' Felty said.

Both brothers stopped working. It was Willie Mack who replied. "Knowing and proving's two different things. I know they ain't got shit on us, pal. If they did, they wouldn't have tried to pull that two-bit deal last night. If they had anything, they woulda just come on after us. Ain't I right? So whatdaya think of our little hideout?''

"It's a mine,'' Felty snapped. "Christ, somebody's gotta know it's here.''

Didimus giggled. He was always giggling. The sound had a high, feminine quality that imbued it with an out-of-sync sort of evil. "Nobody who's alive knows it's here.''

"He's right,'' Willie Mack said. "Our family dug it way back. My grandpa made a pretty fair livin' selling the coal. My paw, he used it to make some of the best 'shine in these parts, so he kinda kept it a secret. Hate to disappoint you, fella, but little brother's right . . . dead right, you might say. The only folks, other than family, who know'd about it are six feet under.''

"Why did you take me?''

"Insurance,'' Willie Mack said. "Just in case we got hung somewhere and needed somebody to protect us. There was another reason. I like to set examples. In our business, it pays. You might say you're gonna be an example.''

"You don't know a lot about cops,'' Felty said.

"I know they die just like ever'body else does. Speaking of that, lemme show you something.''

The big man splashed down the shaft and vanished around a bend in its course. Several moments later he returned with a gallon-size plastic bag full of smaller bags containing a white powder.

"That's coke, man. There's a lot more of that back there. You know where I got it?"

Felty's rage began to fester. "I've got a pretty damned good idea."

Willie Mack grinned, revealing a brace of yellow teeth behind the forest of his beard. "Compliments of your brothers, the way I hear tell it. The word we get is that those guys from Carolina were your brothers."

"You murderin' asshole!" Felty was tied so tightly to the chair that he couldn't even wiggle.

Willie Mack studied Felty's angry face. "Not much of a family resemblance. We dealt with your brothers on several occasions. They weren't too smart a lot. If looks don't run in the family, then stupidity surely does. Look at you, all strapped in that chair . . . all ready to die."

"Fuck you!" Felty bellowed.

Willie Mack grinned, brandishing the large bag of coke.

"Nope, I'd say you're the one that's gonna git fucked. Them cops can come to the house all they want. I won't get uppity with 'em. They ain't gonna find nothing. We'll just lay low for a while, maybe move some of this stuff a little ways up north. No big deal. Is it, Didimus?"

"No big deal, big brother."

"That's where you turn in to Willie Mack's place," Barker said. He had stopped Whit's car and was pointing to a muddy morass of a road that turned off the hardtop. An old mailbox sat atop a wooden post beside the road.

"How far up the road?" Whit asked.

"A mile—give or take."

"Give or take how much?"

"Jesus, Pynchon. I dunno. It's been years since I been up there."

"Years, huh? Can they see us if we're on foot?"

"Sure . . . if they're lookin'. After 'bout a hundred yards up that road, we'll be in clear sight of the house."

Whit studied the hostile landscape. The asphalt road snaked its way up the main hollow, flanked on either side by foothills that had been formed at the base of the mountains. The rain had melted most of the snow on the roadway, but it still blanketed the fields and woodland on either side of the narrow road. Other than the occasional cedar and pine, the leaves had fallen from most of the trees. There would be little cover for the two men as they moved toward the house. To add to the problems, it was continuing to rain. If anything, the slate-gray skies had turned darker since they had left Tipple Town.

"Let's park the car here," Whit said.

Barker shook his head. "You damned fool. You're really gonna try it."

"That's why I came. Park it and give me the keys."

The chief of police backed the car onto the narrow berm of the road. "That's the best I can do. I get any farther off the road and we'll mire up."

"The keys," Whit said, holding out his hand.

Barker turned off the ignition and dropped the keys into the outstretched hand.

Whit had the gun out of his overcoat pocket. He kept it on Barker as he reached down into the floorboard for the oversized rubber boots. "I'm gonna get out of the car," he said. "You stay put until I tell you to get out."

"You're in charge," Barker said. "Leastways, for now."

Whit eased out of the car and quickly pulled the boots over his shoes while still holding the gun. It wasn't easy, but Barker was still under the wheel of the car.

Whit trusted in the fact that the Tipple Town chief couldn't move too quickly.

The drops of rain felt like small pellets of ice as they struck Whit's head and hands. Other than the soft patter of the rain, the only other sound was the dull roar of an unseen stream. Even the birds were silent.

Once the boots were on, he ordered Barker from the car. "You mighta least let me bring my boots," the chief said.

"I apologize for the oversight. Let's start up the road. I warn you. One wrong move and I won't hesitate to shoot."

Barker's jaws rippled as he clenched them. "What the hell is this, Pynchon? Have you gone starry bonkers or something? I ain't done nothin' to deserve this."

"Move it," Whit said.

"Not till you tell me what this is all about. You think I'm in cahoots with the Smiths?"

Whit nodded. "Yeah, that's exactly what I think."

"Jesus fucking Christ! You're wrong, friend. Dead wrong."

"If so, then I'll apologize."

Barker's eyes were flaming. "You'll do a helluva lot more than apologize. If I have my way, you'll do life for kidnapping."

As soon as they neared the juncture of the paved road and the dirt road going up to the Smiths, the sound of the roaring stream became more pronounced. The road to the Smiths, in fact, followed the stream as it furiously coursed down from the mountain foothills.

"It's almost out of its damned banks," Barker said. "If it rains much more, it's gonna wash out this here road."

"Just keep moving," Whit said.

Barker was right, though. The muddy water was cascading down from above, its volume swollen by the runoff as well as the incessant rain. Once the ground became thoroughly soaked, the water had no place to go but down—down the ravines and gullies, down the roads that followed them, down until it reached the Tug River. If it didn't find a path, it made one. At that point in time, the volume wasn't so great that it couldn't squeeze through the massive metal drain running under the paved road. At least its roar would cover the sound of their approach.

Both men tried to stay off the actual unpaved road itself. The huge chunks of lavalike red dog that covered the road showed little respect for the strongest ankles. Gradually, as tires crushed the mine waste, it would turn into gravel and eventually dust, but for the moment it was still composed of large enough pieces to make walking at the best unpleasant and at the worst dangerous.

They reached a tight curve in the road. Barker stopped. "Soon as we round that bend, the house'll be in sight. We will, too."

Whit shifted the pistol from one hand to another. "So? Do we have a choice?"

The police chief's steely eyes locked on Whit's. "Yeah, we can turn back."

Whit smiled. "Think again, friend."

THIRTY-THREE

A FLEET OF POLICE CRUISERS was gathered in the parking lot of the Raven County Courthouse. The men themselves—state troopers and deputy sheriffs—assembled in the covered garage that served as an outside entrance to the jail. The prosecutor stood with Sheriff Ted Early at the rear of the group as Ross Sinclair spoke to the small army from atop a fruit basket. He was outlining the situation and the strategy.

"Pynchon shouldn't get away with this," Sheriff Early complained.

"He's just trying to help Felty."

"In the process, how many of these guys are gonna get hurt—or killed?"

"Maybe none," Tony said. "Let's listen to Ross."

Sinclair had provided the officers with their destination. "We've got to move in fast, fellas. From what we know of the terrain, we'll be in plain sight as we move up toward the house."

A trooper raised his hands. "Why in the hell don't we wait until the special-weapons guys get down here from Charleston?"

"We don't have time to wait," Sinclair said. "If we don't move now, we might find the roads washed out."

Early nudged Tony. "I still don't see why we don't get Barker. He knows that territory."

"Forget Barker," Tony said. As did Whit, he suspected that the Tipple Town cop had tipped the Smiths about the plans the night before. From what Anna said, Whit had intended to latch on to the police chief anyway, but Tony kept that to himself.

"And don't forget," Sinclair was saying. "If these are the guys we're looking for, they're loaded for bear. I wouldn't rule out grenades or even bazookas or something like them. There's no doubt but what they have some automatic weapons and artillery."

"What if the roads are flooded?" someone asked.

"Pardon the pun," Sinclair said, "but we'll cross that bridge when we get to it."

No one laughed.

Sinclair checked his watch. "We roll in ten minutes."

The men started toward their cars. Tony had made arrangements to ride with Sinclair and was easing his way through the grumbling officers when someone came up from behind him and put a hand on his shoulder.

He turned to find Anna behind him. "What are you doing here?"

"I want to go," she said.

"No way," Tony said. "We might end up in an all-out firefight out there."

"I'll stay out of the way."

"No!" Tony snapped.

"I'll follow you," Anna said. She was dressed in a dark blue rain slicker and jeans. Her face remained tense from fatigue and worry.

Tony threw up his hands. "Damn, you and Whit are going to drive me to an early grave. Okay, you can ride with Sinclair and me, but you have to stay with the car when we get there. Agreed?"

"Agreed," she said.

"Let's find Sinclair."

Tony scanned the garage. It had emptied in a hurry

as the officers headed for their vehicles. He turned to look back at Sinclair's car. It remained parked at the opening of the garage and was empty.

Early was to ride with the captain, too, and he was standing at the garage door. Tony, with Anna following, went to the sheriff. "Where's Ross?"

"He went to call home. I gather his wife had a pretty rough night. Poor bastard. I don't see how he keeps his mind on his job." The sheriff then turned toward Anna. "What's she doing here?"

"She's going to ride with us."

"Like hell."

"Not as a reporter," Anna quickly said. "I'm worried about Whit."

The sheriff shook his head. "You're one of the few."

"I don't think they've seen us," Barker said.

Whit wasn't so sure. They had kept within what little cover the leafless trees provided as they moved up on the farmhouse. As they neared it, they were able to stay behind a line of pines that had grown along a fence row running along the house.

"Maybe they're just waiting for us to step out into the clear," Whit said. "Let's get closer."

"And then what?" Barker asked.

"You can tell me where they're most likely holding Felty."

Barker laughed. "Hell, I don't have the foggiest."

"Sure," Whit said.

The row of pines ran within fifteen feet of the front porch. Barker, urged on by Whit, moved to the point closest to the house. They had just come to a stop when a tall figure rounded the house.

"That's Jimmy Carr," Barker whispered.

The cold metal of the gun barrel touched the chief of police's cheek. "Don't make a sound."

At that moment, the door to the farmhouse opened up, and a bulky woman, dressed in a pale blue housecoat, stepped onto the cluttered front porch.

She was intercepting Carr.

"Go on back up to the mine and tell Willie Mack that the law's on the way. 'Fact, be on the lookout 'cause one of them might be here now."

Carr's head swiveled immediately as he looked around the snow-covered landscape.

The woman was still talking. "Sinclair said he didn't have much time, but he said for Willie Mack just to come down to the house and play it cool. He said they ain't got nothing on us, so not to make no trouble."

"Is the house clean?" Carr asked.

"Spotless," the woman said.

"I don't like it," Carr said, still looking around.

"Just go tell Willie Mack. Let him decide."

"I thought it was you," Whit said, his face stricken with disbelief.

"Yeah, and goddammit, I tried to tell you."

"Jesus Christ. Ross Sinclair. I can't believe it."

"So what are we gonna do?"

Whit was surprised. "You'll help?"

"Hell, yes. You got me here. I sure as shit wanna get out in one piece."

"Quick. Let's follow him."

The two men moved around the opposite side of the house and caught sight of Jimmy Carr moving quickly up the wooded slope toward the mountain ridge itself.

"Is there a mine up here?" Whit asked.

Barker shrugged. "Not that I know'd of."

The snow through which they trudged was little more now than icy mush. The rain itself had let up some and was just a drizzle as they moved through the trees.

Whit was studying the tracks. "It looks to me like

they come up different ways all the time, just to avoid making a single path."

It was true. The floor of the sloping forest was covered with tracks. The two men stayed low and, because of that, had difficulty keeping Carr in sight. Several hundred feet farther, he vanished completely. The mountainside itself was becoming almost too steep to climb.

"It's gotta be just up ahead," Barker was saying.

Piles of rocks and granite outcroppings dotted the woodland floor. They moved from one to the other as they tried to find the entrance to the mine.

Whit saw it first . . . or what he figured was it. Cut pine branches were piled between two pillars of rock. "I bet that's it."

Barker looked to where Whit was pointing. "I'd say you're right. Looks like they tried to camouflage it."

"It's gotta be where they have Felty."

They moved closer. The overhead rim of the mine's portal became obvious.

"You head back down," Whit told Barker. "Warn whoever comes about Sinclair. I'll keep these guys here."

"You think you can?"

Whit brandished the lever-action carbine. "I can until I run outa ammo. I hope they aren't too far behind us."

"See, you shoulda let me bring a weapon."

"Just get back down there," Whit said.

The police chief scooted back down the slope toward the farmhouse. Whit jacked a shell into the chamber of the weapon and settled down behind a low ridge of rocks. Almost at once, the moisture from the melting snow seeped through the protection of his clothing. He started to chill.

* * *

Sinclair's cruiser was at the head of the police caravan as it snaked along the road up the hollow toward the Smith farm. The captain saw the river of water rushing across the road, but Early still cried, "Watch out!"

He slammed on the brakes. In the rear seat, both Anna and Tony stuck out their hands to brace themselves as they were catapulted forward.

"What is it?" Anna said, breathless from the sudden stop.

Sinclair's eyes were on his rearview mirror, concerned that his sudden stop might cause a rear-end collision back in the caravan. The Eagle station wagon immediately behind managed to stop.

"The damn creek's over the road," the sheriff said.

"How close are we?" Tony asked.

"It's still several more miles up the road," Sinclair said.

Anna was looking at the water as it rushed over the hard top. "It doesn't look deep to me," she said. "Can't you drive through it?"

"No way of knowing how deep a gully it has already created where it's running across the road," the sheriff explained.

The prosecutor sat back. "Give it a try, Ross. We don't have a choice."

Sinclair jammed the car in gear. "Be ready to abandon ship if we start to sink."

"110 to 100," the radio blared. "Why'd we stop?"

The sheriff grabbed the mike and keyed it. "Just sit tight back there. The road's washed out. We're gonna try to ford it. If we make it, the other units can follow. And stay off the radio."

"Should we get out?" Anna asked.

"Like the sheriff said, just sit tight," Sinclair said. "I think I can make it."

* * *

Barker had just gotten out of sight when Whit noticed a movement at the mouth of what he believed to be the mine. Sure enough, two heads poked into view. One of them was Jimmy Carr and the other the imposing form of a gargantuan man. Whit pegged him at once, based on nothing more than his size. He was the man who had gotten the drop on them inside the Four Leaf Clover— the man who had killed Al Downing. Whit leveled the sights of the carbine on the rock just to the right of the man he believed to be Willie Mack Smith. He let out his breath and, ignoring the pain in his wounded hand, squeezed the tight trigger. Sparks flew from the rock. Willie Mack grabbed the side of his face and fell back toward the opening of the mine. Jimmy Carr went for the ground. The gun's explosion seemed to echo forever from one side of the valley to the other.

"*Police!*" Whit bellowed. "Come out with your hands up. We have you surrounded."

It was a believable lie, he hoped.

His answer was an ear-shattering series of explosions from the mouth of the cave that sent double-ought lead pellets peppering through the woods. None came too close to Whit, indicating that they didn't pinpoint his position on the basis of his single shot. He stayed undercover.

"It's no use," he shouted. "Give it up!"

"Fuck you!" a voice replied.

"Either way," Whit cried, "you won't escape."

A second shotgun barrage was loosed from the mine. This time Whit heard the buckshot pinging against the rocks behind which he was hiding. Whoever had the automatic shotgun had laid a sweeping arc of death right at him. Whit rolled to the edge of the rock pile and let loose with two shots of his own. The automatic shotgun cut loose again. He rolled back to cover.

* * *

Lenny Barker, though well out of range, dove for the ground when he heard the staccato *whumps* from behind him. He had heard all kinds of gunfire and had been the target of more of it than he cared to remember, but he had never, ever heard anything that sounded as deadly as the throaty endless rumbling of that automatic shotgun.

He was on his feet, moving as swiftly as his aging legs would allow across the front yard of the Smith home, when the sound of the feminine voice stopped him. He turned.

Willie Mack's wife stood on the porch, a small bow and arrow in her hand.

"Chief Barker, what are you doin' here?"

"Just take it easy, Jeri—" He had a nodding acquaintance with Smith's wife. Everyone in Tipple Town called her Jeri.

The shotgun exploded again.

"What's all that shootin'?" she demanded to know.

There was no doubt that the object in her hand was some kind of weapon, but Lenny Barker had never seen a woman who could handle any kind of a gun worth a damn. And he was a good thirty feet away from her. That improved his odds.

"I'm just gonna ease on down the road there, Jeri. You just watch that contraption in your hands."

She raised the thing in her hand. "You're gonna stay put, Lenny Barker!"

"Now don't do nothin' you can't set right." He had been moving backward, feeling more secure with each foot that he put between the woman and himself.

She lifted the weapon to her shoulder.

The chief of police whirled and had gone two running paces when the pain knifed right between his shoulder blades. The razor-sharp blade of the arrow sliced through flesh and muscle, glanced off a rib, and broke through just under his chin, gleaming red with his blood. His face turned cold as his legs crumpled underneath him. He tried not to fall facedown. She had already done enough damage to him. If he fell facedown, with the arrow sticking out . . .

But he couldn't help himself. Facedown he went, not even able to scream away the burning agony in his chest and head.

THIRTY-FOUR

"WHAT ARE WE GONNA DO, Willie Mack?" Didimus was dancing around the mine shaft in a state of pants-wetting panic. "They know about the mine, Willie Mack. What the hell are we gonna do?"

Willie Macks's dinner-plate-sized hand struck an open blow on his younger brother's face. "Settle down, ass-hole. We ain't done in yet. Just be sure you go fetch the cash."

Carr's sweating face reflected his own anxiety. "The emergency exit?" he asked.

"Yeah, and we blow those charges we got set just as soon as we get out." Willie Mack wiped the blood from his face. The bullet had ricocheted harmlessly off the rock, but a chip of the granite itself had sliced a two-inch cut across his forehead.

"What about all the merchandise?" Carr asked.

"Hell, man, let's hope to hell it gets buried forever. There's always more where that come from."

Didimus was sniveling, pushing himself up from the mucky floor.

Willie Mack drew back his foot. "Get up! Get the money like I said."

The smaller Smith brother scooted away down into the mine.

"And that cop back there?" Carr was asking.

"Same thing, I hope. He gets buried forever. Go on

back there and cut him loose . . . but be damned careful with the son of a bitch.''

"You know they'll dig it up.''

"Maybe,'' Willie Mack said. "And maybe it won't do 'em no good.''

Didimus reappeared with a metal box. Willie Mack placed it on one of the metal shelves. "Okay, little brother, you take this here shotgun and get up to the mouth. You hold them off. You hear me?''

"Me?'' Didimus asked.

Willie Mack's hand wrapped around his younger brother's neck. "Yeah, you. If you fuck up, them cops won't get a chance to kill you. I'll do it first . . . and I'll make it hurt.''

"What about all this stuff in here?'' Didimus said. "If a stray bullet hits something, it'll take the whole top of the mountain off.''

"Just keep 'em pinned, and it won't happen, asshole.'' He jammed the heavy shotgun in Didimus's hand. The young man scrambled toward the mine opening.

"What are we gonna do?'' Carr asked.

"Carry the dope down to that sinkhole near the end of the shaft. They ain't gonna be able to dig it out of there. We'll carry the fuckin' cop back there, too. Think about it, Jimmy. What the hell they gonna have on us?''

Carr hiked his eyebrows. "Hell, Willie Mack, we been shootin' at 'em.''

"The fuckers shot at us first. That's just self-defense. 'Sides, long as we don't hit 'em we're okay, and we don't gotta worry about Didimus hittin' any of them, right?''

Carr managed a weak smile. "Yeah, right.''

The overlapping blasts of the shotgun shook dust down from the roof of the mine.

"We best hurry,'' Willie Mack said.

* * *

Sinclair pulled his cruiser just past the turnoff to the Smith farm. "I'll park here," he told the sheriff. "We'll let the Eagle head up first. It's got four-wheel drive. We'll just leave the rest of the vehicles where they are now."

Early nodded his agreement. "Sounds good to me."

Sinclair got out and directed the Eagle that was behind him to turn onto the unpaved road. The stream that ran alongside the road had already spilled out of its banks, and the tires of the Eagle pushed the large chunks of red dog deep into the developing mud. It stopped to wait for the leaders of the assault team.

Early, Anna, and Tony were out of the car.

"You stay here, Anna," the prosecutor said.

"Do I have to?"

Tony pointed a finger at her. "We had an agreement. Remember?"

"Okay . . . okay."

The two sheriff's department officials and the prosecutor piled into the four-wheel drive. It proved a rather useless gesture. As soon as the Eagle started up the road, its tires buried up. The driver—a deputy—managed to rock it free, but it mired up again on a second try.

Sinclair exited the Eagle. "Okay, fellas, out of the cars. We go up on foot."

That's when they heard the thunder—or what at first sounded like thunder.

"What the hell is it?" Tony asked.

Sinclair's face was pale, his lips trembling. "I don't know."

But the other troopers and deputies were unholstering their weapons. "I'd say it's that automatic shotgun," the sheriff said. "Christ, listen to it echo."

* * *

Whit didn't dare leave his place of cover. Instead he decided to try to stall them. "Smith? You hear me?"

There was no answer. "If anything happens to Felty, the same thing's gonna happen to your wife."

Still no reply.

"Did you hear me?" Whit shouted.

"You can't do that," a high-pitched voice answered. It didn't sound like the same person who had been talking before.

"Try us," Whit said.

"You're cops. You can't do that."

Whit was on his back in the snow, his head pressed against the rocks. In that position, he was looking back down the mountain toward the farmhouse. He caught a flash of pale blue. Had reinforcements arrived already? He doubted it. Lifting his head a little, he squinted down at the rows of tree trunks. The figure moved from one tree to another.

The woman!

Willie Mack's wife . . .

What the hell happened to Barker?

The woman was trying to reach the mine—or him. She hadn't seen him yet. As she came closer, he had several opportunities to shoot her, but it never crossed his mind. Instead, he abandoned his place of cover and tried to intercept her.

Didimus had noticed the flash of blue, too, moving from right to left—from tree to tree. In fact, it was the first movement he had seen.

"Gotcha," he whispered, lifting the hefty shotgun to his waist.

He could see a wisp of the blue peeking out from the edge of the tree, but he waited, knowing it would move again from right to left probably.

He was right. The figure broke away from the tree.

Didimus jerked the trigger, bracing himself so he could keep the barrel from rising as it fired off a succession of ten quick shots.

In the haze of smoke, he saw the figure in blue drop.

Sinclair and Tony were the first to reach the front yard. They saw Barker, facedown in a pile of snow. A river of blood trickled out from underneath him.

Tony rushed to him. A small spot of blood was centered in his back. The prosecutor put a hand to his neck to check for a pulse.

Sinclair came up.

"He's still alive," Tony said. "Help me turn him over."

Sinclair hesitated. "I dunno. Maybe we oughta just leave him as he is. We might make it worse."

"Dammit, man. Give me a hand."

Tony put a hand underneath his bulky body. He looked back at Sinclair, who was holstering his pistol. "Come on, Ross. Lend a hand."

Gently, they turned Barker over.

"Jesus Christ," Tony said. The razorlike head of the arrow protruded from his chest.

Barker's eyes were open. His lips were moving. His left hand came up, the finger outstretched, pointing toward Ross Sinclair.

"Lay easy," Tony was saying. "We'll get you help."

Barker's lips continued to move.

Sinclair backed away. Other officers were there, forming a circle around the fallen chief of police.

"What's he trying to say?" Sheriff Early asked.

Barker's extended hand dropped to the ground. His legs twitched; blood bubbled from his mouth. His eyes became fixed on the sheriff department's second-in-command as the light of life vanished from them.

* * *

Whit was bending over the mutilated body of the woman. The double-ought buckshot had peppered her face and upper torso. One of the buckshot had burst her left eyeball; the other one stared at Whit, seeing nothing. The blood from the wounds dotted the pale blue housecoat.

"Nice work!" Whit shouted. "You just killed your wife!"

THIRTY-FIVE

"I DIDN'T MEAN TO," Didimus cried. "I swear to God, Willie Mack, I thought—"

Willie Mack's powerful hand shot out and down, grabbing Didimus in the crotch.

"Oh, sweet Jeeesssuuusss!" the younger Smith wailed.

Jimmy Carr cringed. "Maybe the guy down there's just lyin' about it, Willie Mack."

But the leader of the Smith clan could see enough of the body to know. He'd given Jerilyn the pale blue housecoat two Christmases before.

Carr edged forward. "Did you hear me, Willie Mack?"

Carr didn't even see the blow coming from Willie Mack's other hand. It caught him right on the nose and drove him back against one of the rocks that flanked the mine portal. He crumpled to the floor, blood pouring from his nose and mouth.

Didimus's cries were echoing between the mountains. Willie Mack released his grip on his brother's testicles and wrapped his huge fingers around the thin throat.

"Please," gasped Didimus.

Willie Mack squeezed.

Carr had brought out a grimy handkerchief and was pressing it to his nose. He wasn't about to interfere again. To his rear, Curtis Felty, his hands still bound but free of the chair, was creeping toward the mouth of the mine shaft. Carr had just cut the cop free from the chair when they'd heard the cop outside shout the news about Willie Mack's wife. In the ensuing confusion, both Willie Mack and Carr had forgotten all about him.

During the initial confrontation between the Smith brothers, the automatic shotgun had toppled back into the mine shaft. With his hands still bound, Felty reached for it and was gathering it into his hands when Carr, hearing the noise, turned.

"Willie Mack!" Carr shouted.

With a quick flick, the older of the Smith brothers snapped the neck of the younger, just as he had the neck of Poo Kerns.

Felty had the gun in his hands and managed to get his finger on the trigger of the oversized weapon. It unleashed two shots before the recoil wrenched it from Felty's hands. The second shot spread into the air, but the first—all nine pellets of it—smashed into Jimmy Carr's chest. The impact propelled his body out of the cave.

Whit saw the figure flying over the pine-bough camouflage and lifted his rifle to fire. The body, though, was turning, and he saw the splotch of red on the chest. He held his fire and sighted his weapon back at the mine portal.

There were two men, struggling. Whit used the opportunity to make a break toward the opening of the mine. When he was within thirty feet of it, he saw that Felty was in the grips of Willie Mack. The bear of a man had his arms wrapped around Felty's chest.

"Let him go!" Whit shouted.

Willie Mack spun around so that Felty shielded him from Whit. From nowhere, the barrel of the shotgun was lifted into view. Whit jumped for cover as the gun exploded once more, spraying death over the mountainside.

In firing the gun, though, Willie Mack had eased his grip on Felty, who broke loose and dove away from the big man's grasp.

Whit brought the carbine up and pointed it at the massive stomach of Willie Mack Smith. The crack of the rifle was lost in the continuing echo of the automatic shotgun. Its bullet, though, struck home, burying itself in Willie Mack's ample gut.

He reeled backward, the shotgun still in hand. His broad finger, out of nothing more than reflex, remained curled around the trigger and locked tight as he fell back into the portal. The gun started to fire, its pellets ricocheting around the interior of the mine, striking the boxes stored inside.

The initial explosion was little more than a puff of white smoke erupting from the shaft, but a second blast followed, which threw dirt and rock high into the cloud-filled sky. The concussion sent stabbing pains into Whit's ears. He buried his head as debris cascaded down on him.

"Take cover," someone shouted.

The assault team had been moving slowly toward the sound of the gunfire when the first plume of white smoke shot from a point several hundred yards up the slope from where they were.

The cops dove for the ground. The next thing they heard was a momentary rumble. The ground beneath them shivered. Then the mountain ridge in front of them vanished in a billowing tower of smoke, dust, and fire.

Tony actually found himself trying to dig his fingers into the icy ground as the explosion fed on itself. He didn't even notice that Sinclair, who had been a few steps behind him, was stumbling and falling down the slope, away from his fellow cops.

Anna had waited a respectable period of time before she started up the road. When she heard the first explosion and saw the puff of smoke, she had reached the four-wheel drive. The concussion from the second explosion started her so that she fell backward into the chilling mire of the road.

Occasional bits of leaf and dust were still falling from the sky when Whit found Curtis Felty. The cop's face was torn and blackened. The initial blast had sent his body rolling away from the mine shaft. The second blast, so much stronger, had bruised and battered his insides. Blood seeped from his nose and ears.

Whit cradled him in his arms. "You shoulda gone back to North Carolina."

Felty managed to smile. "We got 'em. That's all that matters. It was because of the baby, ya know."

"I know," Whit said.

"Will you tell my wife?"

"Tell her what?" Whit said. "That you're gonna be fine?"

"I know better, Pynchon. My insides are messed up bad. I can tell. I can—" He grimaced in pain. "I can feel 'em moving."

"I'll tell her," Whit said, " . . . whichever way it goes."

"The day before I came up here—," Felty said, stopping to suppress a cough.

"Don't talk," Whit said.

"I gotta. The day before it happened, my brother had agreed—"

This time, the coughing wouldn't be restrained. Felty's face contorted with pain until the spasm passed.

"My brother had agreed . . . had agreed that we could have custody of the baby."

Tony and a state trooper found Whit and Felty. Whit was running a comforting hand over the cop's face. "You never told us that."

"Then the bastards . . . they brought the kid up . . . here."

"Take it easy, Curtis."

"Poor kid . . . never had a chance . . . never had . . . ''

His body went slack.

Whit eased him back to the ground. "Did you get Sinclair?"

"Sinclair?" Tony said. "He's here somewhere."

"Didn't Barker tell you?"

"Barker's dead. What was he supposed to tell us?"

Whit sprang to his feet. "Dammit to hell, Sinclair's the one, not Barker."

"Oh, shit." Tony looked down the slope. "I bet he's headed back to the cars."

Whit sagged. "He won't get far."

Tony, though, was starting down the debris-cluttered mountainside. "But Anna's down at the cars."

Anna was trying to brush the mud from her clothing when she saw Sinclair coming down the road. "What in God's name blew up?" she asked.

"The whole mountain," he said. "I need to radio for some help."

"Is Whit okay?"

"I have no idea."

He opened the door to the four-wheel drive and saw the keys still in the ignition. "Do me a favor, Anna? I need to clear a path in here. Help me back this thing out of here."

"Did you even see Whit?"

"Oh, yeah. I saw him. He's fine."

"But I thought—" Sinclair had such an odd expression on his face. She wondered if he had been injured somehow in the explosion. "Are you all right?"

"I'm fine . . . just shaken. Guide me out, okay?"

"What do you want me to do?"

Sinclair, though, had been looking over Anna's shoulder. She saw his nostrils flare, his eyes become wide. "What on earth is it?" she asked.

He reached out and grabbed her. The pistol came from nowhere and was jammed against her neck.

"Stay right there, Pynchon!"

He then whirled Anna around so that he had her from behind. She saw Whit charging down the road.

"I mean it, Pynchon. Don't come a gawdamned step closer or I'll kill her."

For the moment Whit stopped. "How come, Sinclair? What makes a cop like you go bad?"

"You know what it costs . . . cancer, I mean. The insurance runs out. When that happens, the doctors stop caring."

Whit was easing closer, one cautious step after another. "A lot of other folks go through the same tragedy. They don't become dope dealers and killers."

"I'm not a lot of other people. You take one more step and she dies."

"So what happens to your wife now, Sinclair?"

Several other officers were coming up behind Whit. When they saw the situation, they stopped.

"I don't know."

"Give it up, Sinclair. That way, you can spend a little more time with your wife."

The corrupt cop laughed, but there were tears in his eyes, rolling down his face. "For what? So I can watch her die?"

Sinclair shoved Anna into the open door of the Eagle.

Whit lifted his rifle, but before he could fire Sinclair was inside the car, his pistol again against Anna's temple. The engine came to life.

"Wait!" cried Whit.

Sinclair slammed the car in reverse and gunned the engine. The wheels whined, spinning, throwing mud and red dog in all directions. Eventually, the treads found some traction, and the car started easing backward.

Whit moved forward just as the tires rolled into another soft spot.

Inside the car, Sinclair had the gun in the same hand that he was using to work the floor shift. He was jamming the car from reverse into first, trying to rock it free. Anna eased her hand to the doorknob, praying that it wasn't locked.

"Move, damn you!" Sinclair shrieked, venting his frustration on the car.

Anna saw her chance. She slammed her fist against the gun, knocking it into the floorboard. Then she wrenched up on the door handle. The door flew open. She flung herself out into the snow, water, and mud.

Sinclair's hand found the gun almost at once, and he lifted it up, aiming at her out of the door. Fifty feet up the road, Whit was bringing the barrel of the carbine down toward the windshield. He fired.

EPILOGUE

"I NEVER THOUGHT I'd be thankful for snow," Whit said. His arms were around Anna. Together, they were leaning against a state police cruiser. Tony stood with them.

"It's a good thing that windshield broke," Anna said, watching as two of the troopers shoved a bloody Ross Sinclair into another cruiser. "I hate to have to depend on your marksmanship."

"I didn't mean to hit him," Whit said.

Anna smiled. "Sure . . . sure. Ask Tony if he buys that."

"I'm still trying to get over the fact that it was Sinclair," the prosecutor said.

"I guess the burden of his wife's illness pushed him over the edge," Anna said.

Tony shook his head. "They made him an offer he couldn't refuse . . . isn't that how it goes? Everybody's got a price. The guy that says he doesn't just hasn't been made the right offer yet."

A deputy came down the road from the Smith place. He was brandishing a charred tin box. "Look what we found in the debris just outside that mine."

He handed it to Tony, who opened it. It was stuffed with cash.

"Anybody count it?" Tony asked.

"Yeah," the deputy said. "We figure there's a hundred grand there . . . maybe more."

"Like you said," Whit said, "an offer he couldn't refuse."

The deputy's attention remained fixed on the money. "That would be enough to make any cop go bad."

An ambulance crew was loading a body bag. It contained the remains of Curtis Felty.

"Not any cop," Whit said. "Maybe not that cop . . . I'd like to think so anyway. That reminds me, Tony. I've got to head south."

Tony exchanged looks with Anna and then sighed. "Are we gonna go through this again, Whit?"

The remark caught Whit off guard. "Whadaya mean?"

"I mean, is this another threat to retire and become a beach bum."

"Oh, no. Not this week anyway. I have to deliver the bad news to Felty's wife."

"We can call his department," Tony said. "I'm sure they would handle it for us."

But Whit was shaking his head. "I've gotta do it myself. I made a promise."

"Can I go with you?" Anna asked.

Whit was surprised. "What about this story?"

Anna took his hand. "Somebody else can write this one."

ABOUT THE AUTHOR

DAVE PEDNEAU is a former reporter, columnist, and magistrate court judge. His novels include *D.O.A,* *A.P.B.*, *Dead Witness*, and *Presumption of Innocence*. He lives in southern West Virginia with his wife and daughter.